MR. BLOOMSBURY

LOUISE BAY

LOUISE BAY

Published by Louise Bay 2022

ISBN – 978-1-910747-77-3

BOOKS BY LOUISE BAY

The Mister Series

Mr. Mayfair

Mr. Knightsbridge

Mr. Smithfield

Mr. Park Lane

Mr. Bloomsbury

Mr. Notting Hill

The Christmas Collection

The 14 Days of Christmas

This Christmas

The Player Series

International Player

Private Player

Dr. Off Limits

Standalones

Hollywood Scandal

Love Unexpected

Hopeful

The Empire State Series

Sign up to the Louise Bay mailing list at
www.louisebay/mailinglist

Read more at www.louisebay.com

ONE

Sofia

So far, London was a lot like New York, except without my mom's meatballs on a Sunday. Of course, I was enjoying the red buses and accents, but some problems didn't disappear just because I crossed an ocean. I still didn't have a place of my own, any savings to fall back on, or even a job. I was just short pound coins rather than dollar bills now.

But I had to focus on the positive. I was in *London*, the land of Mary Poppins. The home of Battenberg cake and tea. The place of princes and palaces.

As much as I longed to go out and have a cocktail at a fancy bar, or explore the parks and the museums, most of my days were spent inside, sitting on my best friend's couch, scouring the internet for a position. I'd lowered my salary expectations from when I was sitting in lecture theatres at Columbia, surrounded by the other members of my MBA class. Some of them already had jobs to go to when we finished our studies, but most of us were still searching. The number of unemployed shrank as we approached graduation, and McKinsey, Bain, and Google all picked the cream of the crop. Only about five percent of my year were without an offer when we posed for photographs in our caps and gowns.

I was one of the five percent.

I snapped my laptop lid shut and took a deep breath in the way my meditation app had instructed in order to stave off a panic attack. Two counts into my four-count exhale, my friend of fifteen years—and the owner of the couch I was sleeping on—burst through the front door. Natalie slammed the door behind her, pulled off her beautiful moss-green Mulberry bag, threw it down on the floor and kicked it. And then kicked it again.

There was only one explanation: Andrew Blake.

"What has he done now?" I asked, clearing my pool of papers up to make room for her on the couch.

She kicked her bag a third time and then screamed.

Wow. Her boss must have been even more of an asshole than he usually was, which was saying something. The way she described their interactions—like he was Prince William and she was a scullery maid—was awful. And that was when he did speak to her. Apparently he'd go for days without uttering a word. I stood and headed to the fridge. She needed more than deep breathing exercises. She needed wine.

I set two glasses on the counter—I wasn't going to leave her to drink on her own. She had to have moral support. I glanced at the clock. It was a little after three.

Three in the afternoon. Natalie never got home before eight.

"Nat?" I raced to the hallway where Natalie had moved on from her bag and was now kicking her coat. "Why are you home so early?"

"I need alcohol. Immediately!"

Holy shit, had that dick fired her?

I scampered back to the kitchen and filled up both glasses, time of day be damned.

Natalie wore a glazed expression and was slumped on the couch when I returned.

I pushed a glass into her hand, tucked one leg under me, and sat next to her. "Tell me everything."

She shook her head like some kind of confused nodding dog. Then, as if suddenly realizing that she now held wine, took a large gulp. "I've had enough. He didn't speak to me at all yesterday or this morning. When I asked him whether he'd looked over the research I'd given him, he just completely ignored me. And then after lunch, I hadn't even taken my coat off before he burst out of his office and started to yell at me for—" She paused. "You know, I don't actually know what his problem was—apart from the fact he's got severe personality issues and is the most unrelenting asshole I've ever met in my entire life. Which says a lot, seeing as I grew up in New Jersey."

"You don't know why he was mad?"

"No idea. And the worst thing is, he doesn't shout or scream. When I say he yelled . . . He does it in this unmistakably Andrew Blake way. He goes quiet and his eyes go dark and his voice drops two octaves. It's like he's possessed. It's awful."

I shivered at her description. "It's amazing these men are so successful. Why can't they just act normally? At least they should *pretend* they're regular members of society, even if deep down they're psychopaths."

"I'm done. I've taken as much as I can take. I don't care about the six-figure salary. I told him to shove his job up his ass and I walked."

"Good for you," I said, half meaning it and half wondering whether Natalie had savings to cover the rent until she found another job. And then I registered what she'd just said. "Six-figure salary? As in, he was paying you over a hundred thousand dollars a year?"

"Pounds," she replied. "A hundred and twenty actually. But two hundred wouldn't be enough to deal with his stupid ass."

A hundred and twenty *thousand* pounds? I did the calculation in my head. That was over a hundred and fifty grand a year. "What exactly was your job?" I asked.

She groaned. "To do anything Andrew asshole Blake wanted me to do."

"Like what? Be specific." We'd never gotten past how much of an asshole her boss was for me to understand the detail of what it was she did. "Were you getting him coffee?"

She sighed. "You know what? That was the one thing I didn't do. No dry-cleaning or making personal appointments either. Like, *nothing* personal. It was almost as if he didn't have a life outside work. Like he was a robot or something. A rude, stupid robot."

Most assistant positions that I knew about involved a lot of coffee making and dry-cleaning retrieval. A friend of mine once had to break up with her boss's girlfriend. How bad a boss could Andrew be if he kept things strictly professional and paid a hundred fifty thousand dollars a year?

I grew up in New York with a single mother who worked three jobs—or two and a half, if my participation in the weekend office cleaning job at the office above the CVS on 113th and Broadway counted. I could put up with a rude, demanding, spoiled boss for a hundred and fifty grand. Hell, I'd deal with his dry cleaning for that.

"You're definitely not going back?" I asked.

"Absolutely not," she said, taking another gulp of wine. "No freaking way."

"Sleep on it," I said, my mind racing through the options of when would be a good idea to ask her if she thought I'd be a good fit for the role.

"I've slept on it plenty the last three months. I can't do it anymore. Did I tell you the last person in the role only lasted a day? Not even—she didn't come back after her lunch break."

"You've done amazingly to stick it out. But a hundred and twenty thousand pounds is a lot of money."

She glanced over at my laptop. "Still nothing?"

"Nope." Jobs were scarce. "It will happen though. And we're not here to talk about my lack of job."

"No, now we can talk about *my* lack of job."

I offered her an *I'm-sorry* smile of solidarity.

"Don't feel bad. Tomorrow morning I'll feel elated that I don't have to deal with that jerk anymore."

There was no time like the present. If she was completely sure she wasn't going back, I needed to take the bull by the horns. "And if you do, then we can talk about whether or not you think I'd be good to take over as Andrew Blake's assistant."

Natalie's beautiful, saucer-round eyes widened. "You. Want. My. Job?"

"Well, no. Not if it's still your job. But if you're done with it—really and truly can't take any more—then it's got to be worth a shot?"

Natalie shifted sideways in her seat and grabbed my shoulder with her wine-free hand. "No, Sofia. It's not worth a shot. He's awful. Truly awful. And what he does for a living? He basically ruins peoples' lives. And *you* help him ruin people. It's really not worth it."

I loved Natalie. But she'd grown up in a wealthy suburb in New Jersey. Not trust-fund wealthy, but definitely no-student-loans wealthy. We-have-great-healthcare wealthy.

Natalie's mother hadn't worked one job since she and her brother were born, let alone three. I didn't resent it. It was just a fact that she couldn't understand what it was like to be truly desperate.

"Natalie, I'm running on empty and at this rate I'm going to have to go back to New York with less than I left with. And when I get home, my mom is *still* going to need a knee replacement I can't pay for. I still won't have managed more than an awkward 'How's things' phone call with my father. I'm a tough cookie. I'm sure I can handle Andrew Blake for a couple of months. Until I find something else at least."

Her gaze hit the floor like I'd just told her that her cat had died.

"But seriously, I'll only go for the job if you're really done with it."

She sighed. "Honestly, I'd almost rather go back than have you exposed to the horror. But I don't think I can take one more day with that man."

I was sure I could deal with one day with Andrew Blake. I was sure I could do three months. Maybe even a year. Whatever it took to keep me in London long enough to build some kind of relationship with my father and get the money I needed to fix my mother's knee. I was just going to have to suck it up.

TWO

Sofia

The sky was as black as it ever got in a big city. If the darkness didn't give it away, the chill in the March air trumpeted that it was way too early to be standing outside the Blake Enterprises offices.

It was five fifteen in the morning.

Natalie had said that she once got into the office at six and that Andrew looked like he'd been there a while. I needed to catch him arriving. From what Natalie said, it wasn't going to be easy to get access to him if I didn't. That's why I'd already been here for twenty minutes.

When I'd finally convinced Natalie that me going for her job wasn't the worst thing that was ever going to happen, she pulled up a picture of Andrew so I'd know who I was accosting in the middle of the street. At first I assumed that she'd pulled up the wrong shot, because how could anybody so handsome be such an asshole? He was better looking than every male member of the Avengers cast—combined. Like someone had stuck John Kennedy Junior's

hair, chin, and signature smirk on Chris Hemsworth's bod.
Jesus, Mary and Joseph, if I hadn't wanted a job from the
guy, I think I'd still be outside his office at five a.m. to catch
a glimpse.

I stood on my tiptoes, trying to see down the street for
the flash of headlights coming in my direction. Nothing.
Not even a delivery van. Across the street, an early-morning
runner headed in my direction in a gray hoodie, his face
obscured by the hood. A car going by caught my attention
and when I looked back to the jogger, he was crossing the
street toward me.

Adrenaline pushed into my hands and I got out my cell.
Shit. I was out here on my own. I was just about to press call
on Natalie's number when the runner stopped and pulled
down his hood.

I'd seen that pretty face before.

"Andrew Blake?" I didn't need to ask. It was obvious.
His   John-Kennedy-Junior-had-a-baby-with-Chris-
Hemsworth thing was in full swing. He was just missing the
smirk—and thank God, or my vagina might have caught on
fire. The man was even more gorgeous in the flesh.

He snapped his head around at my question and met
my gaze, his disapproving frown burrowing under my coat
and heading between my legs. He was still hot, even when
he looked like he was about to bite me.

"I'm Sofia Rossi." I held out my hand.

"So?" Ignoring my hand, he pulled out a bunch of keys
and unlocked the gray door I'd been waiting in front of.

"So I'm a graduate of Columbia University. I'm a hard
worker. I'm creative and organized and *super* flexible. And I
want to be your assistant."

"You're American," he said, almost spitting the words

out as if he couldn't possibly fathom a worse idea than having an American as an assistant.

"New Yorker. I'm tough as nails and ready for anything."

He unlocked the final lock. "Not interested." He pulled the door open and went inside.

I wasn't giving up that easily. I caught the door just before it closed and followed him up the stairs, glancing at the elevator and wondering why we weren't using it.

What was it about guys' asses that they always looked at least thirty percent better in track pants? It was all I could do not to reach out and cup his perfect butt cheeks to see if they were as rock hard as they looked. "I heard your assistant quit. If you hire me, you don't have to go to the trouble of finding someone else."

He didn't respond.

We stopped at the second floor, where Andrew bent to unlock the bottom lock of the double glass doors.

"I'm here, ready to work immediately."

Still ignoring me, he unlocked the top lock, pushed through the doors and then switched on the lights, revealing a white, bright lobby area. I glanced around, taking in the clean, modern furniture that looked like it had never been sat on.

"I'm an early riser and—"

Andrew headed left into a small office, which seemed a bit cramped for a dick-swinging life destroyer, but as I followed him in, I realized there was a door on the other side of the desk he was heading toward. I chased after him.

But he disappeared behind the second door just before slamming it in my face.

Okay, that could have gone better.

But at least I was in his office. And he wasn't trying to escort me off the premises.

I leaned on the desk in the outer office and caught sight of Natalie's raspberry cashmere scarf on the coatrack behind the desk. She could afford cashmere, given her salary. All money I could use to get myself off her couch and into an apartment of my own. I wasn't about to be beaten by Andrew Blake's bad mood. No sirree.

I took a seat behind the desk and switched on the computer, then looked around at the papers on the desk. Some of it was covered in squiggles that looked remarkably reminiscent of a cartoon Natalie holding a cartoonishly large chef's knife. There was a small stack of research on a magazine called *Verity, Inc.* At the bottom of the pile was a paper calendar. How charming. I pulled it open and found the right page. It didn't look like Andrew had any appointments until noon. So what was he doing in the office at this hour?

I resolved to hang around until he came out and I could convince him that hiring me was the best decision he would make this week.

I stood, pulled off my coat, and hung it next to Natalie's scarf, took out a notebook from my purse and started to look around. The first thing I could do was tidy up. Not that the place was a mess, but judging by the fact that the entrance lobby looked like it was ready for open-heart surgery, I guessed that Andrew liked everything just perfect. Yes, I'd *show* him, not just tell him, how helpful I could be. Prove to him that there was no task too menial.

I set about clearing the desk. I took Natalie's coffee cup and went to find the kitchen. It was completely spotless. I dunked the cup into the dishwasher and set about making myself a coffee in a fresh cup. Something told me that winning Andrew over was going to be a marathon, not a sprint. For a moment I thought about making Andrew a coffee, but he didn't look the type. With his bod, he probably only ever drank glacier water and protein drinks.

"Can I help you?" a man asked from behind me.

I turned to find an older man looking at me like I was an errant schoolgirl. My heart began to scamper in circles around my chest. I was at a crossroads.

Not much defeated me, but I would struggle to make up a believable story even if a lifetime supply of Ferrara's cannoli was at stake. It was why I'd initially started spending Saturday mornings emptying trash cans with my mother rather than doing whatever it was that eight-year-olds did on the weekends. I'd told her I'd finished my math homework. My mom could tell from a mile away I hadn't been telling the truth, and for the next five years, my Saturday mornings were lost. Swift and severe punishment had always been Mamma Rossi's style.

But now it was sink or swim. I needed this job, and I wasn't a kid anymore.

"Good morning," I said like I'd known the stranger in front of me our whole lives. I beamed up at him. "I'm Sofia, Andrew's new assistant. I've taken over from Natalie." Was it technically a lie if I was *going* to be Andrew's new assistant but I just hadn't been hired yet?

He stepped back. "He recruited someone new already?"

I shrugged. "I started this morning. Can I get you a coffee?"

He pulled his eyebrows together. "You don't need to do that. We get our own coffees around here." He pulled off a checked hat that made him look like an old-school private investigator and headed out of the kitchen. "But . . ." He turned back. "Next time you go in to Andrew, could you take some data I have on—You signed an NDA, right?"

I nodded, trying my best to look convincing.

"Some stuff on *Verity*." He pulled open the bag he was carrying and brought out some paper. "It's a complete disaster and I need Andrew to see it."

"Sure, no problem." I took the three sheets of numbers from him.

He nodded but didn't move away. "A word of warning. He won't like what you're giving him, so hand it over and . . . duck. Or run."

I kept my smile firmly fixed on my face, wondering whether or not I was about to be a victim of a 217—assault with an intent to murder. "No problem," I said. "Leave it with me. Should I tell him who it's from?"

Too late. The man in the hat had disappeared. Apparently, my storytelling had levelled up some time in the last twenty years. I scooped up my coffee cup and headed back to my desk—or what would be my desk once I actually worked here.

After I'd finished tidying the office and brewed my second cup of coffee, I called Natalie to get the password to the computer. Despite the fact that she begged me to come home and offered to lend me money to get me through the next month, she relented. She gave me the password (go_2_He11_BLakE) and a truncated list of her day-to-day duties, and explained where she kept her electronic to-do list. I skipped over the part where Andrew hadn't yet agreed to have me as an employee. I was manifesting hard enough to rip a hole in the universe, so I didn't need to dwell on the fact that it hadn't happened *yet*.

I'd not heard a sound from Andrew's office and half suspected he wasn't there at all. Maybe his office was three miles away through a maze of endless corridors, and I was sitting in front of an empty room.

Each of Natalie's saved folders were organized by company. She had said something about how Andrew went into companies that were facing collapse and fired all the workers and made lots of money. From a brief Google search last night, I'd worked out that he was a turnaround specialist. He *turned around* failing companies. Natalie had made him sound like a monster, but surely if he stopped companies going to the wall, he was saving, not destroying, jobs.

If the hat guy had given me data on *Verity*, maybe that was a company Andrew was considering saving. I pulled up Natalie's file and read all the documentation. *Verity, Inc.* began as a serious, journalist-led magazine at the start of the last century—like a British version of *The New Yorker*—but had been reinvented at some point. Now it was more like the *National Enquirer*.

It didn't take an MBA to spot falling profits and plummeting circulation on the papers Hat Man had given me.

The company was ripe for a turnaround.

This must be Andrew's next project. I just needed to figure out how to get him to hire me, so I could help turn *Verity* around.

THREE

Andrew

Didn't people understand that I wanted peace? I cancelled the call from Tristan flashing on my mobile and minimized my email screen, turning back to the *Financial Times* and the article about Goode Publishing.

For the most part, Bob Goode was good at what he did. He was managing to buck the trends with rising profits and increased circulations with most of the magazines he owned, but *Verity* was the exception.

My phone started to buzz again. Fucking Tristan. I stood—what I always did when I wanted a call or a meeting to be as short as possible. Just as I was about to accept Tristan's call, there was a knock at the door.

I ignored it. My first meeting didn't arrive until one and my team knew better than to bother me before midday.

I pressed accept. "Andrew Blake."

"Honestly, Andrew. I'm calling you. I know it's you. You know it's me. Have you ever thought of starting a phone call with a simple hello?"

I had no intention of replying to Tristan's bullshit, but even if I'd wanted to, I wouldn't have gotten a chance. Despite me ignoring the knock on the door, another one followed, and then the girl from this morning appeared with papers in her hand.

I cancelled the call with Tristan and watched as the woman grinned at me, marched over to my desk, and put two sets of papers down.

"The older gentleman with the hat asked me to bring you these," she said, pointing to the papers on the left. "And this is your mail." She pointed to the papers on the right. "Which I've opened and put in order of priority."

Why was she still here? And why was she acting like she worked for me?

"Get out," I said, my tone low and serious.

"No," she replied. It was like she'd hit me with a hammer.

"Excuse me?" Bloody Americans.

"No, I won't get out." She folded her arms and looked me square in the eye. "I'm going to stay and be your new assistant. I don't expect a better package than the last assistant you had, and I'll work just as hard and be just as dedicated."

"Dedicated?" I asked, skipping past the fact that not only had the woman in front of me refused to leave, she was now demanding I pay her. "My last assistant left. If you can't be more dedicated than her, you should *definitely* leave."

I sat and brought back up my email account, clicking open the folder on *Verity* and scrolling through to bring up last year's financial results.

"She quit because you're difficult to work with. Not because she's not dedicated."

I didn't say a word. There weren't many people in my life who spoke to me like that. Certainly no one who worked for me. They didn't need to. I worked with a talented, dedicated team who got paid handsomely.

"I've got a thicker skin than her," she continued, lifting her chin.

That sounded like a challenge. I didn't deliberately try to run off my assistants, but they couldn't handle the pressure. Since Joanna retired, they'd all been sacked or left before they hit the six-month mark. Some hadn't even lasted six hours. They obviously wanted handholding and platitudes, while I just wanted to get on with my job. I wasn't interested in office banter and chat about whatever water-cooler show was on Netflix. But according to Joanna—who I'd called on average once a week to try to persuade her out of retirement—that's what I needed to be doing.

She called it "soft skills."

I called it bollocks.

"I'm way over-qualified for this job. I have an MBA from Columbia. I'm clever, organized, and not afraid of hard work. You're lucky to have me." She was speaking as if she already worked here.

"Then why do you want the job?" I asked, intrigued despite myself. Getting accosted outside my offices before six in the morning wasn't new. I'd made a lot of cuts in my career, fired a lot of people. And although I'd done it so a business could survive and so not *all* employees lost their job, some people didn't see it that way. Some people blamed me rather than the incompetent management who'd brought me to their door. All I did was clean up someone else's mess. But I hadn't ever been accosted in the street because someone *wanted* to work for me.

"I'll be excellent at it. Just you see. If you disagree, you can fire me." She hadn't answered my question about why she wanted the job.

"How do you even know there's a vacancy?" I'd not yet called the recruitment agency. I hadn't even so much as thought about finding a new assistant.

"I'm Natalie's roommate."

They shared a room?

"I'm sleeping on her couch. She thinks you're an asshole. I think I can handle you."

It took a little effort not to laugh. At least the woman in front of me spoke her mind. It was an essential component of a good working relationship in my experience. Maybe she'd make a decent assistant after all.

If she had an MBA from Columbia, why on earth did she want to be my assistant? She must be bullshitting. "What was your favorite class at Columbia?"

"Favorite or most useful?"

"I said favorite. I don't say things I don't mean."

"Globalization and Markets. Joseph Stiglitz and Bruce Greenwald's class."

Okay, so she was either very prepared with her lie or she'd legitimately studied at Columbia. I'd read some stuff by Stiglitz and knew he taught there.

"What's the worst that can happen?" she asked. "Give me a shot. You won't be sorry."

I supposed she was right. It wasn't as if I had anyone on hand to replace Natalie, and finding someone else would take a few weeks at least. I didn't have a lot to lose.

"Don't talk so much. Don't disturb me before noon, and make sure no one comes into my office unless my door is open. Which it never is."

A grin unfurled on her face. "I'm Sofia," she said.

I ignored her and sat back behind my desk.

"Is there anything you need?"

What I needed was for Bob Goode not to be such a dick. But that wasn't going to happen any time soon. "Leave me alone."

At least Sofia had the sense not to argue. She turned on her heel and left. I pulled out the latest copy of *Verity, Inc.* from the top drawer of my desk and felt the temperature of the blood in my veins rise as I read the headline asking, yet again, *Is Tom Cruise an Alien?* My grandmother would be turning in her grave at the sight of her once-respected publication talking about potential celebrity aliens. There was a time when the magazine she'd led had reported on women finally being allowed to have mortgages without a male guarantor at the beginning of the seventies, the coal strikes and gerrymandering in the eighties. *Verity, Inc.* used to be a magazine that cared about the rights of ordinary people, and keeping the people in power in check. Now it cared whether or not Tom Cruise was from outer space, and whether Taylor Swift was secretly *also* Nicki Minaj.

And now the magazine was losing subscribers and readers, which meant that it was losing money. The entire justification Bob Goode had given me when he started the spiral of ridiculous tattletale gossip stories was that he couldn't make money covering "issues," as he described it.

Well, he wasn't making money now either. Why couldn't he just take my advice? Let me and my team behind the wheel. I could get *Verity* back on track, and when she was healthy, I could put a new, better team in place.

Bob called me a meddler but I was just trying to help. He was just a stubborn old goat who didn't like it that the two women before him—my mother and grandmother—had done a better job running the magazine than he had.

I stuffed the magazine back in the drawer and looked at what Sofia had put on my desk. *Verity*'s latest financials, which I'd already seen but no doubt Douglas wanted to make sure I didn't miss. They were diabolical. Any other company, I'd be content to sit back and watch it burn, but I couldn't do that with *Verity*. It would destroy my mother to lose my grandmother and the publication she founded within a few months of each other. I had to save *Verity, Inc*. I just didn't know how yet.

FOUR

Sofia

I peeled off my coat and hung it on the hook, holding on to it a little longer than I should have. I was exhausted despite doing so little on my first day at Blake Enterprises.

Natalie hadn't been exaggerating when she said that Andrew refused to speak to her, and his reticence was surprisingly tiring. There wasn't even a curt nod or a "see ya' later" when he'd left for his meeting at Canary Wharf. I'd ordered him a car but hadn't had a chance to tell him before he was out the door. I had to run down the stairs after him, bellowing, but he acted like he couldn't hear me. Then Douglas, who had finally introduced himself so I didn't have to keep calling him Hat Man, told me that Andrew didn't require a car. But when I asked whether or not he walked or got the tube, Douglas didn't answer. Was it top secret how Andrew travelled? Did he teleport? Flush himself down a toilet?

Being ignored was irritating. I would certainly take the money for doing nothing, but I wanted to work. I enjoyed being productive and I wanted to get some experience under my belt to prove that I could do the things I already knew I was capable of.

At just past seven, when I'd read almost every file stored on my computer and I was about ready to start pulling out my fingernails to keep myself busy, Douglas put his head around the door to tell me that Andrew wouldn't be back.

Had he called Douglas and not me? Did that mean that he was going to fire me? I couldn't remember if he'd actually hired me or just stopped telling me to leave.

Natalie called out from the kitchen. "Want a glass of wine?"

"Is the Pope Catholic?"

I kicked off my shoes and shuffled two paces to my left, where I collapsed onto the sofa.

"On a scale of one to ten, how awful was he?" she asked.

"I'm not sure I saw enough of him to judge," I replied.

"Does that mean you didn't get the job?"

"I don't think so." We settled down with our wine and I used my last drops of energy to relay the whole sorry day.

"Honestly, it doesn't sound that bad. If he didn't want you to stick around, he would have had you thrown out. I think you can assume you have the job."

That was a relief. Kinda. The wine was like pure liquid energy. I felt myself coming back to life little by little with every sip.

"I'm sure I haven't seen the half of it yet, but I think I can handle Andrew. I mean, he's rude and curt and has mommy issues or something, but like I said, I have a thick skin. I think I'm just going to learn to tune out what he's saying and focus on what he looks like, because holy moly he's hot."

Natalie blew out a breath. "Yeah, there's no doubt he

got lucky in the gene pool lottery. But I bet he's really selfish in bed. Like, expects it all his own way."

"Well, it's not like I'm ever going to find out. I just need him to sign my paycheck."

My phone began to ring and I pulled it out of my pocket.

All the liquid relaxation of the wine froze in my veins. "It's Des."

"As in Des, your father?" Natalie asked.

"Is there another Des?" *Technically* he was my father, although considering the fact that I'd only spoken to him once in my life, I wasn't sure if that particular shoe still fit.

"It's not like he calls all the time," she said, peering over at my cell screen. "Or ever. Answer it."

Yeah, I should accept the call. It wasn't hard. And I needed to speak to him. Needed to create some kind of relationship with him before I asked him for a favor.

I should definitely answer.

I took a breath and swiped to accept the call. "Hello?"

"Sofia?"

"Hi."

"It's your—it's Des."

"Hi," I replied. My mind went blank and I glanced at Natalie as if she was going to be able to save me.

"So . . . I said I'd call," he said.

The one time I'd spoken to my father, I'd called him to say I wanted a British passport. It had been an excuse. I'd needed a reason to call him.

However much I resented him, he was also the solution to at least eighty-five percent of my problems.

"Hi, yes. Thanks." When I'd spoken to him to ask about the passport, he'd sounded happy—delighted even—to hear from me. Which was weird, because if he'd wanted to speak to me, he could have picked up the phone sometime over the last twenty-eight years and called. It wasn't like the phone had just been invented. But I didn't say any of that, because I needed him. Or rather, his money. I had to keep my mouth shut and my eye on the end-game.

"You're in London now?" he asked.

I'd messaged him when I'd gotten my UK cell number and he said he'd call. I just wasn't prepared for him to *actually* pick up the phone. What did you say to the man who was half your genetic make-up but who you'd never met before?

"Yes. Kilburn." I was supposed to be friendly, supposed to lay the foundation for some kind of relationship. I just didn't know what to say.

"And you've got a job?"

"Yes, in Bloomsbury."

"That's good," he said.

I gave myself a mental kick. I needed to woman up. My mother's health and welfare was at stake. I didn't know anyone else who had the kind of money that could pay for a knee replacement out of pocket. So I had to be nice. Friendly. Persuasive. I needed to convince him to pay. My mother's insurance company had denied her the replacement because she could still walk. When I'd enquired about self-pay options, I'd been told we would need to budget nearly fifty thousand dollars once my mother's medication and physical therapy were factored in. Not even working for Andrew Blake was going to get me that kind of money any time soon. My mother was in pain all day, every day. She wasn't going to be able to keep her job much longer without a new knee.

My father was the only person with the money I

needed. But before I could ask for it, we needed some kind of relationship.

That was the whole reason I was here.

"Yeah, I'm enjoying it so far. Do you . . . work?" I asked. It seemed easier to ask questions rather than answer them.

"I do. And I'm often passing through Bloomsbury. Perhaps we could meet? Have lunch, or even a coffee?"

He sounded nice. Friendly. Hopefully he could be easily persuaded that leaving my mother pregnant and penniless at nineteen, then never paying child support, constituted a string of piece-of-shit moves that warranted reparations. My plan was to convince him that he could make amends by paying for my mother's knee replacement. And in my dream of dreams, foot the bill for some decent health insurance for her going forward. At least until I was earning enough to pay it myself.

"That would be . . . nice." Would it? How would I avoid launching myself across the table at him and trying to strangle him?

"Have you been to the British Museum yet?" he asked. "It's in Bloomsbury and it has a nice restaurant we could go to."

"I haven't," I said, starting to worry about how I was going to be able to leave the office to go get a coffee without getting fired.

"Well, we could try there? Or somewhere else if you'd prefer?"

"What about a Saturday? My working hours are a little . . . unpredictable."

"Yes," he said, sounding enthusiastic. "You could come to the house if you wanted. Or maybe that wouldn't be a good idea. I don't know. It's up to you."

I swallowed. When he said "the house," I presumed he

meant *his* house. His house, where he lived with his *actual* family. The woman he married and had two children with. All while my mother and I were struggling to pay our rent. But maybe if I met his wife and his other children, that would help? Maybe they would directly or indirectly help me win my argument, which presently amounted to "this is a debt you owe me and my mom because you were a complete douchebag twenty-eight years ago."

"Sure. That would be great."

"I can't do this Saturday. What about the following week? At half eleven?"

"Eleven thirty? Absolutely." At least I would have been at my new job more than a nanosecond. Hopefully I'd be able to tell him a little more about what I did by then.

"I'll text you the address."

"Great."

I ended the call but kept staring at the phone. Could I really handle having lunch with the man whose absence had meant my mom had to work three jobs? The man who could have saved me from a childhood of plugging holes in the floor so the roaches couldn't get in?

"We're going to need more wine," Natalie said.

"Or fifty thousand dollars," I replied.

She stood. "Wine it is."

FIVE

Sofia

Day seven at Blake Enterprises and I'd opened up the office at five thirty this morning. I was on my third cup of coffee and it wasn't even seven.

Andrew swept through my door, his hard, high glutes flexing merrily in his jogging bottoms. Instead of pretending I didn't exist, he stopped dead in front of my desk. "Don't come in before eight."

Before I had time to respond, he breezed into his office and slammed the door shut. Was he trying to be nice? I mean, he was telling me I didn't have to get in so early. Scratch that—he was *ordering* me not to come in so early. But his tone and his manner suggested it wasn't for my benefit. Maybe my ass-ogling was a little too obvious.

"Good morning, Andrew," I bellowed after him. I wasn't going to let him get to me. Not today. Yesterday had gone by without him speaking a single word to me. He'd forwarded me three emails with the single word "Deal" on each of them. He'd passed me sitting at my desk at least six times and not made eye contact once. Still, he hadn't shouted. Hadn't thrown anything. I had to think of the upside.

As usual, Andrew spent the entire morning behind his door, not a sound coming from his office. Consistent with every other day since my arrival, Douglas appeared at noon and knocked on Andrew's office door. Jeez, this was a man who liked routine. Both the electronic calendar and the paper one that I kept on my desk were all scored out until midday. What was he doing in there? And why was I running two identical calendars?

When Douglas came out, he was grinning. Andrew must be in a good mood. This was a chance to give him back some of the work he'd been giving me.

I gathered up my papers and knocked once, didn't wait for an answer, and walked in.

Andrew glanced up. He didn't speak but didn't order me to leave, either. I took it as a win.

I set a three ring binder on his desk. "This is the research on the publishing industry that you asked me to do," I said, without even saying hello. If I couldn't beat him, I reasoned, I could join him. "It's all summarized at the front of the pack. Jane Cohen called and wants you to call her back. She said you'd know what it was about. And the real estate trends figures you asked for are there, too. I've set it all out on email as well if you'd prefer to deal with it electronically." Finally, I pulled a card from under my arm. "There's this. An invitation to the opening of a building in Mayfair."

The invitation was the only one to get his attention. "It was delivered here?" he said, taking it from me.

"This morning," I said, stupidly delighted that he'd spoken to me. *Out loud.* "Shall I RSVP on your behalf?"

"No," he said, his voice sharp.

"Fine," I said, and turned to leave.

"It shouldn't have been delivered here." He sounded angry. Like an invitation arriving at the office was the worst thing that could possibly happen. "It's from a friend."

What a weirdo. Who would get their panties in a bunch because their friend had delivered an invitation to their work address? But I shouldn't complain. He'd spoken to me. Even made eye contact. Though he was a total asshole, he hadn't directly complained about what I was doing.

"Will I get paid tomorrow?" I asked. Natalie told me I'd get paid at the end of the month, and all I could think of was going out with Natalie and my new pay check to a fancy London cocktail bar. I wanted the chance to feel like I *lived* here, not just existed.

"It's the end of the month," he said.

"That's not an answer."

"Everyone who works here gets paid at the end of the month."

I sighed and rolled my eyes. I just couldn't take it. When I looked back at him, he wore an expression that said, *"Oh really? You want to sass me?"* Shit. It was kinda sexy. And kinda frightening at the same time. Part of me wanted to push him just a little bit more. He looked like he might put me over his lap and spank me if I said another word. I wasn't sure I'd object.

I managed to pull my sensible hat back on and got it together. I was going to have to try harder not to piss him off. I couldn't lose this job. "I just mean that I don't technically know if I'm on the payroll. I haven't had a contract. Or a job title."

"A hazard of barging in and sitting at a desk without an invitation."

I chewed the inside of my cheek. This wasn't going well. If I wasn't employed and earning, I had wasted a precious week and a half of job hunting.

"You'll get paid tomorrow," he said, holding my gaze for slightly too long. What was he about to say? Why were my cheeks burning like someone had set them alight? And why hadn't I noticed how his eyes were an inky purple color?

"Get out," he said, his words vile but his tone a little softer than usual.

Embarrassed at having overstayed my welcome, I almost ran out of his office and went straight to the restrooms.

I hadn't turned into one of those women who found overbearing, domineering men who treated them badly attractive, had I?

There was no doubt Andrew was overbearing and domineering. There was no doubt he was rude, arrogant, surly, and demanding.

And there was also no doubt that I definitely, absolutely, and completely found him attractive.

SIX

Sofia

I couldn't wait to get home, pull out the one very short, very tight evening dress I'd brought with me, and fantasize about the fancy drink I'd order when Natalie and I hit the town tomorrow night. We'd drink, flirt with some inappropriate guys. Maybe I'd take someone home. It had been a while since I'd had sex and I wanted to know if British men were any closer to finding my G-spot than their clueless American counterparts.

"I'm back," I called as I closed the door behind me. The coat rack seemed emptier than usual. Natalie must have been clearing up in between job hunts.

She appeared in the doorway of the kitchen, looking like someone had died.

"What's the matter?" I dropped my bag on the floor and followed her into the sitting room.

"I have some news you're not going to like."

My mind started flicking through possibilities. Before

my imagination could do more damage than whatever reality held in store, I took a breath. "Tell me."

"Promise you won't hate me?"

"Of course not." I grabbed her hand and held it in mine. "What's going on?"

She lifted her gaze to mine, wincing as she spoke. "I'm going back to New Jersey."

My heart dropped out of my ribcage and fell right through the floor, screaming on the way down. "You are? Why? You'll find another job quicker than me. You have great experience and—"

"It's not that," she said. "I'm homesick. I miss my mom and dad, and driving on the right, and decent hotdogs and Twinkies and—"

"I've never seen you eat a Twinkie in your life."

"I know. But if I wanted a Twinkie, I wouldn't be able to have one."

"We can get some shipped over. Just on the off-chance. I get my first paycheck tomorrow. We can start going out and doing fun stuff—all the things we talked about when I first told you I was coming over. I haven't even seen Kensington Palace yet."

"It's really pretty," she replied, her voice wet and wobbly.

"Exactly. I need a tour guide. And a wingman. I want to see some of the nightlife London has to offer."

Natalie nodded. "I know, but honestly, I don't. I just want to go home and see fire hydrants and the New York skyline and . . . I just miss it. London's great and everything but . . . I'm a New Jersey girl. Work had been keeping the sads at bay, but now that I've stopped, I can't ignore it anymore. I want to go home."

I slumped back on the sofa, devastated that my best

friend was leaving me just when things were looking up. Now I didn't have to worry about finding a job, we could have so much fun together. But the look on her face told me her mind was made up. I knew that expression, because it was the same one I wore when I decided I was going to come to London, find my father, and make him pay for my mother's new knee. "When do you leave?"

"Friday night."

"Tomorrow?" I groaned. "We don't even have one last weekend together?"

"I'm sorry. I told my mom, and within an hour my dad had booked me the first flight he could get me on. They can't wait to have me back."

I got it. I missed my mom really bad. I missed being in our cramped apartment, sharing three-day-old pizza and watching reruns of *The Mary Tyler Moore Show*. But I *had* to be here. Natalie didn't. "I'm going to miss you," I said. "Don't forget about me."

"How could I forget about my best friend?" She pulled me into a hug. "The good news is that there's two months' rent paid up on this place. At least you'll have a bed to sleep on."

"I'd rather have you here than a good night's sleep."

We started to laugh.

"I'm going to miss you so much. I just can't handle being so far away from home. You've just got to promise me one thing. Don't take any shit from Andrew Blake."

There was no way I was going to be able to make that promise, because I was certain I couldn't keep it. I couldn't do anything but eat whatever Andrew served up. Now more than ever, because I had to worry about paying rent and bills.

"And whatever happens, don't start thinking the guy's attractive. He's a douchebag."

"I'm afraid that ship as sailed."

She pulled back and squinted. "You can't possibly. He's awful."

"His *personality* is awful. If he never talked, he'd be god-level hot. It's not like I want to marry him and have fifteen Italian babies. I just like to ogle. His good looks are actually helpful. I try to tune out what he says and just look at him. It's a good distraction. Better than being turned to stone by his icy stare, or ignored to death."

Andrew was rude and demanding and arrogant as hell. But he was paying me, and that was all I needed from him. The Blake Enterprises salary would keep a roof over my head and the possibility of helping my mom on track. That's what I had to focus on. Natalie leaving wouldn't break me. It couldn't.

SEVEN

Andrew

Bob fucking Goode. I scrolled up to the interview he'd just given to *Times Money*. Every time he was within a fifteen-meter radius of a journalist, he mentioned my family's connection to *Verity, Inc.* just to wind me up. It was like he thought there was still some connection to the publication of integrity that my grandmother founded and the gossip rag he'd reduced it to. The only thing the two had in common was the name. I'd tried more than once to get him to change it.

I'd put in three calls to him this month and he hadn't returned one. Arsehole. Fourth time might be the charm. I pressed Call. Usually, I checked in on him once a month. I offered to take him through some strategy ideas or offered to come in and do a ground-up consultant's report. Sometimes he'd agree to a lunch but as soon as the conversation turned to *Verity*, he found an excuse to steer us in another direction. I thought I'd have my hands on *Verity* months after I started Blake Enterprises. It was one of the reasons I'd gone into business for myself at twenty-five. That, and the fact I never wanted to put myself in a position where I could be fired again.

My grandmother's death six months ago had renewed interest in my family's connection to *Verity*. It was mildly embarrassing to me professionally, but I could shrug that off. It was the way Goode continued to sully my grandmother's brilliant career and then my mother's continuation of the legacy that I had a problem with. Verity Blake wasn't the founder of a meaningless source of gossip. Her reporting had changed the political and social landscapes in Britain. Now the magazine that had meant so much to her and her readers was reduced to peddling celebrity gossip.

Short of taking out a hit on Bob Goode, I didn't know what to do. I rose from my desk and turned, facing the window and St. John Street below. Fuck. I needed some inspiration. I shoved my hands into my pockets and tried to think.

A knock on the door stopped my Thinking Time before it could start. I checked my watch. It was only ten to twelve. Who the fuck was bothering me? I didn't need to wait long to find out. Before I'd answered, my door was flung open and Sofia appeared.

"I know it's not twelve but if I leave it, Douglas will be in here and I can't risk you flouncing out as soon as he leaves."

Flouncing? I never flounced anywhere. My eye was drawn to her chest. The buttons of her blouse had come undone and her bra was on display. Was it deliberate? Was she coming on to me? She seemed borderline contemptuous most of the time, which was fine as long as she did her job. But it confirmed my suspicion that her wardrobe malfunction wasn't deliberate. A good thing, since it would save me the trouble of telling her I wasn't interested. I never mixed personal and professional, never shat on my own doorstep. I'd learned my lesson the hard way. The women who worked for me were as non-sexual as a loaf of bread. That was the way it ought to be.

I didn't know much about Sofia, but I knew she was book smart. And she came across as a little more street smart than most of the assistants I'd had before her. Surely she was too good at reading people to believe coming on to me was the right idea. That meant she was *accidentally* showing off her bra to everyone she met.

I mentally went through my options.

If I told her, she'd think I was an arsehole for taking a peep. Already, my gaze had lingered a little too long where it shouldn't have. Bronzed flesh pushing against black lace, bulging over it, visible through it . . . For a flash, Sofia was more than bread. If I had less self-control, less-strict rules about how I saw women in the office, I'd be salivating.

For just a moment, the sight of her transported me out of the office and into some far-away hotel room, a beautiful woman at my side. I'd strip her naked and trail my tongue across her skin from ankle to temple before fucking her. Hard. Long. So deep I might never come back.

"Andrew," Sofia said, and I snapped back into the present. *Loaf of bread. She's a loaf of bread.* "Bob Goode returned your call."

Fuck. How had I missed that?

"When?"

"About an hour ago."

"Fuck. You should have put him through."

"Are you actually kidding me? You've glared at me like a fucking cobra for daring to disturb you at eleven fifty-five.

If I came in here an hour ago, you might have cleaved my head off."

Did cobras glare? What a weird analogy.

And *cleave*? That was an oddly poetic expression. Why not just say bite?

Also, did she just use the F-word with me?

This woman was—where was my focus? "Get Bob back on the phone."

"Okay. For future reference, if he calls while you're doing your morning downward dog—or whatever it is you do in here from six to twelve—what should I do?"

Downward dog? She was off, but not by much.

"Just put him through. Bob is the only reason I'm to be disturbed before midday." I turned back to my desk.

"I'll make sure everyone else takes a seat. Even your mom. Figures."

I didn't even want to know what she meant by that. I got the gist. She wasn't dishing out compliments. But she could keep the attitude in check. What she thought of me rang out loud and clear. Again, I didn't care so long as she did her job.

The door slammed on her way out and I waited by the phone. Bob Goode calling me back. What could be made of that?

Without so much as a cursory knock, my door flew open again.

It was Sofia, her cheeks burning red and her blouse now done up, right to the top button. "He's busy. I've left a message for him to call back." She held one of those Starbucks insulated cups with the word "London" around the rim.

I nodded but kept my eyes on my computer screen.

"And—Unbe-fucking-lievable."

I snapped my head up at the profanity. Sofia had apparently thrown the entire contents of her drink all down her shirt.

She clenched her jaw and pretended that whatever was in her cup wasn't dripping down her front and onto her shoes. "I just wanted to say sorry about my blouse."

She didn't say any more, just shut the door, which was just as well, because I had *unbreakable* rules. I didn't need to think about her peeling off her shirt and toweling down her body and—

I jumped at my mobile ringing. It was Tristan.

I swiped accept. "For once you have good timing. What do you want?"

EIGHT

Sofia

I groaned and lowered my forehead to the shiny mahogany bar. What a day. I finally had money for a fancy cocktail and now I had no one to drink with. Natalie had left the country and I was officially friendless in a foreign land. But there was no way I was *not* having a cocktail. Not after a day like today.

Noble Rot seemed like a very strange name for a wine bar, but it was two blocks from the office and boasted an inventive cocktail menu, which meant it fulfilled all the necessary criteria. I passed the place every morning on my way from the tube, and I'd always wondered what it was like inside. Turned out it was a perfect place to drown my sorrows.

Alone.

The bar only had three stools at it and I took the one on the left. At least the place had a buzz about it as people congregated around the small wooden tables set out on the dark, planked wooden floor to celebrate the start of the weekend. Thank God for the weekend. Two days of not seeing Andrew after I flashed him.

I groaned again.

"It can't have been that bad," Tony, the barman said, taking away my empty glass. I'd drained my Vivian Leigh cocktail a little quicker than I'd planned. It was just so good. Probably because I hadn't had a cocktail in about seven weeks. Not since I'd left the states.

"It was worse." I lifted my head. "Get me another. Quick as you can." I needed to blur the edges of my truly horrible day.

"Same again?"

I squinted at the menu. "Next one down on the list." Mixing my liquor seemed to be the easiest way to oblivion.

"So you said the F-word in front of your boss. Who cares?"

"It wasn't just that I dropped an F-bomb. I did it naked."

Tony chuckled. "If you went into your boss's office naked, then swearing was the least of your problems."

"Not completely naked. Just semi-naked. And it wouldn't be so bad if he wasn't the best-looking man I'd ever laid eyes on. His ass is so . . ." I lifted my hands and made a squeezing motion with my fingers. "Tight. And hard. And he looks like John Kennedy. I mean he's fucking on-fire hot."

"Surely better to flash a good-looking man than an ugly one. And if that's your deal, I'm happy to volunteer my services as your flashee. Anytime. Any day of the week."

I smiled. He was trying to make me feel better, but it didn't lift the utter humiliation that had cloaked me since I'd come out of Andrew's office and looked down to see my boobs on display.

He must have thought I was a lunatic. Either I couldn't

dress myself or—I groaned again. He wouldn't think I'd done it on purpose, would he? Like I was coming on to him? Sweet baby Jesus, I needed a do-over. Tony put the fresh cocktail down in front of me and I scooped it up, barely tasting the flavor but feeling the burn of the alcohol as it slid down my throat. *Please make it better.* I sent up a silent prayer and made the sign of the cross before finishing the last of my cocktail.

"I think it wouldn't be so bad if he'd said something. Like, 'you're having a wardrobe malfunction' or 'your blouse seems to have come undone.' But he acted like nothing happened, which is ten times worse."

Tony shrugged. "Is it, though? I mean, sounds like he was being professional."

I guffawed. "Are you kidding me? This guy is not professional unless you mean he's a professional *asshole*. He's an absolute dick."

I put my head back on the bar, wondering how I could salvage the situation. I should call Natalie when she landed and see if she had any ideas. The only problem was I didn't want her to be right. I wanted to *nail* being Andrew's assistant. She'd warned me against taking the job and I'd honestly thought I could handle it.

But I had to admit, he was getting to me.

Tony picked up two drinks and headed out from behind the bar.

"Do you know he can go days without uttering a word to me?" I called after him. My mom tried to tell me that Andrew not talking to me was better than him yelling at me, but I wasn't buying it. The silent treatment must have been thought up in some kind of prison camp—a form of torture. It was like pouring salt on a snail. It made me shrivel up into my shell and start questioning everything. Was he mad at me? Had the research I'd done disappointed him? Had I missed something? Should I be doing something I wasn't? I'd turned into a paranoid freak who walked around with her shirt undone, throwing drinks on herself. The more I assured myself I was doing a good job, the more doubt kept creeping in, and the louder Andrew's silence became. It was like two summers ago when I swore off cannoli for three months. I ended up eating double the amount I usually would because all I could think about was cannoli. The more Andrew didn't speak to me, the more I thought about what he wasn't saying. And, apparently, the more idiotic I became.

This was all Andrew Blake's fault.

Tony reappeared behind the bar, the drinks dropped off at one of the tables behind me. "So, he sends you to Coventry. Let him."

I glanced up at Tony to check he was talking to me. "He's not sending me anywhere. I barely move from behind my desk. I said he doesn't speak to me."

Tony chuckled like I was being cute. He was clearly missing a beat. Or I was. I glanced down just to check my blouse was done up. I was going to have to start making hourly trips to the restroom to make sure I was dressed properly.

"And when he does speak to me, he's monosyllabic or rude or both." I pushed my empty glass toward him. "Next one on the list," I said, realizing a second later that Tony had moved off to serve someone the other side of the pillar to my right.

"Cocktail number three coming up." He flipped the shaker around on his arm a couple of times and I pulled my mouth into a smile. Why did men think juggling was cute?

"You know what I've always done when I've been unhappy with my job?" he asked.

"What?" I said, moving closer so I didn't miss what he was about to say.

"Found another job."

It was the obvious answer but not so easy when I had to make rent and bills. Plus, if my father didn't stump up all the cash for my mom's entire operation, I'd need to squirrel away all I could to pay for it myself. "Yeah, but I can't find another job and I don't have anything to fall back on. Believe me, if there was anything else that paid just as well, where my boss wouldn't be a total asshole freak, I'd be—"

I stopped midsentence as I heard a familiar voice beside me say, "When you've got a minute, Tony?"

It couldn't be.

This couldn't possibly be happening.

Could it?

Andrew Blake was standing right beside me, facing the bar. Holy mother of God, had I just called my boss an asshole to his face? Or at least . . . the side of his face?

"Ready to settle up, James?" Tony asked Andrew.

Wait. Who was James? My head was entirely too fuzzy for this to be happening. I must be hallucinating.

In my alcohol-induced haze, I turned to face Andrew, leaning on the bar next to me, just to make sure I was definitely looking at who I was looking at.

He didn't flinch. He didn't even turn his head to acknowledge me. It was like I didn't exist. Of course, because why would he have had a complete personality change in the last hour and a half? "Yes, please," Andrew said, pulling out his wallet.

Tony set down one of those coaster-sized silver trays and the check. It said one hundred and eighty pounds.

A hundred eighty pounds? How was that possible? Things started slotting into place. He must have been here for some time. Sitting at one of the tables. Had he heard everything I'd said? Every complaint I'd lodged about him?

Andrew slid a bunch of notes onto the tray. "Keep the change."

Tony's eyes lit up. That was one of the cute things about the UK that Natalie had told me about. Bar staff didn't expect tips. I was surprised Andrew was being so generous. I thought he'd be the type to ask for a refund on everything that wasn't entirely perfect. "Thanks, James. I really appreciate it. See you again."

Andrew nodded and slid his wallet back in his pocket, then turned and started toward the door. Just as he came level with my seat, he paused and leaned toward me.

"You know, your boss sounds like a real arsehole."

All the blood in my body sank to my feet. I gripped the barstool to stop myself from toppling over. Before I could think of what to say in return, he left.

I slumped back on my stool like I'd been shot. I should remember not to ever tempt fate by saying that my day couldn't get any worse. Tonight was proof that however bad it was, there was always a path down further into the gutter.

"A Kate Winslet," Tony said, sliding a drink toward me. I tried not to gag. What had just happened?

"That guy," I said, nodding toward the door that Andrew had just gone through. "His name is James?"

"Yeah," he said. "A regular. Why? Did he say something to you?"

I shook my head, entirely confused. "You're sure he's *James*?"

Tony laughed. "I'm sure. You just heard me call him James. Twice."

Why on earth would Andrew be going around calling himself James?

"You think he heard me complaining about my boss?"

Tony shrugged. "I guess. I mean, he was at the table directly behind you."

I turned on my stool to see exactly how close Andrew had been when I was describing him as a prison camp guard. My heart hitched itself up into my mouth. There was a two-foot gap between my stool and his table. There was no way he *couldn't* have heard.

"And he was there for how long?" I didn't know why I was asking. He'd managed to run up a hundred-eighty-dollar check. He must have been there a while. I just wanted to understand exactly how much he'd heard.

"He was there before you, wasn't he?" Tony asked. "Or maybe he came in just after you. I can't remember. But don't worry about it. Plenty of people have sat on that stool and complained about their boss. It's not like he'd care."

I pushed my fingers through my hair. This was horrendous. I needed to get home and crawl into bed and hopefully wake up and realize this entire day had been the worst dream in the history of dreams.

"I need my check, please," I said. More alcohol wasn't going to help. Nothing would. Not only was my boss an asshole of epic proportions—he also knew that I thought so. Was it even worth going into the office on Monday? He was bound to fire me. I wasn't sure why he'd waited. Why hadn't he fired me on his way out? Probably so he could torture me a little more by making me come in and face the music.

Today had been a disaster. I might hate Andrew Blake, but I really needed this job. Maybe if I apologized, this time without throwing my beverage down my front. I could explain that I was just disappointed about Natalie leaving and feeling a little sorry for myself.

Nope. That wouldn't work. Not on a man with an ego like Andrew Blake's. I was going to have to come up with a miraculous idea between now and Monday morning or face the prospect of unemployment again.

NINE

Sofia

If waking up and realizing that I had bitched and complained about my boss for at least an hour with him two feet away wasn't enough, my cocktail-mixing hangover was in full swing.

And if the threat of unemployment and a hangover wasn't bad enough, I was about to meet my father for the first time. Kill. Me. Now.

All I wanted to do was take a sleeping pill, crawl back into bed, and wake up sometime next June. Instead, I was wandering around, Google Maps open on my phone, trying to find my father's house, where I was going for lunch.

I checked my phone to make sure that the address he'd sent said number seventy-one. Yup, this was definitely the house. Most houses in London had an intercom and eleventy million buttons, one for each apartment cramped in behind the door. But this one had just one button. Of course it did, because my father was rich as sin. And that's exactly why I was here.

"God forgive me for the lies I'm about to tell. I'm trying to make my mom better," I said, glancing at the sky and making the sign of the cross. I took a deep breath and hit the bell.

I didn't have to wait long before I heard locks being unbolted and the door swung open to reveal a man in a red sweater. He had the exact same cheekbones as me.

"Sofia?" he asked and shook his head. "Of course it is." He opened his arms and made a sweeping gesture, inviting me inside. "Thank you so much for coming. We're all very excited to meet you."

"Is she here?" a girl squealed from further down the entrance hall.

A child raced toward us wearing an old-fashioned, green-and-blue-checkered dress and blue velvet headband.

"I'm Bella," the girl said, outstretching her hand. "Very nice to meet you. We're half-sisters, you know."

I shook her hand, a little dazed by her confidence. I was somewhat prepared to see my father—the man who'd always been the missing piece of the puzzle as I was growing up. And of course, he'd told me that his two chil-dren would be there. I just hadn't really thought about it beyond numbers sitting around a table. But Bella was right. We were related by blood. We were sisters.

"Bryony is just coming." She turned to the bottom of the stairs. "Bryony?" she bellowed.

"Shhh." A woman appeared in the hallway just as Bella ran off back up the stairs. The woman was very British-look-ing. Tall and thin lipped, with a neat row of pearls sitting just on top of the neck of her camel-colored sweater that was no doubt one hundred percent cashmere.

"How do you do?" she said to me, giving me a wide

smile as she offered me her hand. "I'm Evan. So pleased you could come to lunch. Please come this way."

I glanced at my father, taking in his pale skin and light hair, which wasn't anything like mine, and his amber brown eyes that looked like they'd been stolen from me. He was grinning like he'd spent the afternoon at Serendipity and was high on sugar.

I was led into a room at the bottom of the stairs that looked like something out of Downton Abbey. There were huge old-fashioned portraits on the wall and flowery wallpaper that actually looked like fabric rather than paper, and those old-fashioned chairs I associated with France and long-assed wigs on the guys who wore pointy satin shoes. There were flowers everywhere, crawling from the drapes into the rug and couch.

Bella slipped into the room like a cat burglar, holding the hand of a slightly shorter girl who was wearing exactly the same outfit. "This is Bryony."

I waved and Bryony waved back. Bella led her little sister over to what looked like a footstool underneath one of the huge, Georgian windows. They both sat down, legs crossed at the ankle, hands placed gently in their laps, like one was the shadow of the other.

I almost burst out laughing, everything was so goddamn weird. I bet these guys had servants and ate those teeny tiny sandwiches on tiered plate stands. It was a whole other world from the tiny two-bedroom apartment I grew up in and still called home, with its yellowed walls and a toilet that had to be flushed twice after six in the evening or it got blocked.

This was the home of someone who'd had a very different life.

"You have a beautiful home," I said, glancing up at the

crystal chandelier that hung from the ceiling, raining down refracted light.

"Thank you," Evan said, sitting and patting the cushion next to her. "It's Des's family home that we took over after his parents' death."

My grandparents. I hadn't known they'd died. But then again, I hadn't known my half-sisters were called Bella and Bryony.

There was a lot I didn't know.

I took a seat, and as soon as I had, wished I hadn't. This was too odd. I should have taken up his first suggestion of a quick coffee, just the two of us. Now I was here among the chandeliers, watching him in his normal life that was so far from normal to me. It was the life I might have had, if he'd chosen a different path and not run off and left my mother to figure it out—pregnant and as poor as a church mouse.

"Shall we have a drink before lunch?" my father asked as a young boy, no older than twenty, entered the room. I smiled and said I'd have water. The boy wrote it down, along with everyone else's requests, like we were in a restaurant.

"How are you enjoying London?" Evan said. It seemed like only seconds had gone by and the boy was back with my water—complete with ice and a slice of lime—along with everyone else's drinks. I took a sip and hoped my voice didn't come out as a croak.

"I'm really enjoying it," I said. "I haven't gotten the chance to see an awful lot because I've been so busy at work, but I can't wait to wander the parks and explore the museums."

"We love the natural history museum," Bella said. "Don't we, Bryony?"

Bryony nodded diligently.

I laughed at their double act. They should be on Broadway. "The natural history museum was a favorite of mine too when I was your age. As well as New York Public Library." The library had been a babysitter to me. My mother often left me there among the books while she went off on a shift at her main job as a manicurist. It didn't seem odd at the time. She said she thought it was safer than getting a local babysitter, which carried the risk of a crack addict boyfriend making an appearance. She reasoned that bad actors generally didn't spend loads of time in the library and besides—it was free. We always started at the children's section, where I picked out some favorites, and then my mom would tuck me away in the corner of the biology department where no one would wander. If anyone did happen to pass by, I was instructed to say that my mom had just gone to the restroom and would be back soon. No one ever did. I was left alone but I felt safe, surrounded by the books that were age appropriate and the ones that were less so.

I bet Bella and Bryony had never hidden in a library when their mom needed to get to her job. I wasn't sure if I was envious or felt sorry for them.

Either way, it was impossible not to compare their lives now and what mine had been at the same age. We had the same father, after all.

I needed to snap out of feeling intimidated or maligned in some way and focus on the prize. Today was just a building block. A foundation stone to a relationship in which my father was more likely to give me the money I needed when I asked him for it. I had a job to do, and I had to get to work.

When we'd had more small talk and finished our drinks, we moved into the dining room, which was full of more chandeliers and floral wallpaper, and an antique dining table and chairs. I wondered whether or not the British used silverware in the same way Americans did, or if I'd end up making a complete fool of myself. I should have Googled this shit.

"How's the new job?" my father asked as we took a seat.

I was seated next to Bryony. When she took her napkin from her plate and placed it in her lap, I followed her lead. Yes, five-year-old Bryony would be my etiquette coach, whether she knew it or not.

"It's good. I'm learning a lot."

"Andrew Blake has a reputation for being demanding," Des said. "I hope he's treating you well."

I shrugged. "I'm a New Yorker. I can handle Andrew Blake." Hopefully the heat that burned my cheeks didn't show. I didn't want to talk about my job or Andrew. There was a ninety-nine-point seven percent chance I was getting fired on Monday, and Des didn't need to know that. I wanted him to think he'd missed out on seeing his clever, charming daughter grow up, not dodged a curveball. I needed to provoke regret in him, not relief.

As much as I was here for a reason, my curiosity about my father and his history poked at me. "Did you like New York?" I asked. I wasn't looking to embarrass him. I wanted to know. He was half my DNA and I was curious about which parts of me, apart from my cheekbones and eyes, had come from him.

"I haven't been in a long time, but I enjoy city life— although I think I'm more suited to the country."

I didn't know anything *but* city life. That was okay. I loved New York. I knew every crack in the sidewalk, every scuffed fire hydrant, every Duane Reade from the Apollo to Battery Park.

"We have a place in Scotland," Evan said. "We go in the summer."

Summer in New York was a challenge. Over the past few years, I'd spent the odd few days on the Jersey shore with Natalie, but because of jobs and studying, for the most part my summers were spent in the searing humidity of the city. Like the rest of New York, I'd try to hop between air-conditioned buildings in order to avoid the feeling of being bathed in the drunk breath of an old man staggering out of a dive bar at three in the afternoon. I imagined Scotland was a little different.

"And sometimes at Easter," Bella said. "I like horses."

"We all like horses," Bryony said, speaking for the first time.

"Do you like horses?" Bella asked.

It was a simple question and one I imagined most of Bella's circle would easily answer. The problem was the question *and* my answer betrayed much more than equine preferences.

"I don't *not* like horses," I replied.

Before the confused frown on Bella's face could be translated into further questioning, Evan interrupted. "I have a few friends who've done their MBAs at Columbia. It's a very good course, I hear."

"I enjoyed it a lot." For the first time in my life, being surrounded by the other students at Columbia, I'd felt like I'd been rubbing shoulders with the elite. Sure, I still felt like an outsider, but I knew I wasn't dumber than the people around me. Just poorer. It had fired my ambition and given me a dose of confidence I'd sorely needed. "It's exciting to be able to face my future with that kind of qualification. It feels like a world of possibilities opened up for me."

I glanced at my father, who looked away. It seemed

there was nothing I could say that was both authentic to who I was and comfortable for my father. My mother's answer for most things was to be myself. She prized honesty over most things. "Non ho peli sulla lingua," she would say, after telling me some truth I didn't want to hear. The problem was, I didn't know how to be myself sitting around a table with my biological father's family. The situation was so alien to me. Everything from their sofa to their napkins felt like it came from a different world. Where did I fit in?

"It's an incredible opportunity," Evan said. "I'd be extremely proud if Bella or Bryony ever went to Columbia to get their MBA."

A grateful smile curled around my lips and I nodded. She hadn't needed to be so kind.

"You have to work hard," Evan said, addressing her daughters. "Your sister has blazed a trail for you. This is why you have to do your homework. Isn't that right, Sofia?"

"Homework's definitely important." Evan's obvious effort at including me in Bella and Bryony's world and addressing me as their sister was touching. It gave me hope that despite my father's discomfort, he might want to continue to build our relationship. And that maybe Evan, Bella, and Bryony might just prove to be a lovely perk of my deception.

TEN

Andrew

I'd not made it to a night out with my close circle of friends for weeks. When I was in the midst of a turnaround, things were often far too busy and demanded enough focus and dedication that I couldn't do anything but work and sleep. So I'd been looking forward to tonight.

"Tristan," I said, taking a seat at the Mayfair pub we always ended up in when it was Beck's turn to choose our venue. "Gabriel."

"Do you want me to get you a drink?" Gabriel asked.

I shook my head. The barmaid here knew my order. She'd bring my drink.

"So you're here but not drinking?" Tristan asked. "What use is that?"

"I didn't say I wasn't drinking."

On cue, the barmaid approached and put down a pint in front of me. "The Benediktiner Helles," she said.

She'd remembered.

"Thanks," I said, picking it up and taking a sip.

"How do you do that?" Tristan asked. "How do you get people to do what you want them to do without even asking? Are you a wizard in your spare time?"

"I don't have spare time," I replied.

"That doesn't answer my question—"

"What's happening?" Dexter said as he took a seat. "What's Tristan moaning about? Beck, can you get me a Guinness please, mate?"

And like so often with Tristan, he never got an answer to my question because he was too impatient and way too easy to distract.

As everyone gathered around our table, I cleared my throat. "So, I need your help."

Silence skirted around the group. It was rare that I came to our nights out with a problem to solve or an issue to mull over. I liked to be the one solving problems. Generally, I didn't like a committee to weigh in on my dilemmas. But I wasn't thinking clearly. The ball of lust that had gathered in my gut when Sofia came into my office with her blouse undone was proof of that. I'd had iron-clad walls between my life in the office and my life outside the office since I'd been fired at twenty-five from my first job. Back then, I'd let my personal life and my professional life collide. I'd made sure it hadn't even come close to happening since. The fact that I'd even noticed Sofia as anything more than bread was a sure sign I wasn't my usual, focused self. Listening to her on Friday sounding off about me in Noble Rot had made me realize I had a real problem. Far from smothering the desire I'd felt earlier that day, her smart mouth had reignited it. My iron walls were rusty. I needed a reset from my best friends. They would help me regain my laser focus on *Verity*.

"As you all know, my grandmother died just before Christmas and it's brought things to a head for me."

"With *Verity*?" Gabriel asked.

I nodded. "It's never been easy for me to watch it morph into such a worthless publication but now, with my grandmother gone, all that's left of her is her legacy. And her legacy is *Verity*. I can't stand by and watch it warp and corrupt."

"It's like they've slapped some emulsion on the Mona Lisa and started drawing stick men on it," Tristan said. He was nothing if not passionate on my behalf, which I appreciated.

"So, I need to do something about it."

"Great idea," said Tristan. "You're going to buy it?"

Why did he leap to the wrong conclusions so often? Precisely because he leapt. The man needed to learn patience. "No, of course I'm not going to buy it. It's not my skill set. I don't run companies. I restructure them. I want to find someone else to buy it. Someone with the same kind of skill and passion and determination that she had. I need someone with an investigative journalist's background to build *Verity* back into what it was.

"I've approached Bob Goode a thousand times and offered to turn it around, but he just won't have it. It needs a new owner. And I'd still be completely happy to go in with my team and do the restructuring and transformation piece."

"With someone else's money," Gabriel said.

"Yes, I always do turnarounds with someone else's money."

"Right, but this isn't just any turnaround," Beck said. "And you're looking at restoring a legacy, not putting a business back in the black."

"*Verity* can operate at a profit. There's no doubt about that."

"It will be a challenge," Tristan said. "Magazine publishing isn't a cash-rich business anymore."

"It never was." What the hell did Tristan know about magazine publishing?

"Have you not thought about buying *Verity* yourself?" Beck said. "There's no one more passionate about the publication, and that's what you need when you have such an uphill struggle ahead."

"As I said, that's not what I do. I restructure and turn around. I don't run businesses for the medium and long term," I said.

"I struggle to see how you're going to convince someone to buy it," Beck continued. "Private equity investors might see an opportunity in it, but not if the goal is to turn it back into a highbrow magazine with super-expensive running costs."

That was true. A traditional private equity investor would drive it deeper into the gutter. "So we need a trade buyer," I said. "Someone who already knows the business."

"Like Goode," Tristan said, ever the irritant.

"Look," Gabriel said, resting his hand on my shoulder. "If you were sitting in my seat now, you would look me right in the eye and tell me to get a grip. No trade buyer has pockets deep enough to do the transformation you want to do. No private equity house has the willingness. If you're serious and you want to act quickly, you need to buy *Verity* yourself, turn it around in the way only you can, then stick a manager in. After that, maybe you'll be able to find a trade buyer."

He was right: if I was sitting in his shoes now, that'd be exactly what I'd say.

Irritation prickled at my hairline. I should have been able to see it before bloody Tristan. Before Gabriel. But that's why I'd come tonight. I needed people who knew me to tell me what I already knew.

"Right," I said. I pushed back my stool and stood.

"You're leaving?" Gabriel asked.

"You're just using us for our minds and then dumping us like cheap wine?" Dexter asked.

I didn't respond. I had my answer and my focus back. There was no time to waste. I needed to come up with a plan and act on it. I went over to the bar, dropped a hundred quid to cover my drink and ensure that next time, I wouldn't need to ask for what I wanted either. And I made my way out.

They knew I loved them. I didn't need to kiss them all goodbye.

ELEVEN

Andrew

The glass doors of the Blake Enterprises offices were unlocked when I arrived shortly before six. That could only mean one thing. Sofia Rossi had defied me and gotten in before eight. She seemed to be struggling with the idea that the boss made the rules, and the employee followed them to the letter.

She'd had a shockingly bad day on Friday. At least I was sure now that she'd not been trying to seduce me when she walked into my office half undressed. Listening to her relay the entire sorry tale to Tony at Noble Rot had been the highlight of my week—a fact both disturbing and alluring.

And when she'd realized I'd overheard what she'd been saying about me? Her smooth olive skin had gone bright white.

What she didn't realize was that I didn't give a damn what she thought of me. I wasn't stupid. I already knew, and it was nothing different to what every assistant before her had thought about me—with the exception of Joanna, of course.

I pulled the door open and strode toward my office. I had a lot to do. I'd spent all night strategizing and thinking about *Verity*. I needed to organize my thoughts and come up with a detailed plan.

As I entered the outer office, Sofia, who was sitting behind her desk, shot to her feet.

"Andrew," she said.

"I told you not to come in before eight."

"I wanted to talk to you before twelve. If I'm going to get fired, I'd rather get it over with."

I ignored her and headed to my office. I didn't know what she was babbling on about.

Unfortunately, she followed me inside.

I groaned. I needed space. Time. I needed her to get out of here. Why couldn't she just do as I'd asked?

"So," she said, standing opposite my desk, her hand on her hip.

I didn't care what had happened on Friday. I didn't care about the open blouse, the spilled drink, the character assassination at the bar. None of it.

But despite having regained some focus, it hadn't stopped me looking at Sofia slightly differently. Her open blouse had shifted something in me. Now when I looked at her, I saw an employee but also . . . a woman. A beautiful woman with a mixture of confidence and elegance that—in my experience—only Italian women could pull off. I saw a woman who had a fabulous arse and knew it. I saw a woman who I'd pull onto my lap, spread her legs wide, and torture for hours before feeling her clamp around my fingers and scream my name—if and only if she wasn't my employee.

But she was.

I cleared my throat and tried to focus on what was happening. "What?"

I turned and hung up my suit jacket, then took a seat before firing up my computer.

"I want to know if you're going to fire me."

I sighed. "Why would I fire you?"

Her cheeks were as fire-engine red as they had been on Friday just before she had spilled her drink all down herself. I bet they were that perfect shade just before she came.

Fuck. Had this woman cast a spell on me or something? Why couldn't she just turn back into flour and yeast and get out of my head? I had to focus. There was a lot to do today.

"I just thought that . . . You know . . . because—"

"Get out," I snapped. "Don't disturb me again before midday."

I needed to push Sofia Rossi to the back of my mind and keep her there. I had more pressing concerns that required all my Thinking Time and focus—like how to go about buying *Verity, Inc.* and restoring my grandmother's legacy.

TWELVE

Sofia

I wasn't sure why I was here, but here I was. At Noble Rot on Lamb Conduit's Street in Bloomsbury just two blocks from the office. I was desperate to make sense of what had happened on Friday night and figure out if I was seriously losing it.

If Andrew had heard everything I said, surely he would have fired me. Or at least reprimanded me this morning. I'd given him every opportunity. I knew he'd heard at least some part of my tirade, because he'd delivered that parting shot about my boss being a real *arsehole*.

Was it possible he didn't care? I knew I was a good assistant, but was I good enough to dodge punishment for a 245—assault with a deadly weapon? Maybe my tongue wasn't as sharp as I remembered.

I was back at Noble Rot because I wanted to know I wasn't hallucinating on Friday. The way Andrew had reacted today when I'd asked him if I was going to get fired —it was like nothing that happened on Friday had *actually* happened. Either he was in denial or I was, and I wanted to know which one.

I didn't expect him to be here again tonight. He'd left early for some meeting across town. Which made it easier to do what I was going to do. My plan was to simply ask Tony whether Andrew was "James."

I'd brought up a picture of Andrew on my phone and I was just waiting for Tony to start his shift. Four minutes to go.

"Hey, Sofia," Tony said.

"You're early," I said.

He winked at me. "You've been waiting for me. How sweet. What can I get you? Are you going to keep going down the list? I think the Emma Thompson is next."

I smiled, trying to ignore the swirling in my stomach at the thought of a cocktail—Oscar-winning or otherwise. "Can I just get a glass of red wine? A Barolo if you have it?"

I'd let Tony settle into his shift and then I'd ask him.

Tony placed a glass of velvety red wine in front of me and I took a sip, enjoying the heat that trickled down my throat and pooled in my belly.

"Your usual?" Tony asked. I was just about to tell him I was fine with my Barolo when I realized he wasn't talking to me. I glanced over at the man who'd just slid onto the stool next but one to me.

Fuck. My. Life.

It was Andrew.

"Thanks, Tony."

"My pleasure, James. Good to see you again."

I hadn't been imagining it. Andrew was being called James. Maybe Tony got his name wrong and Andrew was too polite to correct him. I had to stop myself from laughing. Of course that wasn't it. Andrew wasn't polite.

But why was he here? And why was he still pretending he didn't know me?

Tony put a drink in front of Andrew, who nodded in thanks. He turned to me, his glass in the air. "Cheers," he said. His voice was deep and thick with a hint of grit that I felt between my legs. I hated that I found him so goddamn attractive.

On auto-pilot, I lifted my glass. "*Brindisi.*"

We both took a sip of our drinks. As I drank, I watched Andrew out of the corner of my eye. He didn't seem to be laughing at me.

What was his deal?

He slid his glass back on the bar before turning to me once again. "I'm James." He reached out his hand to shake mine.

I took it, a little stunned. "Sofia."

He nodded. "Nice to meet you, Sofia. I hope you sorted it out with your boss."

There was only one explanation—Andrew must have an identical twin. Two explanations—Andrew had intermittent amnesia. Was that even a thing?

Nope, that was the plotline of some ridiculously cute rom-com starring Reese Witherspoon. It was not my life. My life included flashing my boss and breaking the heel of my brand-new shoes. Nothing in my day-to-day was Hollywood-worthy. Except maybe Andrew's face and ass.

Like the man sitting next to me at the bar.

"Not really," I replied. "But I wasn't fired. So there's that."

"You don't seem happy about the fact that you still have a job."

Was this a test? Would James morph back into Andrew

if I said the wrong thing? "Oh, I'm very happy about it. Deliriously happy. *Incandescent* with pleasure."

He chuckled. Chuckled! Like someone with an actual sense of humor. It didn't make any sense. Andrew was a man of few words—I'd learned that quickly enough. But he wasn't just not mentioning the fact that I worked for him, he was pretending we were strangers. A rush of lust licked up my spine and I tried to hide my shiver by having another sip of wine.

"What about you?" I asked. "Do you have an asshole boss?" I told myself the alcohol made me brave, but really, if he wanted to play this game, I was going to see how far it could go.

This time, he turned his entire body so he was facing me and held my gaze, the John Kennedy Junior smirk in full force. "Nope. I *am* the asshole boss that, no doubt, people who work for me sound off about in bars."

Anticipation danced down my limbs. "That doesn't bother you?"

He pulled in a breath and gently exhaled. "Nope. People will always complain about their bosses. And the way I see it, their opinion of me is none of my business."

"That's an interesting way to look at things."

"It's the only way. Your employees are never going to agree with you all the time. I'm not at work to win a popularity contest. It doesn't matter to me whether or not people like me. I don't expect them to. I tell the truth. I don't like to waste time, pander, or play favorites. That tends not to make me especially popular." He shrugged and turned back to the bar.

Was he trying to explain himself? Justify the way he was?

"You're abrupt," I said. He could take it as a question or

a statement—depending on whether he was Andrew . . . or James.

"Yes."

At least he knew himself. He wasn't one of those guys who thought he was something he wasn't. There was something very sexy about a man with a little self-awareness.

"And you think people take things too personally?"

"I'm saying it doesn't matter to me either way. If the people who work for me don't like how I operate, they may leave. I'm busy. I'm focused. I like to concentrate on what matters."

"And people don't matter?" I asked.

"The people who are going to lose their jobs if I don't figure out how to save the businesses they work for matter. The legacies of the people who founded good businesses that have been run by incompetent managers matter. Employees who get offended because I don't chitchat about the latest Netflix show don't matter."

I exhaled a long breath, letting his words sink in. I saw him as curt and rude and demanding. He saw himself as efficient and focused and dedicated.

We were both right.

"I understand," I said.

"Good." He took the final swallow of his drink. Immediately, and without Andrew having to ask, Tony replaced it with a fresh one.

He'd said more to me in the last ten minutes than he had in the last two weeks. And the way he spoke—it was like he'd chosen each word deliberately, so he wouldn't waste his breath on anything superfluous. Like he was in complete control of everything in the universe. If he needed to, he'd stop time before he allowed himself to be rushed. It was completely infuriating in the office but entirely intoxicating under the dimmed lights of this cozy bar. I had the urge to trace the outline of his lips with my fingertips and ask him to keep talking, so I could enjoy the power and vibration of his words against my skin.

I squirmed on my seat and Andrew held my gaze like he could read my thoughts. His eyes burned. Sexual energy seemed to reverberate off him.

"You're very attractive," he said, and it was like he'd sent a thunderbolt of lust straight to my vagina. Such a blunt statement shouldn't be so sexy, but Andrew could pull it off. Or maybe it wasn't Andrew that was making me feel like a thousand bubbles were popping on the surface of my skin. Maybe it was James.

"Thank you," I said. Should I return the favor and tell him I thought he might just be the most handsome man I'd ever met? I suppose he already knew, given my rant about his tight ass and hot AF face.

He looked away from me and drained what remained of his fresh drink.

He placed some cash on the bar and stood up. The heat that had seemed to enclose us in some weird energy bubble drained away. Was he really leaving?

"See you again," he said and swept out.

The man I'd hated so vehemently for the last two weeks had gone. And I'd wanted him to stay.

THIRTEEN

Andrew

I flung open my office door. Sofia was sitting at her desk, typing away. For the ninetieth time, I mentally chastised myself for going to the bar again last night. Why hadn't I just stayed away? Not that I knew for sure she'd be there, but there was a risk. The worst of it was, I'd been fucking delighted when I'd spotted her on her stool, exactly where she had been on the Friday before.

It was like I could feel the iron walls I'd built crumble under my fingers and I was powerless to stop it. Of course Sofia was attractive—beautiful actually. But I'd seen beautiful women before, and it hadn't had me breaking my rules, wanting to do inappropriate things. Over the last decade, I'd developed the self-control of a bloody Jedi master.

So what was it about Sofia?

The one and only time the circles of my personal and professional life had overlapped had ended in disaster. I'd been sacked by the woman I was dating because she didn't like that I'd ended our relationship. Being a junior lawyer fired for sexual harassment, even back then, meant I was toxic. My legal career had been ruined before it had had a chance to get going. For months I lost all self-control. I drank too much. Had a lot of casual sex. Made some shockingly bad decisions. I'd fallen down and was sure I'd never get up again. I'd thought my life was over.

It was only when Gabriel shoved a copy of *Verity, Inc.* under the door that I came to my senses. I knew I had to make something out of my life so I could rescue that magazine from the gutter.

"Can I help you with anything?" Sofia said, jolting me out of my memories.

"Still no word?" I barked, irritated that she had the ability to dilute my focus, even with her back to me. I knew the answer. I'd been tapping my fingers on my desk for the last six hours, waiting for Goode to return my call. I'd have heard Sofia's phone ring, but it had been deadly silent for the last six hours.

"Sorry," she said, glancing up at me and back down as if I might bite.

If only she knew how much I wanted to sink my teeth into her.

Yesterday, I'd asked Sofia to put a call in to Bob's assistant, to try to arrange a lunch—but to no avail. We were told he was working on some "pressing matters" and that nothing was to be added to his diary until further notice. Of course, she was bullshitting, so today I'd decided to take matters into my own hands and call him myself. Twice. And twice I'd been told he was in meetings and would return my call.

Bullshit on bullshit—the worse kind.

"It's after seven," Sofia said. "I think if he was going to call today, he would have done so already."

She was right. If he was going to call at all, he'd use my cell.

"You should leave." I turned back into my office and slammed the door.

Fucking Goode. How was I going to buy his company if he wouldn't even take my call?

A knock at the door interrupted my thoughts and, as usual, Sofia walked in without waiting for me to respond. Was it her defiance that hooked me in and hypnotized me?

"Is there something you need from Goode?" she asked. "Is it something I could pick up from his assistant?"

"No," I snapped.

Instead of sighing and going back to her desk, which was what she normally did when I snapped at her, she came farther into my office. The tendons in my neck tensed and I gripped the desk.

"Andrew," she said. "Tell me what you're trying to achieve. I might be able to help."

It was all I could do not to roll my eyes. She wasn't going to be able to help me buy a company.

Buying *Verity* was my only option. Gabriel and Beck and even Tristan had made me see the truth: there was no way I was going to be able to convince an investor to stump up money for a magazine I wanted to destroy and then build back up again. Buying a company wasn't my normal modus operandi, and I didn't want to fuck it up. But if Goode refused to take my calls, what could I do?

Despite being some kind of Aphrodite, I was more than certain Sofia didn't have the answer as far as Bob was concerned.

"I want a meeting with Goode."

"Yes, that much I figured out for myself. But why? Is he a friend? Connection? Potential investor? And why is he refusing to meet with you? I never have a problem getting time in people's diaries for you—it doesn't matter who it is or how important they seem to be. I swear, I could get a meeting with the Queen if you wanted me to."

"I don't want a meeting with Her Majesty. Just Bob Goode."

"So what's the issue? Did you bang his wife or something?"

Why would her mind turn to sex as the source of the problem? Had she thought about me naked like I'd fantasized about her?

"He's an idiot. Thinks he doesn't need my advice."

"Surely not." She mocked shock and horror and I had to admit, I was slightly amused.

"Can you believe it?"

She smiled, warm like a crackling fire in winter and just as inviting.

I shook my head. "Anyway, I don't want to give him advice. I can admit defeat on that front. I want to buy one of his magazines."

"Wow," Sofia said. "That's exciting. So you wouldn't just be turning it around and giving it back. You want it for keeps?"

"Sort of." I didn't know why I was discussing this with her. She couldn't help. Talking to her was a waste of time when I should be thinking up creative ways of getting Goode to take a meeting.

"Maybe buy it through an offshore company so he doesn't know it's you?" she said.

I glanced up and she met my gaze with wary interest. It was a good idea in theory, but in practice, I was trying to persuade him to let me buy one of his assets that wasn't for sale. Duping him might raise his hackles and set me back rather than make things better.

"It wouldn't work," I said. "I need him to come willingly. Stupid as it sounds, people don't do business with people they don't like. And if I ambush him . . . it's game over."

"Okay. Well, let me think about it. I'm sure we can come up with a plan."

Sofia didn't need to come up with a plan. I did. "Don't worry about it. You should leave." Hopefully she'd go straight home and not stop off at the bar. I wasn't sure I'd muster up my self-restraint by the time I left the office. Though I knew it would be bad for me—and her—I still couldn't guarantee I'd pass up the chance to be the guy who sat next to her tonight, enjoying her smart mouth, flushed cheeks, and the curve of her arse.

She paused, shifting her weight from foot to foot. I was her boss. How long would she defy me? How long would my self-control last? Eventually she sighed and closed the door on her way out.

FOURTEEN

Sofia

Buried deep in research about a company Andrew asked me to report on, I physically jumped at the gentle tap on the office door. Before I could answer, it creaked open and a lady with a silver-gray bob stuck her head around the door.

"Sofia?" She grinned at me.

I stood and opened the door wide. "Yes, can I help you?"

"I'm Joanna."

We shook hands and she glanced over her shoulder. "Hang on a minute." She hunched up her shoulders like we were in the midst of a big conspiracy, her bright smile never dimming.

She scurried away and came back holding a small cake, frosted white with "Happy Birthday" in purple icing. "I put it in the fridge while I was catching up with Douglas. How is he?" she asked, nodding at Andrew's door.

Was this Andrew's mom?

I glanced at the clock affixed to the back wall and smiled. "He's fine. Did you want to—"

Before I had a chance to finish my sentence, Andrew swung open his door, ignored me completely, and almost smiled when he saw who was waiting for him.

"Joanna." His tone was entirely neutral, which was as close to "warm" as I was ever likely to hear in the office. But at least the address told me Joanna wasn't his mother.

"Andrew!" She beamed at him. "Happy birthday!"

It was his birthday?

He swept his hand into his office, inviting Joanna inside. Who was this woman who could come by unannounced and solicit such a welcome? I would have expected any unannounced guests would be seen off with a bazooka or at the very least, a cricket bat.

"What shall I tell anyone who—"

He closed the door before I had a chance to finish my sentence.

Jesus, he could be a prick.

My curiosity was more than piqued. I couldn't make out anything other than a mumble of voices behind Andrew's closed door, hard as I tried to listen in. Who was this woman? A family friend? But he didn't do personal in the office. Who would dare bring him a birthday cake?

I stepped a little closer. Still couldn't make out what they were saying. I glanced over my shoulder, just to make sure the door to my office was closed, and pressed my ear against the door. All I had managed to make out was Joanna's laugh when a sharp knock at the outer door made me jump eleven feet in the air.

"Douglas," I said, pulling my sleeve over my hand to rub at a nonexistent mark on the door jamb to Andrew's office.

"Perfect," I said, as if removing a mark was all I'd been doing, and I hadn't been eavesdropping at all.

"Can you give this to Andrew when Joanna leaves, please?" He put a file on my desk and I sat back down.

"No problem. Do you know if she'll be in there long?"

Douglas shrugged and left.

The mumbled voices moved closer and the door opened slightly. "It was very kind of you to remember," Andrew said. "And if you change your mind, you only have to say the word."

"Wonderful to see you," Joanna replied. She slipped out of Andrew's office, closing the door behind her. Even ten minutes with Andrew hadn't managed to dim her smile. She was an angel sent by Jesus himself.

Now would be a good time to give Andrew the file Douglas had left, but there was no way I was passing up an opportunity to make more sense of who the hell Andrew Blake was.

"Did he like his cake?" I asked.

She laughed. "I don't suppose he did. How are you getting on? Andrew tells me you're new."

He was talking about me? "It has its ups and downs."

"Doesn't it just? I did this job for nearly seven years before I retired."

I shot up from my chair. "You did my job?"

"Absolutely. Loved every moment. He's such a wonderful man."

Everything about Andrew Blake was confusing. His moods. His mode of transport. His tantric masturbation from six until twelve every day. And now here was Joanna, my predecessor, telling me what a wonderful man he was.

"He's . . . a conundrum at times," I said. "But I like a challenge."

"I hope you're still using the info pack I made for him. I called it the Andrew Manual. Did it when I went on holiday the first time after starting." She laughed. "I was pretty sure the temp thought I was joking when I handed it to her."

"The Andrew Manual? If only there was such a thing."

For the first time, Joanna's smile dropped. "You don't have it?" She glanced at the shelves above the cabinet. "Hmmm. Let me check . . ."

She peered behind the cabinet and then the tiny mouse of a woman heaved the whole thing away from the wall.

"Can I help you—"

"Here!" she said, holding up a lever arch file covered in dust. "Oh good grief, you poor girl, you haven't had this to work with? You must think you're dealing with some sort of eccentric monster." She laughed. "He likes to do things in a certain way. If you look in here, I think I covered most topics." She set the file on my desk and checked her watch. "I'm meeting my husband so I have to go, but if you need anything, do give me a call." She opened the file, grabbed a pen from the pot on my desk, and carefully wrote her phone number on the top right-hand corner of the first page. "It was so lovely to meet you. I'm sorry we can't chat more."

"Thank you. Nice to meet you too," I called after her as she shut the door.

A manual for my enigmatic boss? That had to be worth a perusal. I wondered if it mentioned how many of his assistants he found *very* attractive.

FIFTEEN

Sofia

I'd be lying to myself if I said I wasn't sitting at the bar at Noble Rot, hoping Andrew—or rather, James—was going to walk through that door, sit down next to me and tell me again how attractive he thought I was.

How attractive exactly? *Very.* Never before had four letters sent so many tingles down my spine.

Getting to read Joanna's Andrew Manual this afternoon had been enlightening and intriguing. It confirmed that he didn't like to be disturbed before noon, but didn't say why. It noted that he didn't take cars in London but preferred to walk or take public transport. It detailed lots of things I already knew and plenty of things I didn't, like airline preferences, or when he liked things in hard copy versus when he liked email. It would have been a revelation when I first started, and it was still going to be useful. But it didn't tell me any of the stuff I really wanted to know. It didn't tell me why the barman called him James. It didn't say why he lost it when he got a piece of personal mail at the office. It didn't reveal why the man at the bar seemed so different to the man in the office.

He wouldn't come here again. Last night, after he'd given me the best compliment I'd ever had in my life, he'd rushed off like he'd made a huge mistake. Sure, I'd had guys say more gushing things. A few had even dropped the L-bomb. But there was something about Andrew telling me I was "very attractive." He didn't say what he didn't mean, or waste words on things that weren't necessary. Last night, it had felt like he had to tell me what he thought. And he thought I was *very* attractive.

I couldn't be too happy about James's compliment. Today in the office, it was like it had never happened. Like James and Andrew were really truly two different people, and I was living in that Reese Witherspoon rom-com that hadn't been made but definitely should have been.

"A glass of Barolo," I said to Tony as I slid onto my now-usual stool.

"Coming right up," he said.

As he slid my glass across the bar, the bell on the door chimed. I didn't have to look around to know he was here. I could just tell.

Andrew.

James.

Whoever it was who made me shiver and blush at the same time. The man who could turn my knees to water with a half-second-too-long glance. The man I'd been waiting for.

He slid onto the stool next to mine without a word. I wasn't about to strike up a conversation. If he'd wanted to avoid me, he wouldn't have come here. He must have known there was a chance I'd be here. If it was just a coincidence, he could have taken a seat at a table, or left an empty stool between us.

He wanted to see me.

And if he wanted to talk to me, he was going to have to go first.

Without asking, Tony appeared with Andrew's drink. No ice. No mixer—just straight whatever-it-was. Just like him. Andrew didn't come watered down or altered in any way. He wore his edges like he didn't give a fuck if most people would prefer him a little weaker or easier to swallow.

"How was your day, Sofia?" he asked, not even turning his head to meet my gaze.

I took a beat, letting my heart rate settle before I replied. "Good." It had been. For a change. Listening to Andrew explain something of his philosophy the other night made my day a lot easier. I'd always known the way he treated me wasn't personal, but it felt better now I'd heard from him why he was so . . . lacking the usual niceties of working relationships. And then, when I'd gone to him this evening and urged him to share what he was trying to achieve with Goode—he'd done so. I wouldn't go so far as to say Andrew valued my opinion, but he respected me enough not to simply dismiss me. That was progress.

Had my conversation with James changed his perspective about me the same way it had changed mine about him?

"*Good* seems like an improvement," he said. I took a sip of my wine to drown my smile.

"Yes," I replied. "What about you? How was your day?"

Andrew sighed. "Not good. Being here is . . . better."

I tried to ignore the swirl of heat in my stomach. Maybe he was talking about the fact he could get shitfaced, but I was going to take his statement as a compliment. His day was better because he was with me. Although technically, we'd sat about twenty feet from each other all day. But that wasn't the point. In the office, he was Andrew. The man next to me was James. He clearly didn't want to be Andrew right now. Maybe it was because he wanted to escape the pressures and stresses of the office. Or maybe he didn't want to flirt with someone whose paychecks he signed, but he still wanted to flirt with me.

"I'm glad to hear that," I said.

Whatever the reason Andrew had become James, I was happy to play his game. I didn't have to hate this man next to me for how miserable he made my friend and for how obnoxious he was in the office. Because he was James and not my boss, I could enjoy his compliments and the sight of his rock-hard ass.

"Whisky and the company of a beautiful woman are guaranteed to make even a good day better."

Andrew barely noticed me in the office. James, on the other hand, was full of compliments. James was more relaxed, lighter. He seemed to shoulder less responsibility than his counterpart.

"It's good to blow off steam at the end of a hard day in the office," I said. "It's healthy to shrug off the stress and remove the game face."

"Game face?"

Was that phrase just an Americanism? "You know, the armor we all wear at work. The people we are in the office compared to the people we are . . ." I glanced around the bar. "After dark."

He stayed silent and I wondered if I'd blown it. He didn't want to be called out. He wanted to continue our game, no questions asked. And I hadn't meant to push—I just wanted him to know that I understood why he wanted the separation between Andrew and James. At least, I thought I did.

I shifted to face him. My heart was beating a little faster

and my cheeks flushed like a virgin in an MLB locker room. "For the record, I think you're very attractive."

Our eyes locked. "There's a record?"

I couldn't help but mirror his slow smile. "Well . . . in case there is, that should be on there."

His gaze dipped to my drink, then across to my shirt and down, down, down. And then he licked his lips before turning back to the bar and taking another sip of his drink.

"I'm a Catholic," I said. "A bad Catholic but still, I suppose I just needed to confess."

"What else . . . needs to be confessed?"

Lust growled at the base of my spine. What was he really asking?

"I hoped you'd be here tonight," I said.

He didn't reply. I'd gone too far. Said too much. Silence stretched between us. I shifted back to face the bar and gulped down a mouthful of wine. Andrew might like his edges. Mine could do with some smoothing.

I took a deep breath in and as I exhaled, Andrew leaned closer and whispered into my ear, "I want to take you home and make you come."

My pulse pounded in my ears and my heart thumped across my chest. If I'd been standing, I would have fallen, as I'd lost all feeling in my legs.

My asshole boss wanted to get me naked. And the feeling was entirely mutual.

I slipped off the barstool and pulled on my coat.

"You leaving?" he asked.

"I am," I replied. "And you, James, are taking me back to my place to do every last dirty thing you have got going on in your imagination."

SIXTEEN

Andrew

It was inevitable that I'd end up here. I wasn't sure if it was her body and smile or her attitude and brain that paralyzed my self-control and had me crossing every line in the sand I'd ever drawn. Maybe it was all of it. The entire package. I was here against my own better judgment, but I was here nonetheless. If regret was to follow, I would just have to make sure tonight was worth it. The decision had been made. There was no going back.

It was James she'd invited back here tonight. And for a night, maybe I could be James with her, not Andrew. Not her boss. I was going to press pause on reality. Just for tonight. Even if it led to disaster.

I undid the top button on my shirt as I followed Sofia into her bedroom. She stopped and turned to face me when she reached the foot of her bed. Was she second-guessing herself? She certainly hadn't seemed unsure back at the bar. Far from it.

"Do you have water?" I asked.

She padded to her bedside cabinet and took out two bottles of water and handed one to me. I set my wallet on the bedside table and shrugged off my jacket. "Make sure you're hydrated."

She transferred her weight from one foot to the other and nodded. Her anxiety was clear now—I'd never seen her fidget at the office. She took a couple small sips of the water. I took in a deep breath, and cupped her face, watching her amber-brown eyes as they searched mine. Stroking my thumbs across her cheekbones, I bent and tasted her lips before pulling back.

Eventually she opened her eyes. I slid my hands from her face to her collar, then slipped the buttons of her blouse open, one after another, revealing a white lace bra. The contrast with her olive skin made the sight even more mouthwatering than before, and I pushed her shirt over her shoulders, all the while keeping my gaze on her breasts where they pushed against the lace, straining to be set free.

Next, I peeled off her skirt, revealing long, lean legs. I stepped back to take in the whole picture. With clothes on she was a knockout—sexy, curves in all the right places. But naked? She was a fucking goddess. My cock nudged my fly and I pulled in another breath, steadying myself. This was a marathon, not a sprint.

"Are you inspecting me?" she asked.

"Absolutely. You're gorgeous."

"And I'm almost naked. Whereas you are not."

That was just how I liked it.

I moved to sit on the edge of the bed. "Come here."

After barely a moment of hesitation, she stepped toward me. "Where do you want me?"

I growled in response but added, "Everywhere, but for now, turn around so you're facing away."

She paused and narrowed her eyes slightly. Sofia had a temper, that was clear. I'd never had an assistant who was so very visibly irritated by me. She was outspoken and opinionated and certainly no pushover. It was all part of the attraction. In the office, she didn't seem to understand that she needed to follow my rules. Now I wanted her to comply with my instructions. Whether she knew it yet or not, doing so would be in her own best interest.

She half-lifted one shoulder before turning away. I wrapped my arm around her waist and pulled her against me so she was sitting on my lap.

I gathered her hair to one side, exposing her neck and shoulder, and pressed my lips to hot, smooth skin. She smelled so good—jasmine and musk and magnolia mixed with something completely unique. I brought my arms underneath hers and swept my hands over her taut stomach, cupping her mound over her underwear while pressing kisses to her neck. A woman this sexy needed to be explored. A body like hers demanded it.

She twisted her hips slightly and I smiled into the skin of her neck. Her movement stroked my cock and pushed my hand over her clit.

This was going to be fun.

I stroked the fingers of one hand down the material of her underwear and she let out a breathy sigh. My free hand cupped her breast, my thumb finding her hardened nipple.

I started to push my fingers round in rhythmic circles, her hips mimicking the pattern in constrained, jerky movements. She was trying to steal more than I was offering.

To show her who was in charge, I moved both my hands to her chest, stroking and massaging her breasts. She let her head fall back onto my shoulder and relaxed into me. It wasn't just Sofia who was impatient for more. I yanked down the lace cups of her bra and her breasts overflowed into my hands, heavy and smooth and ripe enough to eat.

She tried to turn, but facing away, I could keep her in place. By the time we were done, she'd be more than satisfied.

It was just going to take a while. In all things, I believed a job well done was never rushed.

She groaned. I rubbed her tight, hard nipples back and forward between my thumb and forefingers, the pressure increasing with every stroke until it was just this side of too much; abruptly, I released her and pressed her thighs wide.

I needed room to explore.

I dragged my fingers around the juncture of her thighs, just outside the elastic of her underwear, then dipped one finger inside.

The rise and fall of her chest became more pronounced as I traced the curves and crevices of her folds, up and down, up and down, up and down. I pushed farther and her wetness coated my finger and I used it to oil my path. I avoided her clit, resisted plunging inside her, and instead stroked her up and down, up and down. She arched against me, then snaked her hand around her back, finding my cock, hard and throbbing and ready for her hands.

That wasn't going to happen. I grabbed her hand and took it from my cock. "If you don't behave, this is going to be even more frustrating for you and even more enjoyable for me."

"Why?" she pleaded.

"Because I said so," I replied. "Take a breath and enjoy this. We're not in a rush."

She relented and her body sagged against me. I resumed my exploration of her. Her wetness had overflowed into her folds now, coating my fingers and inviting more. I grazed my thumb over her clit, in a fast, light movement. She groaned like I'd plunged into her mercilessly.

"You see that?" I whispered. "You're making your underwear all wet. Now that won't do." I hooked my thumbs into her knickers and slid them off her so she was completely bare. "You're so fucking wet for me," I said, sliding my hand over her mound. "I bet I could make you come tonight without even touching you." I started to withdraw my hands.

"No," she whimpered. Her timbre reverberated across my straining cock.

I slid my fingers down and into her, grinding my palm against her clit, holding her in place with my arm around her waist. It would last longer like this—less intense, but more frustrating for her.

"Oh God," she cried out, her hips lifting. "I think I'm going to—"

I removed my hands from her. "Do. Not. Come."

She slumped against me. "Isn't that the point? That's what you told me you wanted to do to me." She tried to turn to face me and I maneuvered her back into position, gaze pointed forward.

"You'll get your orgasm. Just not yet," I replied. She continued to squirm and writhe against me, the friction against my cock starting to trip my concentration and blur my vision. Shit. I needed to move or I was going to be coming on her back like a fucking thirteen-year-old boy.

I hooked under her arms and slid her sideways onto the bed before standing and stripping off my clothes. She propped herself up on her forearms like she was watching a show.

"Nice body," she said, looking me up and down.

I chuckled. "Back at you." I grabbed her ankle and

pulled her pussy flush with the edge of the mattress. This way, I could enjoy her without my dick getting in on any of the action.

She lay back and I pushed her knees wide and took her in from this angle. Fuck, she was delicious and I hadn't even tasted her yet. She was all curves and attitude, receptive and desperate. I couldn't wait a second longer.

I pressed my tongue against her clit and pushed down her folds, firm and controlled, licking her juices and enjoying her heat. I'd managed to ignore this woman in the office, walk past her twice in the bar, but there was something about her attitude and body and mind that was so fucking inexorable I just couldn't leave it alone.

And now I wanted my fill.

She was mine to consume from now until sunrise.

I wanted to feast on her.

Her hips danced this way and that way, trying to fight against the hold of my hands and the push of my tongue, but she wasn't going anywhere. Not yet.

As I plunged my fingers deep and my tongue found her clit, she twisted away. What was she avoiding? The pleasure, or my control of it? I pushed her back into position and splayed my hand over her stomach, pressing the heel of my hand to find her G-spot.

She was so close now. Her sharp movements had stilled, as if the enormity of what was about to happen to her had finally dawned. She was about to have the orgasm of her life. And I was the man who was going to give it to her.

Her breaths came in short puffs and her stomach began to undulate under my hand. She was seconds away.

I rocked back onto my knees. Nope. I wasn't ready. I wanted to feel her contract around my cock. I wasn't going to waste this moment. Every drop of her desire was to be savored.

I grabbed a condom from the bedside table and in less than a second, I was paused at her entrance, taking a breath so I didn't boil over the moment I felt her warmth around me.

"You ready?" I asked. She lay like a tortured kitten on the bed, her long, glossy hair splayed out across the bed, her legs open, her lips reddened by her moans and my teeth. *Christ, I could fuck this woman all night long.*

"*Please!*"

I took a breath, held her gaze and pushed into her. My chest pounded like my heart was trying to be set free but I didn't give into the instinct that told me to fuck her quick and hard—anything to relieve this ache in me.

The expression in her eyes turned from desperation to panic as I slid into her.

I smoothed my palm down her stomach. "You can come now, Sofia."

The panic gave way to relief as she cried out silently, arching her back, her body stiffening as she reached her peak. But I wasn't about to stop there. This beautiful, passionate, entirely infuriating woman deserved more than that.

I was coated in her now, and she was warm, slick, and completely boneless beneath me. I began to thrust.

"Again?" She looked at me, fear mixed with confusion in her gaze.

I reached beneath her bottom, tilting her up so I could get deeper.

"Again," I said. "And again. And again."

At this moment, I couldn't think of a minute in my future when I wouldn't want to be fucking Sofia. I wanted to stay in this room for days, weeks, years, just fucking. She was so soft and perfect—compliant with just the right amount of fervor.

"Oh God."

"Yes, Sofia?" I said in answer, and I thrust into her again and again. "I'm the only god that will help you now."

She arched against me as her orgasm crashed through her body. The feel of her shuddering body against mine slashed through my final tether of control, and I emptied myself into her as deep as I could get.

Breathless and swaying on my feet like I'd drunk a bottle of whisky on an empty stomach, I collapsed next to her. I checked my watch. How long until I had to leave? There wasn't enough time. I couldn't just lie here and recover. I'd stepped over a thousand lines to be with Sofia tonight. I wanted to make the most of her before I had to return to real life.

SEVENTEEN

Sofia

I was learning that even the ambient sounds of expensive restaurants were different from the places I usually went to. First of all, everything was quieter. There was certainly no hum of football commentary coming from screens set over the bar. Instead, light piano music barely played in the background of the Mayfair restaurant where I waited for my father. Waiters glided around the space like they were wearing silent electric ice skates; when silverware accidently met glassware, the distinct sound of crystal rang out in harmony with subtle piano.

I sighed, trying to busy myself with the menu and not think about Andrew or James or whoever it was who made me come over and over last night and then abruptly left just before midnight, as if he were in danger of turning into a pumpkin. It wasn't like I expected us to cuddle afterward, but I couldn't help wondering what happened next. Was that it? When I saw him in the office again, would he pretend he remembered nothing about our unforgettable night together? Would work remain business as usual, but would James slide onto the stool next to me again at Noble Rot and continue our game? London was a hell of a lot more confusing than I'd expected it to be.

I wasn't looking forward to another meeting with my father. The lunch at his house had been intimidating despite Evan and the girls making their best effort to welcome me. Still, I'd felt more out of place than a nun at a rodeo. However, I did leave with a genuine fondness for my father's other family. Things between Des and me had been strained, like picking through a minefield of what I couldn't and shouldn't say. Hopefully today would be better.

At least in a restaurant we were in more neutral territory—although places like this weren't exactly a staple in my life. Maybe it would mean that the gap between us wouldn't feel so much like a canyon today. I needed to find some common ground with him. I didn't have years to get the money my mother needed. The doctor had said that if they didn't operate soon, it might be too late to stop her from having permanent damage a knee replacement wouldn't fix.

"Sofia!" my father's voice rang out from behind me.

I turned and he greeted me with a kiss on both cheeks. It seemed so weird to me that a man who should know me better than anyone greeted me like he'd known me forever when we were pretty much strangers.

He sat and ordered something I didn't catch from the hostess, then turned to me. "Thank you so much for coming." He smiled as if he were genuinely delighted to see me. I couldn't help but wonder why, if he was so happy to have me in his life, he'd never reached out to me. He'd had almost thirty years to find me.

"So how was your week?" he asked. "Managed to see anything of London?"

The only thing I'd seen a lot of was my boss's naked body. But I wasn't about to confess that.

"Not much. My job is pretty demanding. My boss is very busy. So I have weekends but mostly, I'm exhausted. Tomorrow, I'm going to take myself off to see some sights." I wasn't sure if that was true. Quite honestly, I wanted to spend the day in my PJs, talking to Natalie on the phone and breaking down the latest episode of *Real Housewives of New Jersey*.

"Andrew Blake still treating you okay?"

"Yup. Just a few weeks into it. But so far so good." Yes, Andrew was an epic dick, but he also *had* an epic dick. It wasn't like the sex made up for how he was in the office, but the James thing and the way he'd been at the bar, the way he was when we were in bed . . . It made him a little more intriguing. He wasn't just an asshole. He was a compelling asshole.

"He has a reputation for being ruthless. Does he treat you well?"

Images of Andrew naked, between my legs, pushing into me, over me, flashed in my brain.

"Yup," I managed to squeak out. "Well, truth be told, he's abrasive and rude, but nothing I can't handle."

A small grin pushed at the edges of his mouth. "I'm glad to hear it."

I shrugged. "I think he appreciates me. He just buries it deep. Lucky for me, I inherited a killer work ethic from my mom. She worked three jobs when I was young." I clammed up when I realized what I'd said. I'd forgotten who I was talking to. Shit, I needed to get the lid back on this can of worms immediately. Everything I said was true, but that wasn't the point. The last thing I wanted to do was to make

Des feel uncomfortable. That wasn't going to encourage him to get out his checkbook.

"A strong work ethic is important," he said. "It's something I worry about with Bella and Bryony. They have so much, they need something more than necessity to drive them. My father always drilled it into me that nothing came for free. Everything was to be worked for."

Nothing came for free? I was pretty sure that great big house full of flower prints and chandeliers was inherited. But I didn't say anything. What would be the point?

"Yup, well it's definitely easier to be motivated when you need to put food on the table and pay the electric bill."

Des nodded slowly and took a sip of the wine I hadn't noticed had been placed in front of us. I'd been too busy wondering if my father understood the definition of irony.

"I have a lot of regrets." He set down his glass and looked me directly in the eye. "Some due to decisions I made, some due to decisions I didn't." He sucked in a deep breath like he was trying to alleviate pain. I was filled with rage at the very idea. He wasn't the victim here. I was. My mom was.

"Like what?" I asked, the Italian blood in my veins jumping all of a sudden.

"Like what regrets do I have?" he clarified. But what I heard was, *"Really? You want to go there?"*

"I don't know. Maybe it would be good to hear them."

Our appetizers arrived and went untouched as my father and I sat in silence for too long to be comfortable.

"I regret not standing up to my father when I told him your mother was pregnant."

This much I knew. My mother had told me that Des's family never wanted anything to do with her, and that he had scurried back to England on his father's orders.

"How old were you?" I asked. I was trying to sound interested but I knew myself better than that. I was bound to seem defensive even in the best-case scenario.

"Twenty. Technically an adult. But . . . my father had a lot of power."

"Because of his money?"

"Partly. And because he was the hub of the family and the family business. I'd always been groomed to take over from him and . . ." He stopped, picked up his knife and fork and took a mouthful of crab.

"I went home to tell my father about the pregnancy and he was very clear. He said I could go back to America and deal with the pregnancy and be with your mother. But he said that doing so would have consequences. I would be cut off from any money he might give me as well as from any contact with my sisters and my mother. Not to mention my future running the family business."

His father—my grandfather—sounded like a real asshole. But Des had been an adult. He was smart, connected, and had his entire future in front of him. He didn't need his father. "So you chose the money," I replied.

Des sighed. "I chose . . . what was familiar. I chose safe."

"For you," I said.

"Yes," he replied. "I put my own needs first. It was selfish and morally unjustifiable, which was why I pushed it away. Pretended it hadn't happened. Bought into my mother's dismissal of your mother as a gold digger."

The hairs on the back of my neck stood to attention, armed and ready for attack. "A gold digger?" I said as calmly as I could manage.

"Of course she wasn't." He slid his hand over mine and I snatched it away. My mother was a beautiful woman who had plenty of men who had promised her a comfortable life in exchange for . . . I cringed at the thought. She'd never sold out. She always put me first and led life on her own terms. The last thing she was, was a gold digger. "I never thought that about her. But my family . . . She never knew how wealthy they were, but my father thought the worst of most people."

"But not Evan," I said.

"I love Evan, of course I do, but she was also acceptable to my family because of who *her* family is."

He was talking like we were living in the Dark Ages.

"So your marriage was . . . arranged?"

"More *encouraged*, because she was suitable."

I gave a half-snort of a laugh. "I'm sure an Italian American woman who grew up in a tenement building in Lower Manhattan wasn't suitable."

He glanced into his lap. "No."

"And they assumed she was after your money. Well, newsflash, she wasn't. Did she ever ask you for anything?"

"I never thought it was about money. We . . . loved each other."

"Did she ever ask you for anything?" I repeated my question. I needed to know he knew who my mother was.

"Never. She even refused the money I offered for—" He cleared his throat. "I'm trying to be entirely honest with you, Sofia."

God, it pissed me off when people expected props for honesty. I dug into my plate of crab, avoiding his gaze.

"I made my choice but I wanted to do something—make it right somehow. I had a small amount of savings of my own left in my American account that I wanted to give to her. I thought maybe she could have . . . a . . ."

"An abortion." I finished for him. My mother had told me he'd offered her a little cash the last time they spoke, but she'd turned it down. My mother was a proud woman so it hadn't surprised me she hadn't taken it, but I'd also resented her for it. Maybe life would have been easier back then if we'd had a little more. But now her refusal made more sense. It was money to get rid of me. There was no way she would have touched it. Not only was my mother Catholic, but she'd always told me that she knew the moment she was pregnant and had loved me from that second, even when I was just a few measly cells. That knowledge had always made me feel safe—completely sure of her unconditional love for me.

"I'm sorry," he said.

I didn't blame him for wanting her to get an abortion. They were young and I was in no way planned. What I had a problem with was that if she chose not to have the abortion, where was the money?

"I was just trying to do *something* and your mother—"

I closed my eyes, trying to shut out the fact he was talking about her. He had no right to. She was a thousand times the person he would ever be.

"She chose to keep her daughter."

"She did. And she's done a great job bringing you up."

I nodded. "She has. But it was hard. And she . . ." My mother wouldn't want me to be talking to Des, let alone describing how we'd suffered. How she'd sacrificed her life for me. She would bat away my questions and tell me there was nothing on earth she would rather do than raise me to be a strong, independent woman. What was I doing here? She would rather cut off her leg than take money from the man who sat opposite me.

"I think I should leave," I said, rooted to my seat, wanting to go and figure out these tangled, confused feelings. Meeting my father and getting to a point in our relationship where I could ask him for money was meant to be like a job. A mission. Get in, get what I wanted, get out. I'd obviously been naïve, but I honestly hadn't expected to enter an emotional maelstrom. I'd always managed to keep thoughts about my father in a box tucked safely away in an abandoned corner of my mind. There was no need to open that box because he wasn't part of my life. My mother was my parent. She loved me. That's all that mattered. My father had been nothing but a sperm donor. But being here in front of him changed things. Now I wanted to understand how he could have walked away from a child—*his* child. Me. I sort of understood that at twenty he didn't have his shit together and didn't want to go against his family. But at some point, he'd become a man.

"I'd really like you to stay," he said. "I know that's a lot to ask. But I'd like to get to know you more."

He'd had a long time to try to get to know me.

"Just tell me one thing," I said. "You left the US at twenty and went back to your family. I get it." I shrugged. I had sympathy for a boy who got a girl pregnant and had his family put pressure on him to cut her off. Not that I excused his behavior, but I kind of got it. "But you grew up, you took over the business, you got married, you had kids, your dad died. Somewhere in all that, you got agency over your life. And you still didn't make things right."

The waiters came to take our plates, top up our wine and water, and as they did, I could see the wheels turning in my father's head.

When we were alone again, he said, "I hate myself for being so weak. I still do."

He paused but wasn't done.

"I'd pushed aside what I had done. When we lost

contact, I wouldn't allow myself to think about what had happened."

It wasn't nice what he was saying, but it was honest. I could see it in his eyes.

"I only allowed myself to think about you a few times. First when I hit twenty-five. Second, before I asked Evan to marry me. I'd told her about you. Obviously, I didn't know if you were a boy or a girl, but I felt like I'd betrayed one woman—I didn't want Evan to be the second."

"Three women," I said, pointing a finger at myself.

He nodded. "And then finally when Bella was born, I thought about . . . you, and what you were doing and . . . I thought you were probably better off without me."

I swallowed. Better off without him maybe. But we could have done with his money. *Still* could do with his money.

"When you called, it felt like I was getting a second chance."

If my mother could see me now, she'd call me disloyal. She'd swear at me in Italian and take to her bed. And not just because I was here talking to someone who'd made her life so difficult, but also because I could feel the ice around my heart weaken slightly. He just seemed so nice. Evan was lovely. Their kids were adorable. And what Des was saying made sense. It felt raw and true and heartbreaking.

I didn't come here to like this guy. To understand him. I just wanted his money. I wanted him to pay his debts. If he turned out to be a nice guy who made a huge mistake, I wasn't sure where that left me.

"This is a lot," I said, setting my napkin down on the table and standing. "I need to . . . think." The man in front of me was weak, but he was also human. I hadn't been prepared for that. I'd been prepared for a monster. Someone

I could manipulate and charm to get what I deserved. Now I wasn't sure what I was doing sitting opposite him.

"Of course," he said. "It is a lot. And I don't want to burden you, but I want you to know the truth. It's the least you deserve."

The only problem was, I'd never wanted the truth. I'd never wanted a genuine connection with the man who was my father. I just wanted his money. Now I was being offered something more, I didn't know what to do with it.

EIGHTEEN

Andrew

I drummed my fingers on my desk like some kind of comic-book villain. How long was this going to take? It had been twenty-four hours since I'd submitted the offer to buy *Verity, Inc.* from Goode Publishing. If Bob had any sense at all, he'd snatch my hand off. He wasn't going to get more than this. The magazine was the only business in his group not making money. Other publications that Goode had were subsidizing *Verity*. This was a clean way for Goode to get rid of a loss-making business and collect some cash at the same time. I didn't understand why I hadn't had a call within ten minutes of my offer landing on his desk.

I stood and pushed my hands into my pockets. Maybe Sofia had been away from her desk when the call had come through. I strode across my office and snatched open the door, half expecting to see an empty chair.

"I haven't heard a word," she replied, without even turning around.

"Have you gone to make coffee or to the loo or—"

"I've left my desk twice this morning to go to the restroom but I had Douglas wait by the phone while I was gone. I haven't missed anything."

I fisted my hands and went back into my office, closed the door, and leaned back on it. Like it or not, Sofia was a pretty good assistant. And she knew how bloody important this offer was to me. She'd even diverted her phone when she left last night. I knew there was no point. Bob wasn't going to respond immediately.

Maybe I'd call his lawyer if I hadn't heard anything by close of business.

The terse ring of Sofia's phone was piercingly loud from the other side of the door. My heart thundered in my chest and I sprinted back to my desk to pick up the call if she transferred it through.

Sure enough, just as I sat, my desk phone rang.

I picked it up.

"It's Goode's lawyers. Shall I put them through?"

"Yes," I said, pulling my shoulders back. This was it. The fish was biting.

"Andrew? It's Charles Whithorn." I'd come across Charles a couple of times in my career. He seemed like a decent enough guy.

"How can I help?" As if I didn't know. He'd called to open negotiations. I wasn't expecting Goode to agree to my terms immediately. But if he came to the table, I knew I could close the deal. And here he was, pulling out the chair.

"It's about this offer on *Verity*. Bob has asked me to call but honestly, I don't know why. He's asked me to tell you that *Verity, Inc.* isn't for sale."

My stomach swooped in my mouth. I must have misheard. "What do you mean it's not for sale? If he doesn't like my offer, let's talk."

"Yes. I suggested we come back to you with some kind of counteroffer—a markup of the heads—but he's not interested. Just kept telling me it wasn't for sale."

He must have got this wrong. There was no way the business wasn't for sale. It was loss making and had no strategic direction. It was a disaster. Of course it was for sale. Realistically, they should be pleased to give it away. I'd offered the cash as well as taking on fifty percent of the debt.

"Have you seen the numbers, Charles? *Verity* is not in good shape. I made a good offer."

"I know," he replied. "I don't think the number is important. He just doesn't want to sell it."

I searched my brain for reasons why he wouldn't want to sell. "Is he trying to sell Goode Publishing in its entirety?"

"Not as far as I'm aware, and I tend to see most of what passes across his desk, even if he's not interested."

"Does he have a plan or a new investor or something?"

"I really don't know. Last conversation I had with him about the business, he talked about the importance of profits. I have no idea why he's not interested in your offer."

"You didn't ask him?" What kind of lawyer was this guy if he wasn't advising his client correctly?

"I did. He wouldn't tell me. But you guys have a history, don't you? Why don't you ask him?"

I sighed. "Thanks for the call." There was no point wasting my breath on chitchat. I needed a new plan. So much for Gabriel and Tristan's brilliant suggestion. I chastised myself for cutting him off. There was no need to make an enemy of Charles. He might prove useful. "I might do that. Thank you."

"Just a thought. You know Bob is a people man. He's old

school. He believes in doing business with people he likes."
I wasn't an idiot. Most people preferred to do business with
people they liked. "Well, he's not said anything—not
recently and certainly not in relation to this offer—but I'm
not sure he's your biggest fan."

This wasn't news.

"The feeling is mutual, Charles. But this is business."

"Business or not, no one wants to feel like a fool. You've
been pretty clear that you don't like the way he runs *Verity*.
And now that it's doing so badly, I'm putting two and two
together and guessing that he doesn't want you proving
yourself right."

I nearly dropped the phone—partly out of shock at the
idea that someone would, through pure pride and vanity,
refuse a great offer for a failing business, and partly as the
reality dawned that I wasn't going to get my hands on
Verity. Not if Goode had anything to do with it.

"So he's going to cut his nose off to spite his face?"

"I'm speculating."

"Well, if your speculations are correct, Bob's a bigger
idiot than I already thought he was." I was frustrated but at
the same time, grateful for Charles' insight. "I appreciate
you being straight with me," I said.

"No problem. You know that's how I like to do
business."

I owed Charles. There was no point wasting precious
time and energy chasing after *Verity*. It was hopeless. He'd
saved me some time and left me with a little heartache. It
looked like my grandmother's legacy wasn't salvageable.

NINETEEN

Sofia

Just because Andrew Blake didn't have a twin didn't mean I couldn't pretend he did. It was the only way I could make sense of him being so different in and out of the office. Last time I'd sat on this bar stool, he'd whispered in my ear about wanting to make me come. This morning he'd barked at me because I didn't have the lights on in my office.

He'd fulfilled his promise during our night together. More often than I could remember. And then the next day, it was as if we were two different people and the previous night hadn't happened at all. Part of me thought it was easier. This way, we weren't about to get caught bent over the photocopier at work. But there was also a part of me that wondered what the fuck was going on. The only way to deal with it was to pretend Andrew had a twin brother called James.

I was only on my second sip of my Vivian Leigh when the bell over Noble Rot's door rang. Though a familiar presence loomed in the doorway, I resisted the urge to look him over.

Something in the air shifted. I knew heads turned as Andrew strode between the wooden tables to reach the bar. I didn't blame them. His confidence seemed to envelop him in an almost-visible bubble. The enigmatic smirk he wore was as compelling as the Mona Lisa's. Everyone's focus was on wherever he was going or whatever he was doing.

I couldn't tear my eyes from him. I couldn't judge anyone else for feeling the same.

He slid gracefully onto the barstool next to mine.

"Sofia," he said, his voice a low, deep growl.

"James," I responded, trying to ignore the fizzle of excitement snaking up my spine.

A drink dutifully appeared in front of him. Tony wasn't on today. It was a new guy who clearly knew the drill. I didn't waste time getting to know the new guy. There was only one man I wanted to talk to tonight.

"How was your day?" I asked. I'd wanted to ask him all day about how he was feeling about the offer and what had happened during his phone call with the lawyer I'd put through to him just before he left the office. But I knew better. Andrew didn't do chitchat. Not in the office, anyway. But I knew he wanted to buy *Verity*. I'd never seen him so agitated at work, waiting for the call.

"I don't want to talk about it," he said. He sighed and dragged his fingers through his hair as if tortured. "I shouldn't be here."

Here was just a bar. But . . . a bar where I was. And then it dawned on me: I worked for him. Maybe finding me *very attractive* was against some moral code or something.

"We don't have to talk shop," I said. "Sometimes it's good to keep work in the office."

"Exactly," he said with a fervor that seemed a little misplaced.

He didn't like the idea of me working for him and sleeping with him. That must be why he was keeping up this charade. "You like to keep your home life and work life separate?"

"Completely," he replied.

Maybe he was worried about abusing his power or position. The MeToo movement hadn't just happened in America, and the British were uptight at the best of times. I could assure him that he didn't have anything to worry about on that score—it wasn't as if this was a long-term gig for me. This time next year, there was no way I would still be working at Blake Enterprises. I thought carefully about how to phrase my next sentence without trampling on our game.

"I suppose when I get my real career going, I might feel the same."

The corner of his lip lifted in amusement. "Your *real* career?"

"Yeah. I don't want to be some big-shot's assistant for the rest of my life. I have an MBA and I'm ambitious. I want to *be* the big shot. The job I have at the moment is a means to an end. I have things to figure out in London. Being an assistant isn't *the* job, if you get what I mean."

"You're not looking for a promotion or—"

"I'm looking for a paycheck until I get done what I need to get done. Then I'll go find myself a career."

Andrew's shoulders seemed to lower and his brow smoothed. "Can we get out of here and go back to yours?"

"We can," I said. "When I've finished my cocktail." I wasn't on the clock. I didn't have to ask how high when he told me to jump.

"I'll make you a cocktail when we get to yours."

I shook my head. "A, no you won't. And B, I like this one."

He spun his stool back to the bar and almost snarled, but he didn't argue, which I appreciated. There was something so completely attractive about this alpha male knowing when not to assert his dominance. Still, I found myself drinking my cocktail a little faster than I usually would.

As we stepped out onto the street, he flagged down a cab.

"I bet you're slumming it coming back to Kilburn. Where do you live?" I asked as the taxi pulled out.

"Old Gloucester Street." He said it like I should know what that meant. "It's just around the corner."

Andrew always had the capacity to surprise. "You live around here? I thought all the houses had been converted into offices."

"They have mainly. But some are still residential."

"I expected you to be in some fancy Mayfair apartment, overlooking Hyde Park or something. Not that it's not fancy around here. Just . . . more low key."

He chuckled. "Yeah, fancy is very much not me. More like my friend Joshua. Pre-fiancée anyway."

"You have friends?" I asked. "Consider the shit shocked right out of me."

The corner of his mouth rose in a half smile. "What I have is a very small, close group of friends. What I don't have is an endless list of people I know. Well, I have that too, but I don't consider those people my friends."

For a second, I imagined Andrew with his friends. Was he as serious with them as he was in the work place? Did he swap jokes and talk about . . . soccer? The weather?

"A small group of friends is nice. Natalie and my mom

are my two best friends. And then I have a couple of girls who I met in college that I see regularly. But . . ." What did I want to confess? That my father's abandonment made me distrustful? That would be too deep. Too much. And now that I was talking to my father, I wasn't sure what the foundations of my approach to life had been built on.

"Natalie," he said, almost to himself. He'd never mentioned Natalie before. I'd told him we were roommates and nothing else had ever been said. His mention of her name was the closest we'd ever come to him admitting that he was Andrew and not James.

"She's an amazing friend. Loyal and fun and super clever."

Andrew stayed silent as we continued our journey.

It wasn't like he was actively denying that he'd ever known her, but he wasn't admitting it either. There were lines he wasn't ready to cross, and I had made my peace with that somewhere around my second orgasm the first time we were together.

It was part thrilling, part downright weird.

"I've only had one drink tonight," I said, half to myself as nerves tugged in my stomach. I wasn't sure if it was the thought of being with him again or our pretense that set me on edge.

The cab pulled up to the curb outside my flat and Andrew paid the driver. "Good."

"Why good?" I asked as I pulled my keys from my purse and pushed them into the lock.

"Alcohol deadens the senses."

Jesus, Mary, and Joseph, if that was true, what could I expect out of tonight? Our first night together was all sensory overload. It had felt like I'd given up complete control of my body to him. There was no way I could feel any more when he touched me.

He followed me up the stairs and hung his cashmere coat on the hanger, next to my ancient North Face that I'd found sophomore year in TJ Maxx at a fraction of the full price.

We headed into the kitchen. In a silent exchange, I nodded to the cupboard where I stored my water and he retrieved two bottles for us.

"You're beautiful," he said, handing me one. I gave him a half-smile, wondering whether it was a line so he could get laid—spoiler alert, he didn't need the line—or whether he thought it was true. Andrew was a lot of things, but he didn't seem like the kind of guy who would say something just for the sake of it. If he really thought I was beautiful, then did he think that when we were in the office? Had he had to hold himself back from touching me? It hadn't seemed so. In fact, if I hadn't been at the bar in Noble Rot that first time, I don't think I'd have ever seen him naked. He continued to stand too close to me while I took a mouthful of water before once again taking it from me and sliding it onto the counter. Cupping my face, he swept his thumb over my cheek. "I've been looking forward to this."

Lust tilted the floor, my knees weakened and I swayed a little, just enough to press our bodies together. "Me too."

Without taking his gaze from mine, he pulled his tie free and undid the top two buttons of his shirt before sliding off his jacket. The incidental grazing of my body with his clothes, combined with the intensity of his stare, was like a warning: I needed to brace myself for what was to come.

He began to undress me, starting with the buttons of my blouse, punctuating my gradual disrobing with sweeps of his fingers, a lingering glance or a press of his lips. It was tortuously slow but I knew better than to try to speed things up. Andrew did what he wanted and how. It wasn't that he was disinterested in my pleasure—far from it. He just thought he knew how to get to it better than I did. And maybe he was right.

My blouse discarded, he smoothed a knuckle down my throat and farther, between my breasts, before it hit the lace of my bra. My nipples were straining for his attention and my breaths were coming short and fast. He glanced from my chest and met my eye. That damn smirk was back—a sign, if ever there was one, that he had me exactly where he wanted me. Part of me wanted to roll my eyes, hand him his clothes, and kick him out. But I didn't move. I just waited. Because he might have had me exactly where he wanted me, but I was exactly where I wanted to be. I knew what came next. His tongue, his fingers, the pleasure he teased out of me like he was some kind of magician. His cock, his hips, the thrusts that went so deep, I wondered whether I'd break in two.

I wanted it all.

TWENTY

Andrew

Sofia's olive skin seemed to glow in the soft light of the kitchen and her glossy hair tumbled over her shoulders. There was no doubt she had a bombshell body.

My cock reared against my zip just from looking at her. I knew the anticipation of touching her wasn't going to be a letdown; Sofia was warm and responsive and passionate. When we were together for the first time, I'd expected her temper to get the better of her. I thought she'd be impatient and irritable at my demands. She'd surprised me. And not many people did that.

I don't think I'd ever come so hard.

"Turn around and hold on to the marble," I said, guiding her hips around so she faced away from me and grabbed on to the kitchen counter.

She bowed her head and tried to steady her breathing.

I bet she was already wet. Already so needy.

I stood behind her, bracing my hands outside of hers,

pressing my front to her back. She shifted her hips, grinding herself back against me.

I chuckled and whispered into her ear. "You need to pace yourself. It's going to be a while before you get my cock."

She groaned and I slid one hand down her stomach and over her mound.

"So greedy." Holding my fingers together, I started to rub big circles over her slit. She pushed against me, trying to feel my fingers in her folds. I moved away. She snapped her head around to look at me.

"You're so wound up," I said. "We've only just started."

She turned. "I want to suck you," she said.

I nodded. "I know. Later. Now you need to turn back around so I can make you feel good."

"I don't think I'm going to last long. It's almost like the less you touch me, the more I want it."

I raised my eyebrows. "That's the point, Sofia."

She sighed and turned back around, placing her hands deliberately on the counter. She remained upright, though, and I curled one arm around her waist, keeping her in place as I slid my hand back down. I allowed just one finger to slip between her folds, giving her just a little more.

"Sex is more than fucking." If it hadn't been for her heat, her wetness, the short, sharp breaths in my ear, I might have been able to hold back. But I yearned for more of her, and I pushed a second finger into her folds and began to stroke, forward and back. "Sex is about feeling, anticipation. About understanding."

She moaned and her fingers curled against the countertop.

"I want to drive you to the brink . . . and pull you right

back. Over and over and over. I'll understand your body then. I'll know exactly how much I can touch, press, suck before you go under. I'll know what you like and how your body responds, and you'll know too." I slid another finger inside her and grazed her clit with my thumb.

She grabbed my wrist. "I'm so close."

I stilled and smiled against the skin of her neck. She got it. Despite her protestations, she wanted it to be as good as we both knew it could be.

"So quickly, Sofia. You're riled up tonight."

She sighed, her body sagging against mine. "For you."

Blood rushed to my flint-hard cock and I swallowed. *Shit*, this woman.

My fingers went back to work, pushing and circling, slow at first and then faster and faster. Sofia's body tensed and I removed my hands. "Breathe," I instructed.

She inhaled deeply, once and then twice, pushing her orgasm down and away. Moments like this were meant to last.

"I'm shaking," she said, holding her trembling hand up to show me. "I feel . . ."

"Lightheaded," I finished her sentence for her. "It's the adrenaline mixed with the anticipation. Take a small sip of water."

As she took her glass, I removed my shirt. Time to switch things up. If I touched her again, however softly, she was going to explode. And I wanted to be inside her when that happened. She watched hungrily as I stripped. I enjoyed her attention on me, my cock rearing under her scrutiny.

"Now do I get to taste you?" Her expression was pleading and I wasn't about to deny her.

I pulled out a chair from the dining table opposite the kitchen island and took a seat.

Sofia didn't take her eyes off my dick as she followed me over and knelt at my feet.

"I don't want a hand job," I said. "I want to feel your mouth, your tongue, and the back of your throat, and that's it. You hear?" If she wanted to suck me then I wanted to be sucked. I never enjoyed a blow job that was more hands than mouth. I didn't like people who didn't commit to whatever they were doing. And I didn't like women who *pretended* to like giving blow jobs. My rule in life was to do something properly or don't fucking bother.

She nodded while securing her hair in a thick knot at the top of her head. A nice touch. Smoothing her hands up my thighs, she caught my crown between her lips and I exhaled.

I bet Sofia didn't know how to give a bad blow job.

A pang of jealousy caught in my chest and it interrupted the feel of Sofia's tongue, just for a second. I frowned. It was a new sensation for me to think about anything when a woman had my dick in her mouth, let alone other lovers she may have been with. Jealousy? That was definitely new. It felt primal and instinctive. But why would I feel jealous? I wasn't some neanderthal who only fucked virgins. I liked women who enjoyed their sexuality. So what was my problem?

The drag of Sofia's almost too-sharp teeth brought me back to the moment. Fuck, she was good.

She glanced at me, and as her eyes met mine, I had the urge to kiss her.

"Sofia," I said, stroking her cheek.

She pulled back, looking at me like a student about to get a critique of their work from a favorite teacher.

"Come here."

I encouraged her to her feet and then drew her toward me. She straddled me, the heat of her rubbing against my hard length. I cupped her head and drew her toward me, snaking my tongue into her mouth and kissing her.

This.

This.

This was what I wanted.

The feel of her entire body against mine, her arms around my neck, her breath mixed with mine.

I relaxed into our kiss all lips and tongue and passion. It felt good. Right. Like the final piece of a jigsaw that had just been found under a wine glass. We clicked together. I felt complete satisfaction, and I wasn't even inside her yet.

Instinctively our bodies began to move together and I grabbed the condom I'd pulled out of my wallet when I'd undressed.

She shifted back on my lap as I rolled it on. Our eyes fixed on each other, she stood astride me as I held my cock at the base. Without breaking our stare, she lowered herself onto me. I gripped her hips and tried not to explode at the friction of her tight cunt.

Fuck. Fuck. Fuck.

"You feel good," she said.

I nodded, unable to add to what she'd said. Saying it was "good" was like saying it rained in England. It was obvious. And the truth. But it was also the biggest understatement I'd ever heard. This wasn't *just* good. She wasn't *just* beautiful.

Fucking Sofia deserved a fireworks display and a sixty-piece orchestra. I needed to take out an advert in the *Times* to tell people how completely fantastic I felt when this woman was naked and on my cock.

I enjoyed sex. Savored it. Made it a priority in my life. But this? Sex with Sofia? I needed to do nothing else but fuck her. The feel of her made me want to give up my job, take her to some deserted island and just fuck her, all day every day.

I began to shift her hips. Slowly, back and forward, in small intense movements so I could make this last. This woman had endured me torturing her until now; it felt selfish to take my orgasm as quickly as I could. I had to fight every urge to flip her over the table and fuck her into oblivion.

"I don't know how long I'm going to last. I'm so full up with you. It's like you're . . ."

I began to move her faster now. Knowing that we were both so close, I couldn't think of a reason to hold back. Her hips moved in perfect rhythm; my cock plunged in and out; my fingertips pushed into her flesh.

We locked eyes.

"It's like you're . . . in my head," she said.

I licked up her throat and took her bottom lip between mine. Our tongues crashed together as she began to climax. I wrapped my arms around her and pulled her close as I erupted into her, the vibrations of our orgasms mixing and binding us closer together.

As we floated back down from the high, the rise and fall of our joined chests began to slow. We sat there with our cheeks pressed together, and I refused to let her go. I wanted to eek out as much from this moment as possible.

"What was that?" Sofia whispered.

I didn't know.

Intense wasn't a good enough description. It was as if the tectonic plates under us had shifted and swallowed us whole. She moved her head and put a small kiss on my shoulder. I closed my eyes, drinking in the perfection of such a small, intimate gesture. It was just what I wanted in that moment.

We stayed that way, embracing, our bodies only moving with our breaths.

"We should move at some point," Sofia said eventually.

"I suppose." I trailed my fingers down her spine.

She looked at me like she wanted to say something but stopped herself, then stood and headed toward the bathroom I remembered down the hall.

I liked that she didn't try to cover up. She just wandered naked to the hallway.

I tipped my head back and reality started to seep back into my thoughts. I was back to square one as far as *Verity, Inc.* was concerned. Maybe I'd go for a run tomorrow morning and try to come up with some new ideas.

"What are you thinking about?" Sofia asked as she reappeared in the doorway.

"You." I stood and headed to the sink to get a drink. "And work."

"Well, me, I know. Tell me about work, James."

I took out a glass and let the tap run ice-cold before I filled it. "I want to buy a company and the owner of it doesn't want to sell." That was the crux of it.

She took a long gulp of her water and I watched her throat as she swallowed. Fuck, everything this girl did was sexy. "He doesn't want to sell or he doesn't want to sell to *you*?"

"He doesn't want to sell to me."

She tilted her head. "So you can't just pretend to be someone else?"

"It's more complicated than that."

She moved around the kitchen island toward me.

"Then make it simple," she said, holding up a condom and placing it on the counter in front of us. She trailed her fingertips around my waist, took my glass from my hand and set it on the draining board. Apparently, she was ready for more.

"Even if I was to set up a Cayman company or disguise in some way where the money was coming from, the owner is old fashioned. He wants to know who he's doing business with. He wants to negotiate face to face—not with some faceless corporation."

She pressed a kiss against my chest. "Then set up your Cayman company and send someone in on your behalf. Get them to pretend to be the buyer."

My cock was responding to her lips and my brain started whirring at her idea. "I don't think it would work," I said. "You can tell a lawyer is a lawyer or an accountant is an accountant a mile away. And the other people in my life who are capable of conducting negotiations against a man like Goode are too busy with their own businesses."

"Really?" she asked, as she took my cock in her fist. "There's no one in your office other than a lawyer or an accountant who's capable of negotiating to buy a business?"

She scooped up the condom, tore it open and, expertly rolled it onto my hard cock.

What was she saying? My mind was starting to cloud over with lust, but was she suggesting *she* pose as the buyer for *Verity*?

She turned around and leaned over the marble counter. All at once, her arse was the only thing I could focus on. "What do you have to lose?" she said.

I trailed my fingers between her legs, feeling for her arousal. I wasn't disappointed. She was dripping with anticipation and need. I nudged at her entrance, coating the crown of my cock with her wetness.

Slow and steady, I pushed into her, relishing the pressure, the drag, the complete fucking perfection of it. She started to tremble under my hands as I drove deeper and I hooked my arm under her, steadying her just as her knees buckled.

"Breathe," I whispered in her ear.

I pulled out just as slowly and then pushed in harder this time, getting as deep and as far as I could go. The curve of her back was so inviting, I wanted to lick long, soft strokes down its length. Her round, firm arse felt like it was made for my hands. "Sofia," I whispered, calling for the woman surrounding me. "Sofia."

"It's too . . ." Sofia's body began to shudder, her legs began to shake, and she slumped forward onto the counter as she tightened around me. "I'm sorry," she said.

She had no reason to apologize.

Gently, I moved and turned her around so she was facing me. "Don't ever apologize to me for coming. Don't apologize to anyone." There was that twinge of jealousy in my gut.

I mentally brushed it aside.

"I know you like to torture me a little more . . ." She lowered her gaze like she was embarrassed.

I lifted her chin so she was looking at me. "I enjoy drawing it out and making you wait, and I enjoy feeling you not being able to control your orgasm even when I've only been inside you a few seconds." It was . . . beguiling how much she wanted to please me. It felt so out of character. Like this was an unseen, private side to herself that she didn't show very often.

"Yeah, you do good work, Andr—"

Before she could finish what she was saying, I grabbed one of her legs and pulled it up over my hip and thrust into her again. "The next time, I'll see it in your face before you lose control."

I pulled her onto my straining cock, sinking with relief as she, once again, surrounded me. It felt like this was how it was meant to be. We fit so perfectly. It felt like this was exactly right.

Bending my knees, I thrust up into her again and again and again. She had one arm behind her, the other on my chest. I was overcome by the thought that I didn't want this to be the last time I fucked this woman. But if she didn't turn up at the bar again, what would I do? Be forced into a situation I didn't want to address. At the moment I was teetering on the edge of my hard and fast rule about the separation of work from anything personal. So far, being James meant I was still playing by the rules. But did it really matter what she called me? This didn't feel like pretending.

She moaned and slid her hand up to my shoulder, then curled her fingers around my neck as she arched back, thrusting her perfect breasts toward my greedy mouth. I bent and grazed my teeth over her nipple, and she screamed in surprise. "We both know how to use our teeth, Sofia." I grinned up at her, then took her breast in my mouth, sucking and flicking one nipple and then the other.

My climax growled awake and I stilled for a second. I was ready to fuck her as hard and as deep as I'd ever been. I shifted us so she was over the counter and then braced my hands either side of her hips. "Are you ready?"

"For anything."

I nodded and thrust into her. Over and over, trying to ignore the sway of her breasts as our bodies slammed together mercilessly. I held onto her hips, making sure I could go as deep as possible, to that part of her that she kept hidden, that I wanted to fuck into the light. Again and again and again, until I saw that look of wonder in her eyes, until I felt that stillness in my body, until I could allow myself to let go that final time, thrusting every ounce of me into her.

TWENTY-ONE

Andrew

I'd thought about nothing all weekend other than the feel of Sofia's pussy when she came and whether or not she could pull off the acquisition of *Verity, Inc.*

Would it work?

Could I trust her?

Would Goode be taken in by her?

The questions went around and around in my head like a carousel, but still I didn't have an answer. It seemed ludicrous that I'd send in Sofia, who I'd barely known a month, to negotiate the most important deal of my career—no, my life. From what I'd seen of her, she was capable, clever, and confident. But that didn't mean she could negotiate against Bob Goode. And it very definitely meant that I shouldn't be sleeping with her.

For years I'd been fastidious in separating my work and social lives. At the moment, my relationship with Sofia out of the office existed in some weird no-man's-land between the office and home; as much as I knew I should keep things professional, there was something about her that made me want to show up at Noble Rot and be James for as long as she'd have me.

My mobile buzzed on my desk and I glanced at the screen. Unknown number. I wouldn't normally pick up, but I needed a distraction.

"Andrew Blake."

"Hi, Andrew, my name's Aryia Chowdhury and I'm writing a book." I was just about to cut her off and when she added, "About your grandmother. I should correct myself. I'm writing a book about women of the last century who tried to shape their respective industries, and I'm planning on including your grandmother's founding of *Verity, Inc.*, as well as your mother's stewardship."

My hand gripped the phone so hard, it was a wonder the screen didn't splinter.

"I was hoping I could set up a meeting to talk about it with you."

"What was your name again?" I wanted to get a complete background check on whoever was writing about my grandmother.

She repeated her name and then offered more information. "I'm a freelance writer. I've written for most of the broadsheets but most often contribute to *The Guardian*. *Verity, Inc.* fascinates me because of its drastic transformation since it was founded."

My stomach began to curdle. I didn't need to hear this from a perfect stranger. And I certainly didn't want a perfect stranger telling thousands of other perfect strangers how something so great had turned into the laughable publication *Verity* was today.

"Do you follow the fortunes of *Verity* and Goode

publishing now? Do you feel any familial connection to the publication?" she asked.

"Is this an interview?" I snapped. I had no interest in being interviewed on the hoof. I needed more information about what this Aryia Chowdhury was doing, and what she intended to say about my family.

"Sorry, no, I got carried away. Could we arrange a time to speak? Perhaps I could take you out to lunch or come to your office or—"

"You'll need to speak to my assistant. How did you get this number anyway? Never mind." I didn't know why I was asking. Everything was for sale. "Call my office and they'll set something up."

"I look forward to it," she said, just before I hung up.

This was the last thing I needed. My grandmother hadn't been dead a year, and now this writer was poking around, ready to tell the world how her work had been wasted because of all that *Verity* had become. It was bad enough that *I* knew how my grandmother, mother, and *Verity*'s important, groundbreaking work had been pushed out to make room for page upon page of celebrity non-stories. Now whoever read this book was going to think my grandmother's life had been wasted.

I sighed and swung my chair around so I could see out the window. My grandmother's passion had been the work *Verity, Inc.* had done. She'd loved it and always been so full of life whenever she talked about it. I didn't want anyone who read about her not to know that. She'd been passionate and dedicated—a trailblazer. Meanwhile, the people behind her were working hard to cover up the path she'd plowed.

I'd have to talk to Aryia. Tell her what the real story was. I needed to be the person who made sure my grandmother's legacy was one of honor and honesty. Of uncovering the truth and pushing for answers. In short, her mission in life had been the exact opposite of everything her magazine had become.

My heart hung in my ribcage like a hunk of concrete.

I stood and stalked across my office and swung open the door. "Get Douglas. I need both of you in here."

Sofia glanced at the clock, probably wondering why I'd finished my "yoga practice" before midday. At least she had the good sense not to say anything.

Less than two minutes later, a grumble of voices was followed by my office door opening and Douglas and Sofia appearing.

They took seats opposite my desk.

"Douglas, you need to get this checked out by the lawyers, but we're going to set up an offshore company owned by some other companies in a country where you don't have to disclose owners or directors. We're going to add layer after layer after layer of companies and directors until no one can trace the original company back to me. Then, when we have that in place, the original company is going to make an offer to buy *Verity*. When Goode requests a meeting—as we know he will—Sofia is going to pose as the buyer."

I glanced at Sofia and then at Douglas and then back at Sofia. Her expression was blank.

"It will be expensive," Douglas said.

I didn't reply.

"And complicated," he added.

"I want it done within the week."

"Then we better get to work," Sofia said. "Douglas, if you work on the structures, I'll work on the offer letter so it looks completely different from last time. I'll also rent office space, organize phone lines, and set up what looks like a viable office. I'll get business cards, an internet address, and I'll update my LinkedIn page. Luckily, I didn't update it when I started working here, so they won't be able to trace me. If it's okay with you, Andrew, I'll use my real name. The fewer the lies, the better. Right?"

Was it me or did she emphasize the word "real"?

"Sounds like you've thought of everything," I said. "I want to submit an offer by the end of the week." Douglas and Sofia stood and headed to the door. "And if Aryia Chowdhury calls to request a meeting, set something up but push it out a couple of weeks."

If I had my way, I'd have signed contracts with Goode to buy back *Verity* before I ever sat down for the interview.

TWENTY-TWO

Sofia

I thought I'd thought of everything, but now that the cell phone I'd put in the name of Andrew's shell company was ringing, I panicked. I didn't have a receptionist to answer the call on my behalf.

"Breathe," I heard Andrew's voice say in my head. I answered the phone. It was a cell number. No one expected a receptionist to answer a cell number.

"Sofia Rossi." Unlike Andrew's gruff, bordering on rude telephone manner, I tried to sound bright and confident.

"This is Mr. Goode's office." I knew that already. They were the only one with the number. "I'm calling to set up a meeting between you and Mr. Goode."

"Wonderful. Let me bring up my diary. When is Mr. Goode free?"

"At the moment he's in the U.S. on business and he's not expected back until the twenty-second."

The twenty-second? Could she mean three weeks away? Andrew was impatient for this deal to be done. He'd been stalking the office like a caged lion since we'd put in the offer yesterday. There was no way he'd survive three weeks. As far as he was concerned, he'd wanted to submit on Friday—but I'd convinced him we should wait for the office space we were leasing to be furnished, just in case Goode investigated more closely.

Waiting three weeks just wasn't an option.

"I'm in New York on business this month," I said. "Perhaps we could coordinate something while I'm over there?"

"Please hold."

Would Andrew kill me for organizing a meeting three thousand miles away? No, this was the right thing to do. He'd gone to so much time, money, and effort to set up this shell company.

I held for what seemed like hours before Mr. Goode's assistant came back.

"Mr. Goode is in New York on Friday. Are you available?"

I held the phone away from me so she couldn't hear my panicked breathing or the thump of my heartbeat telling me I was an idiot for doing this without Andrew's permission.

"I'm free for lunch, if that works?"

"He'll be available at twelve. Please send details of the restaurant."

Shit.

It was only ten thirty, but I had to interrupt Andrew's Ashtanga practice. If I was about to get fired for agreeing to a meeting on another continent, I'd rather know now.

I knocked on the door and just went straight in. I glanced the length of his office, half expecting to see his tight ass in downward dog, before finding him behind his desk, just like he always was.

"I just got a call," I said.

He stayed completely silent while I told him I'd managed to get a lunch in the diary on Friday. In New York.

"So book our flights," he responded.

"You want to come too?" I hadn't thought past hoping Andrew didn't lose it for agreeing to meet Goode in the US. Logistics hadn't crossed my mind. We were going to travel together? Was he going to ignore me the entire time? Or was James, the man who existed whenever Andrew was out of the office, going to accompany me? I supposed I should just be grateful that he hadn't yelled for agreeing to a meeting across an ocean.

"Of course. This is my deal. My money. This *should* be my meeting. I'm not going to leave you to wing it. We'll need to prepare. Debrief and regroup. This is good news, Sofia. But it's only the beginning."

I grabbed on to the back of one of the visitor chairs opposite his desk to steady myself.

Sofia.

Andrew had never called me by name before.

James had. Usually when he was naked and fucking me.

Hearing it from Andrew's lips seemed to tilt the floor and left me unsteady on my feet.

Normally I could separate Andrew from James without any trouble. Andrew was moody, monosyllabic, and downright rude most of the time—even if he had a nice ass and a sexy smirk. James was . . . different. He was considered and deliberate in everything he did. He knew what he wanted and how he wanted me. He was sultry and sensuous and seemed to have put a spell on my vagina.

James saw me. Craved me. Cared about my pleasure.

I wanted to go to New York with James. But I'd be booking a plane ticket for Andrew.

TWENTY-THREE

Sofia

He'd barely said a word to me for the last nine hours.

We'd travelled to Paddington by cab to take the Heathrow Express to the airport. When he first saw me, he'd asked for his tickets. I'd taken it as a good sign. Things were going to warm up between us and we'd have a productive working relationship.

But no. He'd managed to stay silent almost our entire trip, his head buried in his phone, or *The Economist* or *The Financial Times*. I was surprised he didn't have eye strain.

As we arrived at the hotel check-in desk, I turned to ask him for his passport, only to find him already holding it out for me. I pulled my mouth into a sarcastic smile. "Thank you," I said and turned to check us both in. Andrew kept tap, tap, tapping on his phone. No doubt he was up to level three hundred now on Clash of Clans. There was no way he was doing anything useful on that phone.

When the receptionist saw Andrew's passport, she shifted gears entirely.

"Good to have you back with us, Mr. Blake, sir," she said, lifting up on tiptoes to make sure he heard from behind me.

He turned and nodded in her direction. Within seconds, an older gentleman had arrived at Andrew's side.

"Mr. Blake. Delighted to have you stay with us again. Can I accompany you to your room?" He glanced at me. "Your rooms."

"Thank you, Mr. Parker," Andrew replied, sliding the phone into his pocket.

Andrew hadn't lost the use of his tongue then. Apparently it was just me he didn't talk to.

"Miss Rossi," Mr. Parker said as he led us to the elevators, "is it your first stay with us?"

My first stay at the New York Mandarin Oriental? No sirree, I like to come as often as possible, whack down my American Express Platinum card and reeelax. "It is," I replied. "New York is home, so I don't usually need a hotel."

"A native," he said, grinning. "Well, welcome. We hope you enjoy your stay with us. I'm the hotel manager. If you need anything, just ask for me." He handed me his business card.

I'd not stayed in hotels very often, but I was wise enough to know that hotel managers didn't escort every guest to their room.

Natalie couldn't have known about the Andrew Manual. She would have told me. Thank goodness Andrew had a birthday before we travelled to New York and Joanna had found it. It had really helped me make travel arrangements. It told me that Andrew only flew British Airways first class and listed his hotel preferences. That's how I'd ended up sipping a glass of champagne and watching *The Hangover* in my own personal "suite" thirty thousand feet up. And it's how we'd ended up here. I couldn't wait to tell my mom, but I wasn't going to get to see her until just before we flew back tomorrow afternoon. I knew I had to focus until after I'd seen Bob Goode. Then we could catch up for a couple of hours.

"I've taken the liberty of upgrading you to your usual Presidential Suite," Mr. Parker said. "And Miss Rossi, we hope you'll be comfortable next door in the Oriental Suite."

Shit, Andrew had clearly changed his preferences slightly since Joanna left. The manual didn't say anything about the Presidential Suite. I should have thought to ask before I booked.

Wait, what did he say? Next door? To my boss?

"Oh, I'm happy with the original room I booked—"

Mr. Parker raised his hand to stop my objection. "We insist. It's always a delight to have Mr. Blake to stay, and it's nice to welcome home a native New Yorker."

We exited the elevator to find just two doors in front of us. Were our two suites taking up the entire floor? That was crazy. This hotel was huge.

"Your bags are already in your rooms. Mr. Blake, we have George unpacking for you. You know that he is available to you twenty-four hours a day. Can I arrange for some food to be sent up? George can prepare your drinks."

Who was George? Apparently, some kind of multi-tasking Superman who knew Andrew's likes and dislikes a hell of a lot better than I did.

"I'm fine, thank you, Mr. Parker. You and your team always make me feel at home and I'm grateful." He shook the manager's hand. Mr. Parker opened the Presidential Suite door and Andrew disappeared behind it.

Mr. Parker turned to me. "We can arrange butler service for you too, if you'd like?"

I tried not to laugh. "Thank you, but I quite like to unpack myself."

"Can I show you around your room?"

"Honestly, I just want to get into the shower and turn on some American TV. I've missed it."

Mr. Parker smiled and gave a little bow. "Very well. I'm at your beck and call. Enjoy your stay, Miss Rossi."

I slipped into my suite and closed the door behind me. I might be home, but this wasn't the New York I'd come to know and love for almost thirty years.

After a shower so long and so hot I was surprised I didn't shrivel up into a dehydrated version of myself, I called my mom. She delivered a brief lecture on how I should have made it across town to see her this evening despite an eight-hour flight and the obligations of the job paying me to be here. I wasn't sure if I'd have enough time after the meeting to see her, but I promised to make it up to her somehow. Then I dried my hair.

I should have been exhausted, but what I wanted to do was hear some American voices and drink a Manhattan in Manhattan.

I was in New York. Back home. And that gave me more energy than I knew what to do with.

I applied a dash of makeup, slipped on a casual shift dress, and headed down to the bar. There were a thousand places I'd been to in this city, but I'd never made it to the hotel bar in the Mandarin Oriental.

I wanted to try it.

And I wanted to see if James was there, too.

TWENTY-FOUR

Andrew

I saw her as soon as I entered the MO Lounge. She was chatting to the barman, which caused a now-familiar pang of jealousy to twist in my gut.

I didn't want conversation. I'd just gotten off the phone from Tristan, who was also in town. We'd agreed to meet up tomorrow night. I didn't want to drink in the Manhattan skyline; I had a better view from my room.

So why was I here?

I strode across the lounge and slipped onto the barstool next to Sofia.

She turned to me, entirely unsurprised by my arrival.

"Good evening," she said. "My name is . . . Bianca."

She was ridiculous.

The barman slid a glass of my favorite Barolo in front of me. I thanked him with a nod.

"How do you do that?" she asked. "It's like everyone knows who you are and what you want. Is it Jedi mind tricks? Is that the secret?"

"If it was, I'm pretty sure my assistants would have a better turnover rate."

"Oh, he speaks."

I took a sip of wine while Sofia continued to complain and gripe over . . . I wasn't quite sure what exactly. Perhaps she was nervous about the meeting tomorrow. Maybe being back here triggered something for her. Whatever it was, I didn't appreciate the sarcasm. And I didn't appreciate the non-stop noise. She was still in work mode.

I was not.

"Can we not do this?" I asked her. I wanted to relax. I wanted half a chance of sleep tonight. I didn't want to be berated about my lack of social skills. I hated travelling. It was far too easy to waste a day doing nothing when you were in transit, so in every moment that I wasn't walking from one designated area to another, I ensured I was doing something productive—emails, reviewing research, reading articles. Anything but inane chitchat and a rewatch of *Mamma Mia!* Once was more than enough.

"Do what?"

I didn't respond and continued to smooth my fingers down the stem of my glass. Sofia was clever. She could figure out what I was saying if she shut up long enough to think about it. She had a combination of cognitive, social, and emotional intellect that I didn't come across often. Most really clever people couldn't hold a conversation at a party. Those who could read people often couldn't focus on technical details. Sofia had the rare ability to do it all. She just needed to refine her skills, and she'd be unstop-pable. The priority was surely learning to control that mouth.

An image of her on her knees in front of me, my cock in her mouth, slipped into my mind. I glanced over at her and she met my gaze; it was as if she knew exactly what I was thinking.

"Can we go upstairs?" she asked. Her tone had shifted. Like someone had popped her bad mood like a balloon. "I need to . . . blow off some steam."

I'd always been so good at separating my business from my personal life. I made my mistakes big and early and I learned from them, and was determined not to repeat them. But Sofia had put a spanner in the works. I probably should have left when she came into Noble Rot that first evening. I was just . . . amused by her irritation at me. It was entertaining to learn what it was my assistants hated so much about working for me.

I should have left her to it, but something kept me there until the very last moment that I had to leave for a drink with Gabriel. When it came time to pay, I didn't know what it was that made me want to reveal myself to her—to let her know I'd been listening all along. It was only fair. And I wanted her to know that she didn't need to worry. Maybe I was unreasonable. Maybe I was an arsehole in the office. Maybe I was just focused and I expected the same from everyone else. Whatever it was, when I turned to her and she'd heard the barman call me James, it was like she wasn't the employee who worked right outside my office door every day. In that moment, she was a beautiful woman who'd had a bad day. A woman who wore her passion on her sleeve— and I couldn't resist the urge to learn just how deep that passion ran. At least I'd had the good sense to leave her fully clothed. That first time, anyway.

And then when she was there the following night . . . Game over. It had left me with no choice. I had to see her eyes grow hooded as she approached orgasm. I wanted to feel her shudder underneath me as I fucked her. I wanted to smooth my hands over her soft, warm skin and feel her fingers in my hair.

I should have resisted.

I should have walked right past the bar instead of going inside to see if she'd been as tempted to see how this played out between us as I'd been.

Too late. What was done was done. And here I was—here we were—three thousand miles from home and all the rules that kept our relationship in balance. She wanted me again, just like I wanted her. We were still in limbo between my personal and professional lives, but the doors to each world were ajar. It felt like they were about to come off their hinges.

"I'm not sure that's such a great idea." The words curdled in my mouth as I spoke.

Out of the corner of my eye, Sofia took a sip of her cocktail. "Because you're my boss?"

In my head, I could hear doors slamming and car tires screeching to a halt as James and Andrew morphed together in some kind of Terminator-type amalgamation.

"And you like to keep things separate. Hence you freaking out like a bunny in a fox pen when you got a social invitation at work."

"Foxes don't live in pens. The bunny would be in the—"

"You get what I'm trying to say." She swiveled on her stool so she was facing me. "We both know your name's not James. And technically you're my boss but—"

I couldn't keep my chuckle silent. "Technically?"

"Yeah. You're my boss as much as Mr. Romano at Emilio's Cucina was, the summer after freshman year. He thought he was in charge of me, but I was only there for the summer. How much authority did he really have?"

"This isn't about authority." I didn't want to abuse my

power. I didn't want any part of Sofia to think she had to sleep with me because I was her boss or because she thought she might be fired if she said no or if things went wrong. "I'm not Mr. Romano. Everyone has different boundaries."

"Boundaries can be redrawn when crossing them is important. Venice wasn't part of Italy until 1866, and before that Italy was cut up like a margherita and divided between France and Spain and Austria."

"Thanks for the history lesson."

She shrugged. "I'm just saying, boundaries aren't fixed. If it's important, they can shift." She took another sip of her drink and then stared right at me. "You and me? It feels important."

My heart spun in my chest. It felt important to me too.

"Maybe it's just great sex," she continued. "I don't think so. It feels like more. I'm not saying I want you to be the father of my fifteen Italian babies or anything. It's just . . . I think I get you. And I think maybe you get me too. Like you're the yang to my yin, if 'yang' means moody, uncommunicative, and irritating." She grinned at me.

I wasn't sure someone worried about their job security would call their boss moody, uncommunicative, and irritating. I couldn't fault any of her arguments.

"I don't want to shut down something so . . . interesting." She emphasized the last word like the men she usually met were boring. I could imagine Sofia running rings around most people. "I want to see where it goes." Her tone shifted, suddenly bordering on shy.

I'd never broken my rules or moved my boundaries for anyone. The fact that I'd kept going back to Noble Rot had meant something. I'd gone back for *her*. I hadn't been able to keep away. And now she'd dissected all my objections.

I pulled out my wallet and left enough cash to cover our drinks and a generous tip. "Let's get out of here."

I took her hand and we rode up the lift in silence. As we entered the suite, I pulled off my jacket. "Take off your clothes and go stand facing the window."

We both needed to blow off some steam. Whatever else was between us, sex with Sofia was unlike any I'd experienced before. I'd spent too long trying to pinpoint why and come up empty. Maybe this time, I'd be able to figure it out.

"Can people see?" she asked, as she pulled her dress up and off, leaving her in just her underwear. Confident as ever, she unsnapped her bra and then bent to take off her knickers.

Completely naked, she wandered across the living room to the floor-to-ceiling windows that spanned the entire suite. I undressed while I watched her as she hovered a meter or so from the glass.

"There are buildings right there," she said. "Can they see in here?"

She turned as I strode toward her.

I dropped some condoms on the console table she was leaning on and led her over to the window facing a building covered in mirrored glass.

"Maybe," I replied, placing her palms on the glass and moving behind her. "Maybe they can see your beautiful body." I cupped her breasts, one in each hand, and pulled her nipples between my thumb and forefinger. "Maybe they can see me doing this to you. Touching you, bringing your nipples to a peak, squeezing harder and harder until your breaths come a little sharper, a little more desperate." I let go and she whimpered—maybe in relief or perhaps it was because she wanted more.

I wanted more too.

"You think they see you splayed out like this?" I bent and positioned her legs apart. "Your pussy wet, even though I've barely touched you. You think they can see how ready you are?"

Her head fell back and she groaned as I trailed my fingers up her legs and across her stomach. She was spread and eager for me.

"You get to come quickly tonight. You need your rest before tomorrow."

I tore open a condom wrapper and rolled it on my cock. Without ceremony or warning, I slammed into her.

"Jesus," she cried out.

Her fingers curled into fists against the glass and I watched the reflection of her pendulous breasts jutting towards our reflections every time I thrust into her.

"You're so good at fucking me."

She didn't need to tell me how good it was for her. The way she tightened around my cock, requiring me to brace myself on her shoulder as I fucked her, told me this felt just as fucking fantastic for her as it did for me.

"You think everyone's gathered around their windows, watching you get fucked?" I growled into her ear. "Do you think they know how good my cock feels?"

"They couldn't understand," she huffed out in desperate breaths. "Nothing has ever felt so good."

She was right. There was nothing better than what we shared, and there never would be. She knew it. I knew it. It was just the cold, hard truth.

"Do you like being watched, Sofia? Do you like to show off this beautiful body and how it reacts when it's treated just right?"

"I like them seeing me with you." She exhaled and spread her hands wide on the glass, and locked her knees so the next thrust would go as deep as possible. "I think all the women looking are jealous of me." We locked eyes in the glass and her mouth fell open, her lips red and wet and so inviting. "I think all the men watching want to fuck like you fuck."

I groaned as I pushed up into her. At her words, yes, but mainly at the way she met every challenge I lay down for her. And upped the ante. I was used to dominating every woman I took to bed. But Sofia met my controlling, demanding requirements in a way that was never truly submissive.

And there was nothing sexier.

Yes, her body was all graceful curves and smooth flesh. She knew exactly when to push, bite, squeeze. But it was her attitude that made her entirely irresistible.

I pressed a kiss between her shoulder blades and slid my hand down, my fingers finding her clit swollen and needy.

"Andrew, you're going to make me come."

We both froze. She'd never used my name when we'd seen each other outside the office. It was the line that separated the day from the night. The office from the bedroom. The boss from the lover. But the construct had disintegrated. To pretend otherwise would just be fooling myself. And I never did that. Our game was over

I began to move again. Slowly. Deliberately.

"Say it again," I whispered.

"Andrew," she whispered back.

My cock ached with the need to feel her come.

"Again," I said, thrusting up into her.

"Andrew." She screamed this time, as if she couldn't hold back. "Andrew, Andrew, Andrew." She chanted as she bucked and writhed against her orgasm. Her unrestrained movements doubled in front of me—her and her reflection—

sent me into sensory overload. I came and came and came, my orgasm leaving me weak and unable to feel my legs. I fell forward over her back, my hands over hers on the glass.

After a few steadying breaths, I stood and hoisted her over my shoulder. "Once more, and then we both need to sleep."

TWENTY-FIVE

Sofia

Adrenaline was an amazing thing.

From eight o'clock on, Andrew kept threatening to send me back to my room to sleep. He'd finally kicked me out at midnight. We'd agreed I wouldn't see him again until after my meeting. I didn't want any distractions.

Luckily, I slept like a baby—even if it was for only six hours—and woke with a fire in my belly that made me determined to nail this *Verity* deal to the wall. I was going to have Goode eating out of my hand. I'd make sure of it.

I got to the restaurant where we were meeting—some fancy steak place in Tribeca—and checked my phone.

When I woke up, I'd had one message from Andrew. It read, *You know what to do*. It was all I needed to hear.

Maybe some employees would have been pissed at a boss that dropped a message like that before the most important meeting they'd ever been to, but not me. I knew Andrew didn't waste words. He meant what he said.

He believed in me.

I pulled open the door and took in the moss green walls, patterned mosaics on the floor, and the deco light fixtures. It was like a fancy Upper East Side townhouse. When I lived in New York, I could never have afforded to come to a place like this, and now, here I was, armed with a Blake Enterprises company credit card, ready to order the best wine on the menu.

The hostess showed me to my table and I took a seat facing the door. I knew what Bob looked like and I wanted a few seconds of advantage, knowing he was approaching.

I scanned the menu and made my choice. When I confessed to Andrew that I hadn't got a clue about what wine to order, we brought up the wine list on the website and he made a couple of choices. I nearly died at how expensive they were, but he assured me getting this deal done was ninety-five percent confidence—and I needed to reflect that in my wine selection.

I saw Bob enter and faked a relaxed perusal of the menu as he approached. I was certain the entire restaurant must be able to hear my heart beating in my chest.

I stayed seated as Andrew had suggested and set down my menu as my guest arrived at the table. "Ms. Rossi. I'm delighted to meet you." His eyes sparkled as he grinned at me and then took a seat. "Have you been here before?"

"I haven't. I'm a native New Yorker but there are always more restaurants than time to visit them."

"Well said. It's the same in London. And you're based there, despite hailing from this fine city. Is that correct?"

"New York is home. But I have family in London, so it's my adopted city. Don't ask me to choose." Bob didn't need to know that I'd barely seen London beyond the stretch of city between my apartment and Blake Enterprises.

The waitress came and took our orders. As Andrew predicted, we both ordered steak.

"Shall we have some wine?" I suggested. "The 2001 Redigaff merlot caught my eye."

Bob's gaze slid to mine and the corners of his mouth turned up just a fraction. "Excellent choice, Ms. Rossi. Why not?"

I ordered the wine and we handed the menus back to the waitress.

"Please, call me Sofia. If we're going to do business together, I have to feel we have a connection, you know?"

Goode nodded. "I do, Sofia. I do. Business is a people sport, as they say. But you look far too young to be out trying to buy companies. Tell me your story."

I shrugged. "Not too much to tell. I'm a Columbia grad. I'm ambitious and driven, and I'm lucky to have some very rich people's money to play with. My investors believe in me and I believe in *Verity*." I paused, giving Bob time to respond. It would be easier if he was doing the talking, but he passed on the opportunity so I continued. "Truth is, I've always loved celebrity gossip. Grew up on Perez. Still buy all the tabloids, even though most places in the UK don't even carry *People*." I tapped my nose. "I have my secret list of sellers. And now I'm in the UK, I can get *Hello* and of course, *Verity, Inc.*"

"So your plan is to buy it from me and run it yourself."

It was a good question and honestly, one of the few I hadn't rehearsed. "I want to start that way. Ultimately, I want to put a great manager in charge who shares my vision for the business, so I can go out and expand."

"Your vision?" Bob asked.

"Tell me yours. I've been looking forward to meeting you for so long and now I'm here, I'm doing all the talking.

I'd love to know if we see *Verity, Inc.* going in the same direction."

It was as if Bob had been waiting for his cue. He regaled me with stories of how successful the magazine was, despite the slowest circulation of the magazines in the space. He explained how he wanted to keep the paper presence but really focus on the online platform as the medium to break stories. Nothing he was saying was groundbreaking, nor would his strategies pull the magazine out of the massive hole it was in. The market was dominated by online versions of *Page Six* and *Daily Mail*. Pushing a paper version of *Verity, Inc.* was a vanity exercise. Andrew might not like Bob, but Bob wasn't a fool. He was holding back. He wasn't telling me everything.

"Have you ever thought about a subscription model?" I asked.

He lifted his chin slightly, as if I was challenging him.

"What am I saying—of course you've thought about it. You're one of the most successful men in magazines. Well, you asked me about my vision for *Verity*, and that's where it starts. I want to see subscribers sign up for breaking news and blind items. We make the product more exclusive, differentiate ourselves from our competitors, and at the same time, smooth out cashflow."

Bob nodded, looking me straight in the eye as if it were crunch time and he had to make a decision about whether or not he could trust me.

"I wonder if we should swap the merlot to champagne," he said finally. "I've got a feeling we're going to be doing business with each other."

My stomach rose like a wave and then tumbled into a crash.

The rest of the lunch was spent with Bob regaling me

with tales of celebrity encounters. At one point, he asked me about my financial backers and as quickly as possible, I told him I had family money. The fact that he didn't dig any deeper told me that he knew exactly who my father was. It was a relief. Andrew and I had a more in-depth cover story, but I was serious when I'd said to Andrew that the fewer lies I told, the better. The fact was, my father was rich. He just wasn't my investor. Bob had put two and two together and come up with seven. Worked for me.

"Sofia, it's been a pleasure, but I really must head out to another meeting. Shall we catch up for breakfast on Monday?"

It was Friday. Monday was three days away.

"You're in town for a couple of weeks, from what my assistant told me."

"Absolutely," I said, setting my napkin on the table and standing to say goodbye. "On one condition. You tell me whether that recent wedding at the Four Seasons between my favorite Mexican actress and the *Avengers* star was a love match or an Oscar grab."

Bob chortled. "It's a deal." He took my hand in both of his and gave it a hearty shake. "It's been a pleasure. You're a spitfire. I like your offer, Sofia. I have some thinking to do, but I liked your offer indeed."

And with that lack of commitment, he was gone.

I slumped back in my chair and took another swig of the vintage champagne I'd ordered.

What would Andrew say about extending our stay? Did that mean I had a weekend in New York? With Andrew?

Last night when I'd pushed his boundaries, I thought I'd ruined whatever it was we've been doing. But instead, it seemed to have made it better. I couldn't exactly put my finger on it but Andrew was more . . . relaxed. He'd even said that if it wasn't for the meeting, he'd make me stay the night in his bed like he knew there was something between us that wasn't just great sex just the same way I did.

He was right. I'd slept much better on my own without his distracting, rock-hard body next to me. It was the right call, but part of me wondered what would have happened if I'd not had this meeting today. If I'd have stayed. Then what? I could feel myself getting in deeper with him every moment we spent together. Now we weren't playing games, where were our boundaries?

I paid the check, swallowing down my fear that the credit card I was holding was going to malfunction and I'd be forced to spend the rest of the decade washing dishes to pay off the wine. It went through like I was spending ten dollars on an Uncle Chubby at Regina's Grocery rather than almost a thousand bucks for two steaks and a bottle of champagne.

As I stepped out onto the street, I pulled my coat tight around me. A New York spring could be bitterly cold.

"Hey, Rossi," a voice from up the street called. I couldn't figure out where it was coming from. It sounded like Andrew, but it couldn't be, right?

A driver stepped out of a limo to my left and opened the passenger door. "Ms. Rossi."

I bent to see who was inside and found Andrew grinning at me. "Get in, it's bloody freezing."

I slid into the car and the driver closed the door. "You came to get me?"

"How did it go?" He swept my hair from my eyes as if he wanted to see me better and I bit down on my bottom lip in order to hold back my grin at the unexpected contact.

"You never have a driver in London."

He cleared his throat as if he were reminding himself that we were meant to be discussing business. "That's because in London, cabs are more comfortable and can use bus lanes, and the tube has better coverage. Do I have to ask you a second time about how the meeting went?"

"Apparently," I said with a shrug. "There's good news and bad news. I think he liked me. We had chemistry. I think he liked my ideas for *Verity, Inc.*—"

"Your ideas?"

"Yeah, I thought he might ask about my plans, so I'd worked up an answer around subscription models. Anyway, after I told him that, he ordered champagne and told me he thought we could do business together. He wants to think about things and have another meeting."

Oh shit. I was meant to have lunch with Des on Sunday. If I stayed in New York, I'd have to cancel. The entire reason I was in London and had this job was so I could do things like have lunch with my father on the weekend.

"What's the catch, Sofia?"

It was just one lunch. This *Verity* deal needed to get done. I'd reschedule with Des—and I'd get to see my mom.

"There's always a catch. He wants our next meeting to be breakfast on Monday. Right here in Manhattan. But I can stay," I hurried to add, heading off any objections. "You don't have to. I can get a late flight back to London and be back behind my desk Tuesday morning."

"That's not a catch."

"But you hadn't planned on me staying in New York for the weekend."

"It's no big deal. And I'm not flying back without you. This is important. I'm by your side every step of the way."

He glanced at me and then out the window, as if he'd said too much. I knew *Verity* was his deal, and it was in his interest for my meetings with Bob to go well, but I couldn't help enjoying the feeling of loyalty and support he gave me. The yang to my yin.

TWENTY-SIX

Sofia

Being in New York with a few dollars in my purse was a new feeling—one I could get used to. I stepped out of Andrew's limo in my almost-too-tight red cocktail dress and the black velvet coat my mom had kept since college. I headed toward the restaurant entrance where I was meeting Natalie. There were definite upsides to staying in New York for the weekend; I'd get to spend tonight with Natalie and tomorrow night with my mom, who told me in no uncertain terms that Friday was her book club night, and she wasn't cancelling if I was going to be here for the whole weekend.

"Sofia?" a familiar voice from down the street called.

I turned to find Natalie hurrying toward me. She glanced at the car I'd just stepped out of and then back at me.

"Who brought you?"

"Just Andrew's car service. Apparently he hates New York cabs."

"What a snob."

I wasn't sure *snob* was the right word. If Andrew was really a snob, he'd have a driver in London. Plus, he was right about our cabs.

"I'm surprised he let you use his car."

I shrugged and Natalie gave the hostess our name. When we were seated, we ordered our cocktails and I grabbed Natalie's hand across the table. "It's so good to see you. I've missed you so much."

"Me too. Tell me everything. Why are you even here?"

How was I going to explain that I was pretending to be a buyer of a company Andrew wanted to acquire? "Andrew has some meetings. I'm just here . . . you know, assisting."

"Wow," she said. "I'm not sure if that's a perk or not. I can't imagine how awful he is to travel with."

"Yeah, he didn't say much on the way over." I laughed. "Just a few grunts here and there when absolutely necessary."

The waitress arrived with our cocktails and we placed our dinner order. Two meals out in one day, along with champagne and cocktails . . . Whose life was I living?

"That guy is the rudest asshole I've ever met," Natalie said. I'd been hoping our drinks arrival would have changed the subject. I didn't want to talk about Andrew being an asshole because he wasn't. He was curt and sharp in the office, but now I knew a different side of him. "Any other jobs on the horizon?"

Truth was, I hadn't been looking. The job at Blake Enterprises was a challenge, but I'd dealt with worse. "Andrew's not that bad." She gave me a disbelieving look. "And anyway, the money's good."

"You don't mind that he's so rude?"

I shrugged. "It's not personal. He's not everyone else's

chatty best friend except for me. It's just . . . how he's made."

"Oh, so because he's an asshole to everyone, that's alright?"

"He's just focused and knows what he wants."

Natalie rolled her eyes and took a sip of her cocktail. "Does he still bite your head off if you disturb him before lunch?"

Not last time, when I'd had the call from Goode's lawyers. "I just leave him to it."

"What is he doing in there? I saw his inbox—he's not spending all morning answering his messages. Maybe he's watching porn."

Andrew wasn't that guy, although I still wasn't exactly sure what he was doing behind his office door every morning. Now that I knew him better, there were things that made more sense, like the lack of communication—he just liked to be efficient and didn't see the point in small talk. But there were a number of things that didn't: the way he shut himself away in his office every morning . . . and I still didn't know why exactly the barman knew him as James.

Natalie was being ridiculous. "You make him sound like a monster. He's not that bad. He gave me a job when he didn't have to."

"Because he was desperate. He goes through assistants like cups of coffee."

I sat back in my chair. "Wow, thanks, Natalie."

Our appetizers arrived and an awkward silence descended as the waitress needlessly described our food.

"I'm seeing my mom tomorrow," I said, when the waitress had left, desperate to alleviate the tension.

"I didn't mean it like that," Natalie said when we were

once again alone. "You're way too good for him. I just meant that . . . I'm sorry, I just—"

"It's fine. It was a Hail Mary pass going for your job, but it paid off. I'm grateful he took a chance on me and I'm getting a lot more responsibility. I'm even going to a meeting on Monday. I'm enjoying it."

I'd spent my life as the kid from the wrong side of the tracks, trying to do better for herself. Now I was actually doing better. Not many twenty-eight-year-olds were negotiating major deals on behalf of their boss.

"I'm pleased," Natalie said, clearly not wanting to rock the boat.

"And I like him," I said, feeling a little bit braver. "He's got a good heart."

Natalie swallowed her mouthful of Waldorf salad and looked me in the eye. "You like him?" She regarded me with the scrutiny of an NYPD detective sizing up a potential suspect.

"Yeah," I said. "I really like him."

She groaned like I'd just told her I was moving to Ohio. "You have a crush on him?"

"Of course I have a crush on him. He's gorgeous." That was no confession. Every straight woman who ever met Andrew was bound to have a crush on him, or at the very least, appreciate his body.

"Personality matters," she replied.

"Like I said, I think I see him differently than you." Andrew was irritating at work. The way he spoke to me—or didn't—was annoying, but because I'd gotten to see him outside work, his at-work persona was more manageable. It wasn't like we were discussing the meaning of life when we'd spent the evenings together, but it had shown me more of the man I worked for. He wasn't *just* an asshole. He wasn't even *just* an asshole with a tight butt. He was focused and driven and determined to get what he wanted. He was controlling and domineering and he fucked like an Olympic champion.

"Differently? That's for sure. As long as you're not sleeping with him, I don't suppose it matters."

I busied myself with my Caesar salad, ready to move on to something other than how much my best friend hated the man I was sleeping with.

When I looked up, Natalie was staring at me. "You're not, are you?"

"Not what?"

"Sleeping with Andrew asshole Blake."

Despite my convincing performance in front of Goode at lunch, I clearly didn't have Natalie fooled.

"You're sleeping with him?" she whisper-screeched. "Oh my god." She made the sign of the cross and put her hands together in prayer. "Are you kidding me? Did he force you?"

I put down my fork. I'd lost my appetite. "Of course he didn't force me."

"Look, if you need money, I still have my savings. I can—"

The blood in my veins started to heat. "You think I'm sleeping with Andrew for money? What, I get fifty for a blow job and seventy-five for a fuck? What the hell, Natalie?" Jesus Christ, I'd worked really hard to put myself through college, but I'd never done anything like that. Why was prostitution the first place her mind went?

"I didn't mean that. I just know how much you need to be in London and maybe you felt obligated—"

"Andrew and I met outside at a bar by accident. We got to talking. I made a move on him." That wasn't exactly true, but I probably would have, given enough time and Barolo. Lucky for me, when Andrew wanted something, or someone, he made his intentions abundantly clear. "He's fucking phenomenal in bed. Our working relationship hasn't changed at all. I haven't gotten a pay raise. He's still as rude as he always was at the office. And I don't regret a single second. He's hung like a horse and knows his way around a woman's body like it's his job." I stood up and threw my napkin on the table. I was done with this conversation. I didn't want to hear about how it was inappropriate or how I was going to get fired when Andrew was bored with me. I didn't want to sit opposite my best friend while she judged my choices.

"I'm tired. I'm going back to the hotel."

"Sofia!" Natalie called after me but I didn't slow my pace to the exit. I didn't want to listen to a single second of criticism from her.

She caught up with me just as I made it outside. "Come back," she said. "I'm so sorry. I love you and I'm just trying to look out for you."

I'm sure that's how she saw it, but right then, all I could focus on was how she'd assumed sex with Andrew was some kind of gratitude payment. Sex with Andrew was anything but. It was sport, and a way to blow off some steam. It was fun. And it was more than all that. It was easy and intense and I never wanted it to stop.

My anger dissipated, dissolving as quickly as it appeared. "I need to go. I've had a long day." Natalie and I had been friends a long time. We'd get through this. But right at that second, I needed some space.

"Seriously? I haven't seen you for over a month and—"

"I'm here until Monday. Maybe we can catch up for a drink before I leave." I glanced up and saw Andrew's limo at the curb. Was he here? A smile started to nudge at the corners of my mouth. Had he been waiting for me?

"You never told me how things are going with Des." I could see in her eyes that Natalie wanted to mend fences, but the fire in my veins needed more time to burn itself out before we could have a normal conversation.

"I have to go," I said. I pressed a kiss to her cheek. When I stepped toward the car, the driver emerged and opened the passenger door. I dipped to see an empty back seat. Damn. Andrew was exactly the person I wanted to see right now.

As we pulled out into the familiar New York traffic, I leaned forward. "Do you know where Andrew is?"

"I've been parked outside the restaurant. He asked me to wait for you."

Warmth swirled in my belly, and I pulled out my phone.

TWENTY-SEVEN

Andrew

The bar Tristan had suggested was dark and gloomy—almost like someone had forgotten to pay the electricity bill. The hostess was painfully thin, dressed all in black with blood-red lipstick, her hair pulled back into a severe bun.

Had Tristan brought me to some kind of S&M club? It wouldn't surprise me.

The hostess showed me to the table where Tristan was hunched over his laptop.

"How long have you been here?" I asked.

"Couple of hours. I'm working on something. I knew I wanted to meet you, but if I started on this anywhere else, I would have lost track of time."

Made sense. Tristan was like me in terms of his focus once he was in the zone. He was good at pretending he was a little all over the place, but nothing was further from the truth.

"Anything interesting?" I asked, after giving the waitress my drink order.

Tristan snapped his laptop shut and shoved it into his bag. "Yeah actually. A couple of things." Typically, he gave nothing away. Tristan made a lot of money—evident by his address and the kit he always had. Although we all knew he worked in systems security, I didn't exactly know what that meant or who his clients were. Still, I had my suspicions.

"You're not worried someone will steal your laptop when you're working in public?" I asked.

"Nope."

"Why?"

"It's my job to make sure no one can find anything, even if they take my laptop."

"What about hackers?" I asked.

Tristan gave me a sideways squint. It seemed the glare was meant to make me feel stupid. It didn't, but I wasn't quite sure how I'd mis-stepped either. "No, Andrew, I'm not worried about hackers. I'm the best hacker in the world. Which makes me the best person in the world at stopping hackers."

I was used to hearing Tristan talk about how great he was. In our friendship group, he was often the butt of jokes because he was so immodest, but maybe it wasn't boastful if it was true. "But surely, they can unscrew the hard drive and extract the information somehow."

Tristan nodded like I was an idiot.

"Can't they?"

"You tell me. You seem to be the expert."

"You're annoying."

Tristan shrugged. "If anyone tampers with this laptop, the data stored on it automatically deletes. If the camera detects someone in front of the laptop who isn't me, the data deletes. If the keyboard thinks the keystrokes don't follow my typical patterns, or the fingerprints don't match mine, or if someone puts in the wrong password—"

"The data deletes. Okay, I believe you."

"I don't tell you the risks in your business. You don't need to worry about mine."

I grinned at Tristan. He was the youngest of the six of us and we often treated him like a younger brother. But he was nobody's fool.

"Speaking of business, how's it going with Goode?" he asked.

"I'm unusually impatient," I said. "But okay."

"Who did you end up sending into the meeting to pose as the buyer?"

My phone buzzed in my pocket. A message from Sofia flashed up on my screen. Speak of the devil. "My assistant," I replied, as I opened the message.

Her evening had ended early and she was heading back to the hotel.

Without thinking I started to type, *Swing by Bram Bar on your way. If you want to.*

"You mind if she joins us?" I slid my phone onto the table between us.

Tristan fixed me with a stare. "You want your assistant to join our drinks?"

"Is that a problem?"

"You're not one to mix business and . . . anything else."

I shrugged and took a sip of my drink. "It's not a big deal. We're travelling on business. Sometimes the rules change."

"The rules *never* change for you."

I picked up my phone again. "If you're going to make a big thing of it, I can tell her I changed my mind."

"Oh, no. Please don't. I can't wait to meet the woman you're changing the rules for."

I put my phone down and fixed Tristan with a don't-fuck-with-me stare.

Tristan shrugged. "So tell me about her."

I sighed in exasperation, but maybe it would be good to talk things through. Up until this trip, Sofia had been easy to keep in a box.

This trip had well and truly broken that line. I was Italy prior to 1866.

"She's bright, overqualified to be my assistant, and I'm sleeping with her. She's . . ." I took a deep breath, trying to pinpoint exactly what I was trying to say. "I like her."

"Wow," Tristan replied.

"Enough of the sarcasm. I'm telling you what I know." I stopped a waitress and ordered a glass of Barolo and a cocktail, so Sofia had the option.

"I wasn't being sarcastic. Translating what you've said from Andrew language into English, it sounds like you really like this woman."

"Yes. I just don't know what that means," I confessed. I did like Sofia. A lot. I liked her spirit and independence. I liked that she knew when to challenge me and when she just needed to accept what I was saying. I liked her smart mouth and tight pussy and I more than liked having sex with her.

"Does it have to mean anything?"

"I don't think I get a choice." I knew I couldn't freeze time. People talked about living in the now, but that was bollocks. The *now* was past as soon as it was spoken about. *Now* didn't exist more than a second before it was gone. This trip, what we'd shared physically and professionally—it had changed things between us.

"It can't just be an office fling?"

The waitress came with Sofia's drinks and when she set them down, I shifted them so they were in front of the seat next to me.

"There's two things wrong with that statement. The first is that an office fling comes with strings if I'm the boss and she's my employee. It's just a fact." I wasn't an idiot. There was more than one reason I didn't shit where I ate. It made things too fucking complicated. "And the second thing is that . . . she's a big deal."

Sofia in the office had started as a minor annoyance, had transformed into an assistant who seemed to know what she was doing and got bonus points for not letting my attitude and foibles get to her. As a lover, Sofia had started as a woman I wanted to fuck, but had transformed into a woman I couldn't get enough of. Of course she was a big deal.

Before I could say anything further, the hostess interrupted us and Sofia appeared at our table. My breath hitched in my chest and I cleared my throat. She always looked gorgeous, but tonight she looked breathtaking in a tight red dress that covered her arms and cleavage, and hit just below her knee. She was completely covered up but no one had ever worn anything so sexy.

I took the jacket folded over her arm and nodded toward Tristan. "This is—"

"It's nice to meet you, Sofia," Tristan said, standing as he reached out his hand. "I'm Tristan."

Sofia glanced to me for further explanation.

"Tristan is one of my oldest friends." I guided her to sit down and then chastised myself that I'd chosen to sit in a chair so I couldn't be closer to her.

"I thought you must have been joking when you said you had friends." Her expression was like I'd just told her I had a twin brother called James. "How does that work? Do you have to hire them?"

Tristan chuckled from across the table. "I like her."

She turned to me, smiling, and I reached under the table to slide a hand onto her knee.

"I hear you're helping Andrew with this Goode situation," Tristan said. "The guy sounds like he'd cut his nose off to spite his face. You're doing well if you're getting him on side."

"I think it's simpler than that. It's good old-fashioned ego at work with Goode."

"You think?" I asked. She'd never said that to me. I supposed we had never discussed his motivations; we'd always kept to cold, hard facts.

"Yeah, he doesn't want to sell to someone who's going to render useless what he's done with *Verity*—though the irony of that doesn't escape me. He doesn't want to look foolish more than he wants to turn a profit. What I proposed to him today was maintaining his strategies but adding a subscription model—new for this publication, but not in publishing. It's a different approach from burning *Verity* to the ground like *some people* plan to do," she said, throwing an accusing glance in my direction.

I glanced at Tristan and he met my eye. I could tell he was thinking exactly the same thing I was.

Yeah, she was a big fucking deal.

TWENTY-EIGHT

Andrew

Drinks with Tristan had been fine. Good, even. Yes, I knew I'd go back to London and face a subtle inquisition from the rest of the guys, but it was good to see Sofia in a social situation. She was relaxed and charming and so fucking sexy I couldn't wait to get her back to the hotel.

At some point from leaving Tristan to reaching the hotel, something had shifted. Sofia had grown quiet. She was upset.

And I didn't know why.

The lift doors opened on the fifty-third floor and I stepped out after her.

"Now that we're alone, are you going to tell me what's wrong?" I asked.

"Who said anything was wrong?"

I pulled my key card out of my wallet, ignoring her. She didn't have to tell me what was the matter, but there was no point pretending everything was fine.

"Are you coming inside?" I asked, holding open the door to the suite.

"It depends," she said, folding her arms and leaning on the door. What the fuck had crawled up her arse when we left Tristan? I wish she'd just spit it out.

I met her gaze and waited.

And waited.

"I have questions," she said finally. "Questions for you. Things I don't understand."

"Okay," I said carefully. I suddenly felt I was surrounded by landmines, and only complete stillness could keep me from being blown to bits. I hated the coldness in Sofia's voice and the look in her eye that suggested we were . . . strangers.

"You'll answer them?"

She knew me better than to think I'd commit to answer questions before I knew the exact nature of the information requested. "Can we do this inside? I want to change and enjoy the view rather than skulk around in hotel corridors."

"On one condition. No one's getting naked until I've had my questions answered. And maybe not even then, because I might choose to go watch Netflix in bed by myself."

I sighed. Where had this evening gone so wrong? What had soured her mood? "Fine."

"Fine," she said, and slipped past me into the suite.

I toed off my shoes, grabbed a couple of bottles of water from the bar, and handed one to her before taking a seat opposite the New York skyline. I was ready for her questions.

Ridiculously, she sat in one of the occasional chairs opposite me, as if this was an interview.

"What is it you do in your office from six to twelve?" she asked.

Okay, I'd braced myself for questions about Goode, about how much money I made, about how many women I'd slept with or was sleeping with, but my morning office routine hadn't even been on my thousand-mile radar. "Sun salutations, according to you. What do you think I do?"

She shook her head and stood. "I'm leaving if you're not going to take this seriously."

I caught her hand as she walked past and yanked her down onto the sofa next to me. "What the fuck, Sofia? You're throwing your toys out of your pram because I've not told you why I don't like to be disturbed until midday? What's going on?"

She shrugged, but at least she stayed seated. "Natalie just pointed out that—"

"Ohhh, right. Natalie. I think she hated me most out of all my assistants. So tell me, why exactly does Natalie think I don't want to be disturbed before twelve?"

"I asked first."

I shifted around and put my hands on her shoulders so she was facing me. "I want to focus. I want to think. And I want to do that without interruption."

Sofia scoffed. "For six hours every day? Oh, that makes perfect sense."

I let go of her. "If you think me a liar, that's your business, not my problem."

"You're telling me you're in there . . . *actually* meditating? My guess was closer than I realized."

"Partly—though I assure you, there's nothing tantric about my morning routine. Meditation normally only takes twenty minutes right at the beginning of the day. Then I work out my priorities, reassess strategic goals, and go to work. In case you haven't noticed, as soon as midday rolls around, I'm back-to-back meetings, phone calls, and interruptions. If I didn't draw that line in the sand, I'd have no time to do anything of value."

"So you're just working?" she asked, with an expression of frank disbelief.

"Yes. What else would I be doing? What did Natalie suspect? Forget it, don't answer that, I don't even care."

"You're spending six hours meditating and working . . ." It wasn't a question—more like she'd found the solution to a puzzle and was repeating it out loud.

"Next question."

"Why do they call you James at the bar?"

I collapsed back onto the sofa. That one was a little more complicated.

"And I noticed you always pay cash."

"Yeah. That's deliberate. I don't want them to know my real name."

"Why not?"

"For lots of reasons."

"Hit me with your top five."

She wasn't going to let this go. And in her shoes, I'd admit, it looked a little weird.

"First, privacy."

"Come on. Yes, you've been in the financial pages, but you're not Harry Styles."

I chuckled. "I know. I don't mean that kind of privacy. I've run into situations before that staff have Googled my name on my card and figured out who I am and . . . I've made a lot of enemies doing what I do."

She put up her hand to stop me. "Whoa, there, buddy. You're saying that bar staff Google your name off your card?

What kind of—" She stopped herself. "Oh, right. Women. Female bartenders."

I stayed silent. She'd figured it out, as I knew she would.

"And what do you mean, you've made enemies? You're not a child molester."

"No, but I've taken over companies and had to make a lot of very hard decisions."

"To save businesses."

"Not everyone sees it like you. And that's not surprising. I've had to fire people, make people redundant, shut down divisions and product lines. This impacts real people. It's not just a line item on a spreadsheet. It takes away the ability for men and women to provide for their families. It's never going to be a popular thing to do, no matter the reasons behind it."

"But you're doing what's best for the majority."

"I used to think knowing I was doing what was best to keep the entire company from failing was enough. But it's not. People are still going to feel aggrieved if they're laid off. The reasons why don't matter. I learned that lesson the hard way."

"The hard way?"

Even now I didn't like to think back to that night. "I was ambushed in the car park of the office one night. Maybe they thought if they got rid of me, they could get their jobs back. Maybe they were just trying to vent their anger and frustration at the person they saw as making the decisions that were causing them pain. Either way, I ended up in hospital, battered and bruised with a broken jaw. I learned my lesson that night."

"Jesus, Mary, and Joseph, did they find the guys?"

"I knew who they were. But the last thing they needed was to end up in prison. I took my punishment. Not for laying them off, but for not listening to my father. He always said, 'The greatest victory is that which requires no battle.' A real *Art of War* fanatic, if you know the type. Those men weren't to blame. I'd misjudged the situation. Now I handle things differently."

"So you go around pretending you're someone else." She sighed like she got it but didn't like it.

"No. 'Invincibility lies in defense.' I'm not pretending to be anyone I'm not. I use cash and a different name when it doesn't matter—like when I'm having a drink at a local bar. I'm still myself. It's just my way of keeping a low profile."

"When it doesn't matter, huh? I thought you pretended to be a different man with me because somewhere in that head of yours, you could justify being attracted to me if you weren't Andrew Blake—my boss. But if you use 'James' when the stakes are inconsequential . . ."

"No. You were never—that is, what's between us isn't—" I paused for a deep breath. I wasn't accustomed to muddling my way through a conversation. "I'm saying this badly."

She tilted her head and gave me a small smile. "Yes, you are."

"This might sound harsh, but I never saw you as more than my assistant in the office. Not really. I have that side of me switched off completely, out of respect for the men and women who work for me. But then when I heard you talking about me at the bar . . ." I paused, thinking back to that night. "Something shifted. I was entirely attracted to you. From that point, you're right—I needed to not be your boss in order to let myself have you." I'd kept my gaze steady on the skyline out the window while I spoke, but I needed Sofia to hear what I was going to say next—hear it, and know it was true. Finding her eyes was easy, since she was already watching me. "You are not inconsequential to me, Sofia. You matter very much."

After a beat of silence, she shimmied her shoulders like she was shaking off a chill. "Tell me why your boundaries are so tightly drawn." She looked at me with a softness I'd not seen in her before.

"It's easier to keep work separate from my private life."

"But everyone spends so much time in the office. Isn't it natural to form personal relationships?"

"Piranhas are natural. Volcanos. Hurricanes. Just because something's natural doesn't mean it's salubrious."

"Piranhas? We talk about intra-office romance and your mind goes to flesh-eating fish? And *salubrious*? You have an interesting brain, Andrew Blake."

"I'm just saying, sometimes you need to swim against the tide."

"It's an unusual stance. Or at least it's unusual to be so rigorous in adherence to such a rule." She put on a weird accent which I guessed was supposed to be British but actually sounded like an American who'd had one too many limoncellos.

"At the beginning of my career, I got sacked when I ended an affair with a female partner at the law firm I was working for. She wasn't happy and decided revenge was the best way to work through her feelings. I don't want that to ever happen on my watch." It was a long time ago and losing that job had ultimately led to good things, but the situation hadn't been fair. I'd vowed at the time that when I was the boss, decisions should be taken on ability—not personal vendettas or really, personal feelings at all. The only way to ensure the integrity of the work environment at Blake Enterprises was to ensure the office was about work and work only.

"Your boss fired you because you didn't want to be her boyfriend anymore?"

"It was a little more complicated than that, but pretty much."

"Oh, well . . . now I feel like an asshole."

"Don't. I'm unusually strict about that particular boundary." I sighed. "In my head, if I was James, I could give in to my desire to take you to bed."

A small smile curled around her lips.

"How much longer will this interrogation last?" I asked. "I'm just wondering whether or not I need a whisky."

She swung her legs over mine. "I'm done," she said. "Thank you for being honest with me."

I slid my hand over her calf. "Thank you for asking questions and not just assuming Natalie's theory was correct."

We'd had our first fight and come out the other side. It felt like we'd reached a crossroads and chosen the turning together. I just wasn't sure where that turning would take us. Whatever was between us was more than fucking, but we weren't dating—were we? Part of me wanted it all when it came to Sofia, but it wasn't a part I was accustomed to heeding.

"Tomorrow morning, I'm taking you on a tour of my city," she said. "I'm going to show you all the places tourists never get to see."

I shifted and crawled over her on the sofa, laying her on her back as I slid her dress up her thighs. "If we have time. I plan to keep us very, very busy."

TWENTY-NINE

Sofia

He glanced up at the giant ice-cream cones affixed to the side of the Ferrara's storefront. "This is our first stop on the tour?"

"Pre-tour cannoli. Can't hit the sights without proper sustenance."

"Cannoli? Is that pasta?"

I shook my head and laughed. "Absolutely not. You've never had cannoli?" I slipped my hand into his and pulled him into the shop.

The sight of the familiar red-and-white-checkered floor sent a shiver of familiar comfort up my spine as we approached the counter.

"Wow. This is quite the bakery," Andrew said.

Oh, it was so much more than that.

Behind the glass counters were rows and rows of the finest Italian pastries and desserts outside of Italy. Rows of different shapes and sizes of crunchy sfogliatella, over-stuffed cannoli, cassata, frittelle, bite-sized amaretti, crostata, and the only pasticciotto in the city that I'd ever found. "This place is a slice of heaven," I said. "But cannoli has to be the first thing you try if you've never had it."

I approached the counter. "Due cannoli per favore."

"La piccola Sofia, is that you?" Mamma Isabella bellowed out from nowhere. I hadn't seen her when we arrived. I was so used to seeing new people behind the counter, I hadn't even looked very hard. Her red hair popped up around the counter and she threw up her hands. "I didn't know you were coming. Dove sei stato."

"I moved to London, Mamma Isabella. Didn't Mom tell you?"

She didn't respond but called to the back, "Lorenzo, get out here!"

I rolled my eyes. Mamma Isabella and my mom had been trying to get Lorenzo and I to date since we were both born. Lorenzo had a boyfriend and had been out since he was about fourteen. It didn't stop Isabella though.

"Isabella, this is my friend Andrew," I said, turning to Andrew.

She looked him up and down and smiled tightly, then turned back to the kitchen. "Lorenzo, did you hear me? Sofia is here."

I grinned as a huge hulk of a man wearing a white chef's uniform appeared from around the counter. "Sofia!" I turned back to Andrew and smiled at him as Lorenzo came charging toward me.

I squealed as Lorenzo picked me up and swung me around. "It's been a while," he said, setting me back down on my feet. "I hear you've been in London."

"Yeah, I'm just back for a few days. This is my friend, Andrew." I hadn't expected all this fuss when we came in or I wouldn't have come. Most times I came to Ferrara's now, there were a bunch of strangers behind the counter and I could slip in unnoticed.

Lorenzo did an up-and-down sweep of Andrew just like his mother had, but his gaze wasn't disapproving. He turned back to me with a grin. "Nice," he said, before leaning toward Andrew and shaking his hand. "I've known this one since she was in diapers. I have all the dirt if you need any."

I laughed. "You were in diapers too. Like you have anything on me."

After some catching up, a pile of pastries stuffed into boxes, and lots of kissing, we were on our way.

"Sorry about that," I said as we got out to the street. "I didn't expect Mamma Isabella to be there. She can be a lot for an uptight British guy."

He chuckled. "Nothing I can't handle. But I have to warn you, I think she hopes her gay son is going to marry you."

"I know," I said, smiling and shaking my head. "Lorenzo's boyfriend of five years spends the holidays with them. He's out, but they still think he might marry a nice Italian girl. I've stopped trying to convince her it's never going to happen."

"So you grew up around here?" he asked.

"Sort of. My grandma lived around the corner and my mom cleaned at Ferrara's before she went through beauty school. I'd always go with her—even as a baby—so I've known them all since I was born."

He scooped up my hand into his and we walked north "It's . . . nice seeing you in this environment. It's different."

"You mean when you're not snapping at me or we're not naked?"

"I suppose." He looked a little confused, or at least like he was trying to figure something out. I was too happy to question anything. I was back home, among my people, with a man I liked more with every passing day. He was far from the monster Natalie thought he was, and so much more than most people gave him credit for. He was the most open and honest man I'd ever met. He was loyal and kind, and I was going to soak up every minute I was with him.

"How come you went to work with your mum?" he asked.

I shrugged. "My grandma was too old and frail to look after me, and my mom couldn't afford childcare."

"What about your dad?"

"He . . . wasn't around. He was a British guy who left her when he found out she was pregnant."

He squeezed my hand. "I'm sorry. You've never known him?"

"I've seen him a few times since I've been in London," I said. "I'm . . . exploring that."

"Wow. That must be . . ."

"It's a lot of things. Confusing, challenging, sometimes good. I'm just taking one step at a time. A coffee here. A lunch there. I have to check my resentment, you know? He's always had so much, and we never had much of anything."

"He didn't pay child support?"

"Nope." I went on to explain his reasoning. "I get it. But it doesn't change the fact that I went to cleaning jobs with my mom from when I was six weeks old so she could put food on the table. Speaking of, we need to get on the subway. Next stop is the New York Public Library. It's free and safe and full of books—the best place in the world as far as I was concerned as a kid."

We stopped in the middle of the street, strangers rushing by us. He pulled me toward him and landed a sweet kiss on my forehead. "I'm more than happy to go book browsing with you, but I draw the line at a subway ride. Let's use my car." He nodded at a limo on the street.

"You've had your car following us?"

He shrugged, like that was a totally normal thing to do. "We can taste the cannoli on the way."

"You had me at cannoli."

I PULLED in a deep breath as the limo cruised to a stop in front of the library. There was nowhere in this city that felt more like home.

We left the remaining cannoli in the car—Mamma Isabella didn't know what "no" and "too much" meant. Hand in hand, we started up the steps. "Hey, Patience," I said to the huge stone lion on the left. "Hi, Fortitude."

"Friends of yours?" Andrew asked.

"Friends of the city. Friends of the library. And anyway, who doesn't like a stone lion? Do you guys have names for the lions in Trafalgar Square?"

"Not as far as I know. But lions aren't my specialty. I'm more of a penguin man myself."

I started to laugh. "Really? I would have thought you'd pick cheetah or eagle or something. Why penguins?"

"Those fuckers can withstand temperatures of minus fifty centigrade. They survive in the most inhospitable places on earth. They swim at twenty miles per hour, they're waterproof. They're indestructible."

I nudged him. This playful side of Andrew was completely adorable. If only Natalie knew.

"I know it was only built at the turn of the last century, but being in here always makes me feel like I'm in ancient Greece or something." I stared up at the cream columns nudging up into archways that seemed to reach so high, they were holding up the sky. "Come on, let's go to the biology department." I tugged at his hand.

"You think I need an anatomy lesson?"

"Absolutely not. But I have something fun to show you." We wound our way up and down stairs, through doorways, this way and that through rows of books before finally finding the shelf I was looking for. "I want to see if it's still here," I said, my voice a half whisper despite there not being a soul in our immediate vicinity.

"What?"

"I'll show you. Have patience, Mr. Blake."

He glanced behind us then circled his arms around my waist, stopping me where we were and kissing my neck. "Hey, we're in a public place." He relented and took my hand as I led him deeper into the stacks.

"Can I ask how on earth you know your way around the biology department this well? What did you read at University?"

"What did I read? You mean what did I major in? Economics. With a minor in politics. Nothing to do with biology." I scanned the bookshelves, searching for the hidden treasure.

"It's the next one down, I think." I turned right as the shelves broke and saw the table where I'd spent so many hours. "This is it. The plants section."

"Why spend so much time here?"

"It was a reliable babysitter." I trailed my fingers over my desk, searching for the thumb tack embedded in the underside of the wooden table. It was still there, fourteen years later. I glanced up at the shelves and couldn't stop my grin when I found what I'd been looking for.

Among the books on plant biology of the Amazon was a

deliberately misplaced copy of Schaechter's *Mechanisms of Microbial Disease*. I slid it out to reveal my hidden stash.

I couldn't believe it hadn't been discovered: emergency stationery supplies.

"I hid this here just in case I ever forgot stuff from home. Mom would drop me off before her shift in the nail salon started at eleven, and if I forgot any of my stuff there was no hope of going home to get anything. I'd be stuck for hours without being able to write or—"

Andrew rested his head on my shoulder, his hands on my waist, looking on as I rummaged through my rainbow pencil tin. It even had the basketball keyring I'd been keeping for my first apartment. "How old were you when you used to come here?"

"My first time, I was about ten, I think. And then at fourteen, Mom let me stay home by myself." I took the keyring out of the tin, dropped it into my pocket, and shut the case. "I think I'm going to put it back."

"In case you ever turn up without stationery supplies?" He kissed my neck, once, twice, pulling me closer.

"Or in case some other kid does and finds it." I kind of liked the idea that the secret would remain until someone else picked up the baton.

"You're lovely," Andrew said, kissing me again.

He spun us around so my back was against a shelf of books and pressed his lips against mine, prizing my mouth open and slipping his strong tongue inside. His lips were soft and insistent as he woke my lust from its short nap. I reached around his neck, sinking into his kiss when he slipped his hands up my shirt.

I stepped to the side. "Andrew. What are you doing?"

He silenced me with a kiss, sliding me back in front of him and snaking his fingers into my bra. "You like it when you think someone might see." He pressed kisses up my neck and then found my mouth. He pushed his hands over my ass, pulling at my skirt, hiking it further up my legs.

I pulled away. "Andrew," I whispered and pressed a short kiss to his lips. "We can't make out in a library."

"There's no one here," he said, his fingers finding their way under the hem of my skirt and into my panties.

My head tipped back against the books and I shifted involuntarily, giving him better access. He took full advantage and shoved two fingers right inside me.

I gasped, falling forward, my hands braced on his shoulders. "What are you doing?"

His fingers started to twist and turn, his thumb rubbing and pressing against my clit. Would it be obvious what he was doing if someone turned down this row of books? I burrowed my face into his neck, concerned that I wouldn't be able to control the sounds that came out of me if he kept this up. And we both knew he wasn't going to stop until he'd made me come. It was almost as if he felt my orgasm belonged to him now. He controlled it. He decided when I climaxed, and how often. There was nothing for me to do but give in and enjoy it.

An echo of people's voices not far away made us freeze. Shit. If they hadn't already heard us, maybe we were about to be caught. Yes, we were in some obscure section of the library where I'd sat for hours on end without ever being disturbed, but there was a first time for everything.

"Shhh," Andrew whispered, his fingers starting up again, despite the nearness of the voices. "Be very still. Very quiet."

Jesus. Was he serious? He was going to try to make me come with people a couple yards away? What would they do if they saw me like this? Mouth open, breathing labored, legs quivering from Andrew's touch, barely able to stand.

He upped his pace, circling and pushing, rubbing and pressing. I wasn't going to be able to take much more. "You want me to stop?" he whispered, his lips so close they grazed my ear.

The voices had faded, but I didn't know if they'd just been drowned out by the thumping of my heart in my chest and the pounding blood in my ears. I gripped more tightly onto his shoulders. "No," I said through my short breaths. "Make me come."

We locked eyes as he pushed up further, his fingers deep inside, his knuckles finding my folds. He rocked his hand back and forth, pulling my climax from me. A mixture of shock and pleasure spun up my spine and Andrew's face split into a small, proud smile as he held me through the orgasm silently tearing through my body.

Andrew maneuvered me into one of the old familiar chairs to let me recover. "You should check your phone," he said as he scanned the bookshelves. "It went off when we . . . When you were coming around my fingers."

I shot him a warning glance. He needed to lower his voice or we were going to get arrested. "My cell rang?"

He shook his head. "Just vibrated."

Thank Jesus I hadn't been so drunk on lust for Andrew that I hadn't heard my phone go off in a library. I pulled out my cell but there were no new messages and no missed calls. "Must have been your phone," I said. "Nothing came through on mine."

"I just checked mine—"

"Shit, it must be the Goode phone." There was only one person who had that number.

I scrabbled through my purse and pulled it out. There it

was: a missed call and an email. "What does he want?" I asked, Andrew's head peering over my shoulder.

"I suggest you open the email."

I took a breath and opened it, scanning it as fast as I could. "Lovely to meet you, yadda yadda, lunch, yadda yadda . . . loved your ideas about *Verity*. Could I put another offer on the table? I want you to come to work for me —What?"

"Shhh," Andrew said from behind me. "We're in a library." He straightened and I turned around to face him. He shrugged. "Well, at least he liked you." He pulled the phone out of my hand and read the message in full.

"He wants to discuss all possible options with you at breakfast on Monday."

"This is a disaster. He was meant to like me enough to sell his company to me, not give me a job. I'm going to reply."

He pulled the phone away before I could take it back. "No, you're not. Not yet anyway. We're going to take a breath and figure out our next move. No knee-jerk reactions. This is too important."

He was right. We needed to keep a cool head, and I was still reeling from my orgasm. Andrew balanced out my impulsive side, but despite what others might think, he had a wild side of his own. I'd never be able to look at New York Public Library quite the same again.

THIRTY

Sofia

Not even the devil himself was more terrifying than my mom if she thought her daughter was disrespecting her. "We have two minutes to finish this," I said, hopping from one foot to the other. "My mom will never forgive me if I'm late. I'll get a lecture about how I was brought up, and then she'll start asking me how many times I've been to mass since I've been in London. That will snowball into how I could have saved money on a hotel if I'd stayed with her, and before you know it, the whole evening will be wasted."

"Okay, we're done," Andrew said. "You want to read it through before I send it?" He'd drafted a response to Goode's job offer.

"It needs to be in my voice," I said. "Or Goode won't believe it."

He grinned up at me. "So you keep saying. You're more invested in this working than I expected."

"That's because it's important to you." I landed a kiss on his lips. "And you're important to me." I scanned the reply to Goode's email. Andrew was so smart and he'd crafted my voice so perfectly; his focus got me so hot I mentally calculated if we had time to—no, we absolutely did not. My mom would kill me.

He grabbed my hips and pulled me onto his lap. "You're important to me too."

I pressed send on the email. "You think he'll go for it?"

"You were clear and firm in your refusal of any kind of job working with him. But it was polite and you had good reasons—you want to build a business of your own. I don't think he'll try to convince you otherwise. All that remains to be seen is whether *Verity* is up for sale. Let's see if he still wants the Monday meeting."

I turned to him and stroked my finger along his jaw. "How can you be so calm?"

"What's the alternative?"

"You want to come meet my mom?" The words were out of my mouth before I had a chance to think through what I was saying.

Andrew shrugged. "Sure. Will there be cannoli on the menu?"

"You're a dufus. But you're adorable."

"We can fuck in the car on the way over."

I pushed off his lap and went to grab my coat. "Your invitation is revoked. There's no way we're going together." Even if Andrew could keep his hands off of me, and there was no guarantee of that, I was pretty sure I wouldn't be able to keep *my* hands off him.

"Sorry, you can't revoke an invitation once it's given. Your mother wouldn't approve."

He wasn't wrong.

"I'm meeting Tristan for drinks at the hotel bar at nine

thirty, so as long as your mom won't be offended if I head off early, I'd love to come and meet her."

What was I thinking?

As the car pulled out from outside the hotel and headed toward 145th street, Andrew pulled my hand onto his lap and threaded his fingers through mine. We sat in comfortable silence.

"Does your mum know you're talking to your dad?" he asked out of nowhere.

I shook my head. "Please don't mention it to her. It would break her. She wouldn't understand what I'm trying to do. And if she found out, it would all be ruined." There was no way my mother would take money from Des. Not at this point. I was going to have to pretend I'd managed to save fifty grand while working in London. If I made sure all the bills came directly to me, I might get away with it.

"I won't say anything."

"Oh and for the record, you're paying me a lot of money and there's a great big bonus at the end of the year if I stay until December."

"There is? How much?"

"I don't think she'll ask. I just . . . If it comes up, just play along. Okay?"

Silence filled the car, but it wasn't the comfortable silence from before. This one was full of unasked and unanswered questions. "You want to tell me what's going on?" he asked.

"I'm trying to get some money from my father. That's why I came to London. To meet him, convince him to give me what he owes me. My mom needs a knee replacement and her shitty insurance won't cover it. For all the years he didn't pay child support, it's time my father paid up."

"Right," Andrew said quietly.

"If that's judgement in your voice, I don't want to hear it. My father walked out before I was born and my mother worked three jobs to put food on the table. He owes me. And I don't want the money for cannoli. It's so my mom can continue to work two jobs to keep a roof over her head."

"I'm not judging you," he replied.

"Good," I snapped, pulling my hand from his. "I don't deserve it."

"Sounds like you might be judging yourself a little bit."

"I'm Catholic. It's what we do." Maybe confession would help. Not with the money, but with the guilt for trying to establish a relationship with my father just so he'd give me what I wanted. The more I'd gotten to know him, the stronger the guilt became. "I wish I didn't have to do it. I wish the insurer would just pay up. And then I would never have met him and his wife and his perfect family. I wouldn't have listened to his perfectly reasonable explanation for his behavior."

"*Is* there a perfectly reasonable explanation for his behavior? It sounds like his family had more than enough money to help you and your mother."

"He was young. Everyone makes mistakes when they're young."

"Agreed. But at this point he should do everything in his power to put it right."

"Exactly. That's why I'm going to ask him for the money. I'm not going to steal it from him. I'm just going to say I've fallen behind with my student loan payments. Even if he loans it to me and I have to pay him back eventually, that would be enough. I just want my mom to walk without pain."

"Tell him that. Give him a chance to do the right thing.

If you say he's got an entirely reasonable explanation for doing what he did, he'll want to help."

I knew Andrew was sharp and clever, but he seemed hopelessly naïve in this instance. "And what happens if he says no?"

Without missing a beat, he said, "Then I'll pay."

I didn't have a chance to respond before we pulled up in front of my mom's building.

She buzzed us up and met us by the front door, fiddling with her bun as she always did. "Sofia, stella mia." She held out her hands and pulled me close. It had only been a few weeks, but I felt as if I'd been away for years.

"How is your knee, Mamma?"

She released me from the hug and patted me close. "I'm fine. No fussing please. You must be Andrew." Mom shifted me into the apartment as she held out her hand to shake. "I'm glad you came. If I'd had to take the call from Isabella just now without knowing who this man was that you were going about the city with, we'd have had to have a conversation about family, tesoro."

"Smells delicious, Mamma," I said, ignoring her and sending up a little thank-you to God for inspiring the wisdom to invite Andrew along this evening.

"So you work with Sofia?" she asked, taking Andrew's coat and hanging it on the coat rack. Before we'd gotten into the kitchen, the buzzer rang.

"Delivery for Andrew Blake," a voice from the intercom sang. Mom glanced at Andrew but buzzed the delivery up.

"Sorry about this," Andrew said, pointedly ignoring my stare. What was he doing? Had he had some documents couriered over or something? He hadn't said anything about work on the ride over. Andrew opened the door just as the delivery guy arrived.

"Apologies that this has had to come direct," Andrew said, handing my mom a huge bouquet of lilies and roses. "And a selection of wine," he said, lifting the box in his arms slightly. "Italian, of course."

My mother's eyes were bright and twinkly as she answered. "That's very generous of you, Andrew. I hope you like meatballs."

"Mom," I said, shock plain in my voice. "You made me meatballs on a Saturday?"

She took her flowers and swept past me into the kitchen as if she hadn't heard me this time. "When's the last time you went to mass?"

I turned to Andrew and mouthed, "*I told you so.*"

THIRTY-ONE

Andrew

Tristan was hunched over his laptop when I found him in the hotel bar.

"Don't you like American women?" I asked as I took a seat. A hostess followed me over and slid a glass of Barolo onto the table. My taste for red wine had developed since being with Sofia. Soft, plump, and delicious—taking a sip was almost as good as kissing her.

Tristan shut his laptop and looked up. "Not as much as you, apparently. Why do you ask?"

"Just whenever I see you in a bar or restaurant in London, you're chatting someone up, giving someone your number, flirting."

Tristan shrugged. "I'm busy. When I'm this busy in London, you don't see me."

I couldn't argue with that.

"Flirting is just a way for me to let off steam. A distraction. That's all. Most of it never goes beyond that."

"That's because your game is terrible."

Tristan laughed. "Okay, super-stud. If you say so."

One of Tristan's best qualities was he had skin like Teflon. Nothing much got to him—not even his closest friends roasting him on a regular basis. He had an inner confidence and didn't give much of a shit what anyone else thought of him.

"Any news on *Verity*?" he asked.

I winced. "Not really. A potential wrinkle in the plan, but I'm sure we can flatten it out." By Monday afternoon, I'd know either way. "If he's prepared to sell, I want to move as quickly as possible."

"And then what?" Tristan said, quick as a flash.

"And then I'll own *Verity, Inc.* and I'll be able to protect my grandmother's legacy." He must have heard this a thousand times before. Why was he asking?

"But how? You've never run a company for long, Andrew. And when you go into a business, it's not to change their entire business model. Sure you might add in sales channels and close down divisions, shift strategy, but changing *Verity, Inc.* from a gossip rag back to a revered publication with an investigative journalism bent will be a challenge. Even for you."

Tristan wasn't stupid, so I didn't understand why he was underestimating me. "I'm pretty good at what I do. Don't you worry about me."

There had been a nugget of doubt resting at the back of my mind about the turnaround of *Verity*, but I wasn't about to admit that to Tristan. Not when I'd not allowed *myself* to think about it for long. Normally my goal was to make something profitable and sustainable in the medium and long term. It wasn't usually to change course from unprofitable to *really* unprofitable.

"Have you even thought about whether you want to run a business long-term?"

What was Tristan doing tonight? Throwing darts and then when they hit, twisting them to see if he could catch an artery? "I don't think I will. I'll need to get in an MD." I knew I couldn't run *Verity*—it wasn't in my wheelhouse. For me, going in to a failing business was like going into a zoo when all the keepers had gone home and left the cages open. It was up to me to herd the animals back into their pens and shut the doors. Then I had to clean up the mess they'd left before doors opened again. Once the first visitor arrived, it was game over for me. The day to day running of a zoo wasn't what I wanted to do.

"So if you're going to do it in the short term, do you know how you're going to move from A to B—how you're going to move from gossip to politics or whatever it will be? Are you going to shut down current operations, fire everyone, and start from scratch? Or are you going to spin off current operations into an online-only business under a different brand and then build *Verity* back slowly? I mean, what's the plan?"

I had thought about the answers to Tristan's questions but they hadn't been my focus. All my energy had been channeled into getting Goode to agree to the sale. If he didn't do that, there was no point in having a brilliant plan I couldn't implement.

"I'm working on it."

"Is Sofia the problem?"

I frowned and took a sip of my wine to unclench my jaw. Tristan was my friend. I had to remind myself he wasn't *trying* to be provocative. "Sofia isn't a problem."

"You clearly like her."

"Why would that be a problem?"

"As long as it doesn't cloud your judgement, it's not."

Now he was really starting to piss me off. I set my glass down. "Women don't cloud my judgement."

Tristan nodded. "Okay then."

He wasn't going to elaborate? "Why would you think that?"

"Because it's just not like you to try to trick someone into doing business with you."

"But it's like me to do everything I bloody-well can to get what I want."

"You've never struck me as a man who'd compromise who he is to get what he wants. So something's changed."

"Nothing's changed. Nothing's ever been as important to me as getting *Verity*."

"Getting it away from Goode, or making it a success? I'm not trying to be a dick here; I just think you're not acting like yourself. Sofia seems great, and maybe she's not the issue. But something's off."

Tristan was one of my best friends. It was his job to challenge me and take me to task when he thought something was wrong. I had to listen. He was right when he said I was supremely focused on getting my hands on *Verity*, and he was right that I hadn't worked out in any detail what I wanted to do with it when I had it. I knew the end result. I just didn't have the roadmap to get me there. I should have spent more time planning, but my lack of preparation had nothing to do with Sofia. If it hadn't been for her, I wouldn't be within touching distance of actually getting hold of *Verity*.

"Okay," I said. "I've heard what you've said and I'll think about it."

"I'll drink to that." He held up his glass full of who-knew-what. It was fucking green with a yellow parasol in it.

"What the fuck are you drinking?"

"I'm always trying what's new. Don't want to be like you, old and stale."

"Fuck off."

Tristan grinned like I just told him I loved him.

THIRTY-TWO

Sofia

Andrew had been borderline charming to my mother. For him anyway. He hadn't snarled, had talked more than he usually did, and I'd even caught him smiling a couple of times while he glanced between me and my mom as she told me everything that had happened to every Italian-American on the island of Manhattan since I'd left for London. He'd helped clear plates and offered to wash up. That was never going to happen while my mother had a beating heart in her chest—not because Andrew was a man, but because he was a guest.

Now he was gone, my mother had gone quiet.

"What's the matter, Mamma?" I asked her as I put the final clean plate away in the cupboard. "Are you tired? Do you want me to leave?"

She grabbed my hand from where she was sitting on the ripped kitchen chair and pulled me down to sit next to her. "Are you serious about this man? He's so much older."

I shook my head. "Not by so much. Just a few years." I

patted her on the knee and tried to pull my hand away, but she pulled it onto my lap. "What's the matter? You didn't like him?"

"If he's not older, he's more established. He has money and a company and . . . I don't want to see you taken advantage of."

"He's not taking advantage of me," I replied. Is that what she'd witnessed from our interaction this evening? What had been said or done that might make her feel like that? "He's a good guy."

"Bambina, he's rich and good-looking and older. I know these men." She looked me dead in the eye and we both knew she was talking about my father. "These men see you as nothing. As their plaything. They will play with you, make you dance, and then what?"

I went to speak but she held up her palm. She wasn't finished.

"I know you're going to tell me I'm wrong, Andrew's different and so wonderful, but these men are used to getting what they want. At any price. Now he wants you. What happens when he doesn't want you anymore?"

If she'd been talking to Natalie about one of her bum boyfriends I'd be nodding vehemently. Mamma always talked so much sense. She was wise and understood things we didn't. But she was wrong about Andrew, wasn't she?

My gut churned with confusion. I loved my mother more than anyone else in the world. I trusted her and I was entirely certain she only had my best interests at heart. Although Andrew could be surly and rude in the office at times, he was a good man. He'd never done anything to make me think otherwise. Then again, I hadn't known him long.

My mom had been warning me about men like my

father for my entire life. She taught me the importance of independence and how I had to make my own money and live life on my own terms—create my own future. They were all good lessons. But she taught me these things because my father had lied and broken promises to her, and she didn't want me following in her footsteps when it came to men. Andrew wasn't my father. I wasn't even sure Des was quite the monster that my mother described.

"Do you ever wonder what happened to my father?" I asked.

My mother tutted and glanced around her apartment. "I do not. I have enough to worry about in my life right now."

She was right. I was sure her knee would be excruciating after preparing dinner for us all.

"You remember you said he offered you that money when he got back to England?" She acted like she hadn't heard me and went to stand. "You ever think you should have taken it?"

She snorted. "It would have relieved his guilt, that's all. What's with all the questions? You need to think about your future, not your past."

I shrugged. "You made the comparison between Andrew and . . . *him*." I'd always been so savvy when it came to relationships with men. I never gave more than I got, never compromised my plans or dreams. But with Andrew, things felt a little different. Was this a feeling I had to be afraid of?

"Why can't you find yourself a nice Italian boy? Someone like Lorenzo—"

"You want me to date gay men?"

"I didn't say Lorenzo. I said someone *like* him. Someone

with a steady job and a good family. Someone . . . buono come il pane. Someone who will take care of you."

"I can take care of myself. You taught me that. I'm not relying on Andrew." That wasn't quite true. He was my boss. For now. And it wasn't like we were engaged or even thinking along those lines. My feelings for him were unexpected, and stronger than I remembered having for anyone else, but we were still at the beginning of whatever was between us.

"You just need to be careful. Learn from my mistakes. Don't get burned."

Andrew might be rich and powerful and *very* attractive. But he wasn't my father. We weren't kids. He hadn't made any promises that could be broken. "I'm not going to get burned."

She shook her head. "So certain of everything, tesoro. I know that look in your eye. I had it once myself, too."

As much as I might want to, I couldn't dismiss what she was saying. She thought I was following the same fate, falling for a rich, handsome man from England. I couldn't blame her. Was I being naïve thinking that Andrew was different? Special? Worthy of my trust?

I didn't want to believe it, but that didn't mean it wasn't true.

THIRTY-THREE

Andrew

Fucking Tristan. No one made me doubt myself. But I couldn't stop pacing the length of the Presidential Suite, playing our conversation over and over in my head.

There was no doubt I would have preferred to have sat across the table from Goode, written him a big check and told him to go fuck himself when he signed *Verity* over to me.

I couldn't force him to sell face to face, but did I want to "trick" him as Tristan described it?

Verity had been established to uncover lies and corruption and injustice. What would my grandmother think if I got her company back by lying?

I collapsed back on the sofa. I knew the answer to that—she'd tell me it wasn't worth it. If she was alive today, she'd tell me to let go and move on, that her legacy wasn't in the magazine but in the people whose lives she touched.

She'd said the same thing when my mother first went to her with the idea of selling the magazine.

The choice had been made years ago, by the women in my family with a stronger connection to *Verity, Inc.* than I'd ever had. I should never have come to New York in the first place. I'd lost sight of the ultimate aim of restoring a legacy.

My heart lifted in my chest and the tension in my neck and shoulders seeped away. It was the right decision; I could feel it in my body and heart. I could feel it in my DNA, for Christ's sake.

Sofia was going to be pissed off. I hoped she would understand when I explained it to her.

My phone buzzed with a message from Sofia—a screen-shot of a reply from Goode about accepting her rejection of his offer and still wanting a meeting on Monday. Shit. It would have been easier if he'd called to cancel.

I typed her a reply, telling her we needed to talk.

When I opened the door to the suite, I could tell by the way she wouldn't meet my gaze that something was wrong. "What happened?" I asked.

She gave me a one-shouldered shrug. "What do you want to talk about?"

Her mood had soured like month-old milk. We'd had a lovely evening at her mother's place. The food, wine, and conversation had been great. But something had clearly shifted for her.

"You want a drink?"

"No. I need a clear head for this."

"For what?" I said, the tension in my neck returning like a mast being hoisted into position.

"Whatever you're going to say."

I exhaled and took a seat on the sofa. Instead of coming to sit next to me, she perched on the stool for the grand piano.

"I want to cancel the meeting on Monday."

She blinked once then twice, as if she were processing my words. "Just like that, you've changed your mind?"

"I had a chat with Tristan today and . . . I don't like what I'm doing. I don't want to get *Verity* back if it means lying and cheating to do it."

Her head shot up and she stood. "Tristan changed your mind? What happened?"

"We've known each other a long time. It's our job to keep each other in check, and we trust each other to tell us when we're making a mistake."

"And Tristan thinks you're making a mistake?"

I patted the sofa next to me, inviting her to sit. "He pointed out the hypocrisy of me trying to restore *Verity, Inc.* as a bastion of truth when I had to lie to own it."

"Right," Sofia said, plonking herself on the sofa next to me.

"I'm not prepared to sacrifice my character just because Goode's an arsehole."

A small smile curled the edges of her lips. "You always know exactly the right thing to say."

I wasn't sure that was true, but I was all too happy to accept her change in mood. "I'm just telling you the truth."

She nodded. "I know. And I appreciate that." She slid her arms around my waist. I lifted my arm and she burrowed into my side. "I want you to be honest with me. Always. You know . . . for as long as we're . . ."

"I promise."

We sat in silence for a few minutes, just staring out onto Central Park, holding each other.

"Maybe you should go to the breakfast on Monday," she said.

I knew owning *Verity* was hopeless now. There was no point in flogging a dead horse. "It's fine. I've got to move on and honor my grandmother's legacy in a different way."

"Isn't it worth one last shot?"

"I've been on this hamster wheel with Goode for years now. I need to step off, dust myself down, and break out of the cage. It's done. I've made peace with it."

Sofia tapped her fingers against my chest. "Just turn up to the breakfast on Monday—"

"Seriously, it's fine. I'm over it."

She pulled out of my arms and gave me a don't-fuck-with-me look. "Hear me out. You know what I said about his ego? This is information you didn't have before. You can make it work to your advantage. Go to the Monday meeting and confess. Tell him I work for you, what we'd been planning. Then tell him how much your grandmother's legacy means to you."

"He knows, Sofia. He doesn't give a shit."

"I'm not so sure. Like I said, ego drives that man. He just doesn't want to end up with egg on his face. If you go to him and offer to keep him as a partner—"

"I've told you—I've offered a thousand times to go in and manage the business for him, to turn it around."

"Goddamnit, Andrew, stop interrupting me. I'm telling you not to *just* manage the business. Offer to take all the risk by buying out the majority of the shares but keeping him as a minority shareholder. You put all the money in, do all the work turning around—under his minority ownership, at zero risk to him. If it fails, the deal states you have to buy him out—so publicly, it looks like you've sunk the ship. If you're successful, he can publicly participate in the success because he's still a shareholder."

I took in what she was saying. Her suggestion put Goode in a position where he had nothing to lose, and a front-row seat to my humiliation to gain if I failed. That would be hard for him to pass up.

"You might be on to something. I just don't know if he'll be able to get over the fact that I've deceived him by sending you in to bat for me."

"Maybe not, but you have nothing to lose by being honest. We're in New York anyway."

She was right: if I didn't try, I'd always wonder if I'd left a stone unturned.

"I'll try, but you know, Tristan fed me another home truth tonight and it's got me thinking." I explained to her how he made me see I wasn't prepared if Goode actually agreed to sell. "I wondered if you'd be interested in putting together some operations planning in the unlikely event Goode takes the deal."

Wearing a big grin, she shook her head exaggeratedly. "What am I going to do with you? You've come to your senses and realized that not only am I a fantastic assistant, I have a lot of skills you're missing out on."

I shifted her onto my lap. "I want to experience your entire skill set."

"I'm not sure you're ready," she replied.

"Try me."

THIRTY-FOUR

Andrew

Despite it being April in New York City, the heat from the sun reflected off the buildings and felt like August. My phone buzzed and I answered it. "Andrew Blake."

"Andrew, you know it's me calling, just say 'Hi Sofia.' Anyway, what the hell happened with Goode and why haven't you called me already?"

I laughed. "I just stepped out right now."

"I know," she said, "I can see you."

I glanced across at my waiting limo and squinted to see if I could see inside. The window wound down to reveal Sofia. "Get in here," she said, grinning. "I want to hear everything."

I'd been completely honest with Goode. Told him everything—even that Sofia was my assistant. He'd sat quietly as I told him I hated him for what he'd done to the magazine and hated him more for not selling to me, even though we both knew it wasn't turning a profit. His defenses had been up until I talked about co-ownership.

"He wants to do it," I said as we pulled out into traffic. "He'll be a minority owner. We're privately owned, so he can pretend to whoever cares that he still owns it. If it goes well, he can take the credit; if it goes badly, he can blame me. Just like you said."

Sofia grinned. "Holy shit, it worked."

"Honesty is the best policy, apparently."

"Guess that means I'm busy on Monday doing the operations planning. You might have to get a new assistant."

I groaned, an uncomfortable knot lodging in my throat. "No way. I don't like new people who get offended because I don't speak to them."

"We'll figure it out," she said. "New York, you've been good to me, as always." She made the sign of the cross and looked up to the roof of the limo. I was sure she wasn't going to find whatever she was looking for up there.

"What's next?" I asked.

"JFK," she said. "Everything's in the trunk."

"Back to London via the mile high club?" I coughed, trying to dislodge the nodule of disquiet I couldn't quite swallow down.

There was no doubt the last few days in New York had shifted things between Sofia and me, and I wasn't ready to give her up. I wasn't sure if I ever would be. I just couldn't shake the storm clouds gathering in my brain. I'd been here before—sleeping with someone I worked a few paces away from. It hadn't worked then, and it couldn't work now. Einstein wasn't wrong when he said the definition of insanity was repeating history and expecting a different result, but I might already be too far gone to walk away from Sofia.

THIRTY-FIVE

Sofia

Two days after our return from New York, I returned to Blake Enterprises to find it unchanged—but somehow, everything was different. I chewed my lip as I slid off my coat, hung it on the rack, and took a seat behind my desk.

When he thought I wasn't looking, I'd caught Andrew staring at me a couple of times on the flight back to London.

It was like he didn't have anything better to do than to look at me—a far cry from the flight over, when he barely acknowledged my existence. His hand had slid into mine at various points during the flight, and I brushed his hair out of his eyes when he fell asleep. He'd made sure I was hydrated and I'd shared my extra blanket with him.

We'd been in New York less than a week, but something had shifted between us. He'd lowered his guard and I'd let him in. We'd become a couple.

We'd gone straight to my place from the airport, then slept and ate and fucked through Tuesday. This morning, when the alarm went off, he was already gone. I tried to shake off the rolling chill in my chest. I didn't expect us to saunter into the office hand-in-hand, but I hadn't expected him to pull a Houdini, either.

There was so much still unsaid between us.

I immersed myself in work as Andrew's office door remained firmly closed. Even though I had the urge to stick my head around the door and offer him a coffee, I resisted. This was his focus time. I needed to respect that.

At exactly midday, Douglas came through to the outer office.

"Great news about Goode," he said. "This is going to be different for him. You know, running a company in the long term."

I nodded. "Very different. But good."

"We've got a lot of work to do. We won't be able to handle it all. First on the agenda is recruitment."

Douglas knocked on Andrew's door before I had a chance to ask him what he meant. Andrew was going to run *Verity*, I was going to be his assistant, and Bob was going to be his finance guy. The rest of the office was going to do what the rest of the office always did. Who were we going to recruit?

Douglas wasn't in Andrew's office long before he swept out juggling a pile of papers. He always went in looking composed and came out looking like he'd wrestled a tiger.

"Sofia!" Andrew bellowed through his closed door.

Instinctively I jumped up, grabbed a notebook, and went inside.

Andrew didn't look up as I entered.

"Sit."

I wanted to tell him to go get a dog if that's how he wanted to speak to someone, but instead I took a deep breath and reminded myself that his tone was nothing new.

I couldn't expect him to have had a personality transplant just because we were . . . whatever we were.

Even if I had the chance to change Andrew's behavior at work . . . would I? I'd fallen for the man Andrew was outside the office, but I wasn't *not* attracted to the man he was inside it. His intense focus and no-bullshit attitude were sexy as hell. He wasn't cruel—could never be cruel—and I vowed not to start taking his brusque demeanor personally just because things had changed between us outside of the office.

"I have a proposal for you," he said.

I had the wherewithal to feel embarrassed by the part of my brain that screeched *"YES I'LL MARRY YOU!"* I shook my head to clear the rogue thought and mentally slammed the door on every rom-com Natalie and I had ever watched.

"Verity," he said, at last looking up to meet my gaze.

"Verity," I repeated. "I'm working on the plan. The transition from where they are now and where we want to take them is going to be key."

Andrew drew in a long breath and nodded. "I agree. And finding the right person to guide them through that is essential. I need to recruit a CEO."

So that's what Douglas had been talking about.

"You don't want to do it yourself?" The reason Andrew was so attached to this business was because of his personal connection to it. Didn't he want to be in charge?

"Nope. Goode made it a stipulation that I shouldn't lead the change there. And it makes sense. The business is too personal for me. Besides, I'm not sure I need to be in the weeds."

"Shall I reach out to some headhunters?"

"That depends," he said. "My first choice for CEO is you."

I turned my head to the side slightly, wondering if my hearing was going in one ear. What did he just say? "Me?"

"Yes. You're bright, you know the business, and Goode agrees. We both want you to run it."

"Even now he knows I lied to him?"

"Yes. He knows you're on my payroll. I also told him your ideas about a membership model weren't mine. Plus, he knows your CV."

"Then he'll know I don't have any experience running a business." I wasn't trying to talk myself out of a job, but I didn't want to sink the ship before it was out to sea.

"I'll guide you. You have an MBA, so you know the theory at least, and everyone has to run a business for the first time at some point."

"You think I can do it?" It wasn't a question I would normally ask someone offering me a job, but I was overcome by a powerful wave of self-doubt. "I'm just your assistant."

"We both know you're overqualified to be my assistant, and I wouldn't have asked you if I didn't think you were capable. Goode likes that you're a hustler. And I know talent. Remember, my job is to go into organizations, promote talent, and get rid of whatever prevents the company from thriving. I know what you're capable of, and you're more than capable of this. I know you." He looked me dead in the eye. "I can trust you."

This was the break I'd been waiting for. In fact, it was the break I'd thought I'd still be waiting for in five years. It was the opportunity of a lifetime. Things like this didn't happen to people like me. Yes, I got into a decent college and then Columbia, but none of it was easy. I had to work harder, be better. Everything was a challenge. I didn't get handed opportunities like this. It might be the kind of opportunity Bella and Bryony could expect to get when their time came, but nothing like this had ever been on my radar.

"I'll take it."

"There's just one thing," he said.

Of course there had to be a catch. There was always a catch.

My heart boomed like someone was swinging a baseball bat on a kettle drum inside my chest. I braced myself to hear what was next.

"You and I . . ." Andrew sighed and nodded. "We've become close."

I swallowed. A wave of dread surged like an army toward me. I sat powerless against what was next.

"You know how I feel about mixing my personal and professional life."

Heat rose from my stomach and burned hot in my chest. I nodded, impatient for the inevitable.

"With you as CEO of *Verity*, it's important that we keep things professional. The company's success is important to me and I'm going to be your boss long-term. The stakes are high. We need to keep things separate."

"Okay . . ." I said, not quite sure what he meant. Usually there was no clarification required when I had a conversation with Andrew. What was he trying to say— that I should call him James out of the office? "Which means?"

His Adam's apple bobbed and he glanced at his office door like he was willing an interruption. "We should keep our relationship purely professional."

The heat in my chest pushed down out of my limbs, a chill racing down my spine in its wake. I didn't know whether to feel angry or sad. "If you don't want to date me, you don't have to offer me a job that makes it impossible.

You can just tell me you don't want to date me. You're not usually so indirect."

"Sofia," Andrew said in the angry growl I'd come to know.

"I mean it. Don't be a coward."

"I told you, I don't lie. I want you in this job. But it requires a sacrifice. Working together and . . . being together." He shook his head with such certainty it was like he was plunging a knife into my skin. "It's not possible. You'll be great at this job. You have a deep well of creativity, an appetite for hard work, and impressive qualifications. You're perfect for this role. And the money . . . It will make your life a lot easier."

If he hadn't made me an offer I couldn't refuse already, reminding me that the job would come with a pay raise sealed the deal.

I couldn't turn this down. If I didn't get what I needed from my father, I'd have to find another way of paying for my mother's operation. This might be that way. Anyway, I didn't want a man who didn't want to be with me more than he wanted a CEO.

Maybe my mother had been right: Andrew had been playing with me all along. Now he was bored and didn't want me anymore. At least I wasn't pregnant. I supposed I should be thankful for that.

The Rossi women always knew how to look on the bright side.

"Fine," I said. "When do I start?"

Andrew glanced down at his desk, and if I didn't know him better, I could have sworn he wore an air of disappointment. There was no pleasing this man. Maybe it was better things between us were over now, before I got in too deep and realized I'd never be enough for him.

He cleared his throat. "Right away. Liaise with HR. They have the contract details. I want to see your ninety-day transition plan by this time next week."

I stood and smoothed down my skirt, hesitating. Was that it? He was done with me, and now I was dismissed—from his office, his life outside work, and his bed.

THIRTY-SIX

Sofia

I held up my glass, mirroring my father's pose. I was here at lunch with my father in body, if not mind. My mind was all Andrew Blake's. I tried to distract myself and keep busy, but I kept replaying every moment we were together in my mind.

"Congratulations on your brilliant promotion," he said, beaming at me. "So much good news this week. Did I tell you Bella got accepted at the school Evan and I really wanted her to go to?"

"Oh no, I didn't know about that." I needed to focus on the moment right here or I could blow things with my father.

"Yes, it's been a challenge. We want to give her the very best start in life and it starts young, you know?"

My mom had wanted to give me the very best start in life, too. That's why she'd worked as hard as she had.

"The people she goes to school with now will be the

people she does business with in the future. It's such a responsibility."

I stayed silent. If I uttered a word, I feared that my fury and frustration would spill out. How could he be so insensitive, talking to me about the responsibilities of raising a child? To me, the child he abandoned and never made any effort to be responsible for.

"Evan's delighted. We both are."

"Does Bella like the school?" I wanted to steer the conversation onto more neutral territory. Bella was adorable and absolutely not responsible for anything I didn't have growing up.

"Yes, but only because two of her friends are also going to the same school. Anyway, enough me talking about Bella's school. Sometimes I feel that's all I ever talk about. Tell me what you were like at her age."

I shrugged. "Nothing to say, really. The people I went to school with are the drug dealers and gangbangers of today. But my mom was strict and I worked hard so . . . here we are."

Silence pulled between us. "You've done amazingly," he said. "You didn't have anything like the resources that my . . . that Bella has had."

"Nope," I said. "Just a bunch of student loans." And a mother with a knee that needed replacing because she'd scrubbed so many floors.

My feet started to tap against the plush carpet of the restaurant we were in. I wanted to go. Leave. Every time I was with this man, all I could feel was what I'd been missing in my life. What I'd gone without. He'd never taken responsibility—not when he'd grown out of his father's control, not when he got married. He'd had so many opportunities to right his wrong, but he'd never taken a single one of them. If

I'd never called, he would have gone the rest of his life without ever setting eyes on his first daughter.

"I hear college in the US is very expensive," he said.

I nodded. "It is. I'm going to be paying my loans off for decades." It felt good to tell him even a little bit of the impact his lack of support had had, even if it would take days to articulate the full scope. It was too soon to ask him to pay off my debt—and use that money to pay for my mother's surgery—but not soon enough to get him thinking about what he owed me. Yes, I had my salary increase, but it wasn't going to give me the money overnight like a check from Des would. I'd do anything to relieve my mother's pain as soon as possible.

"I suppose you have a great education to show for it," he said. At least he had the decency to sound a little awkward. It had obviously registered at some point that him talking about his daughter getting into some fancy private school was insensitive. I had to keep my eye on the long game and remember that I didn't need to like the man in front of me. I just needed him to like me.

"I absolutely do."

"I have no idea what really brought you to my door, Sofia. I don't know if it was curiosity or something more. But I'm glad you're here. I never wanted to lose all connection to you."

I couldn't help myself—my eyebrows arched of their own accord. "Really?"

"Really. I understand why your mother cut off contact. What she needed from me was money, but I didn't have any to give her."

Had I heard him correctly? "Skip back a beat. My *mother* cut off contact? With you?"

"Yes. You know that, right? After I came back to

England, we kept talking . . . and then one day I tried to call her and the number was dead."

My mouth went dry and my palms began to sweat. It felt like I was chewing chalk. She'd cut him off?

No. He had to be wrong. He'd abandoned us.

"I thought you knew. I shouldn't have said anything."

I glanced up at him. "I want to know the truth. I think I deserve that."

"I can't blame your mother and neither should you. She was protecting herself. I'd hurt her and she was just trying to stop the pain. I get it. I got it at the time."

That made sense, but why hadn't she told me? Not that we spoke about my father very often, but it was a key detail in the story of how we came to be the way we were.

"When I finally hit twenty-five and got access to my trust fund, I tried to contact her again," he continued. "I even flew to New York, though I had no idea where to look. We were students when I last saw her. She'd talked about her mother, but I'd never been to the house. I didn't know where she lived. I went to that bakery she loved—the one downtown with the great cannoli?"

My head was spinning. I wanted to stop the ride and get off. I knew the story. My mother had always been honest with me. She'd told him she was pregnant and he'd fled New York to go back to London. They'd spoken a couple of times and he made it clear that he wanted nothing to do with me. *That* was the truth.

"You're saying it's my mother's fault that you and I don't know each other and that . . ." What *was* he saying?

"Absolutely not. She was doing the best she could. From her perspective, she had a boyfriend who abandoned her as soon as she was pregnant and then didn't help her out. This wasn't your mother's fault. The responsibility lies at my door. I want you to know that."

Sadness welled in my stomach. Sadness for my mother, for the feelings of panic and loneliness she must have experienced as someone she loved slipped away from her. Sadness for my father, for understanding how weak he was and not finding the strength to change. Sadness for me and the life I might have had if both my parents had been . . . different. Older. Wiser.

"Not knowing you has been a huge regret in my life," he said, his voice thick with melancholy. "And now you're back. I want to try to make things right. You should know that I've adjusted my will to reflect the fact that I have three daughters."

It was as if he'd reached down my throat and pulled out my lungs. I didn't have air. I didn't have words. I didn't know how to respond.

"I'm not looking for credit or thanks. It should never have been any other way. I hope we can continue getting to know each other like this, but even if you decide you don't want to pursue a relationship with me, nothing will change as far as my will is concerned."

I have three daughters.

His words rang in my ears. I'd grown up not having a father. I wasn't the only kid in school in the same boat, but my dad hadn't run off with another woman. He hadn't divorced my mom, hadn't gone to prison, been shot and killed. He had just . . . never existed.

"I never expected anything like that," I said, my voice coming out quieter than I was used to.

"I've never given you any reason to expect anything from me. I hope I can change that. You know you can come to me. For anything. Anytime."

This would be the perfect moment to tell him about my mother's knee, but something in me couldn't. I'd spent these lunches and coffees trying to position myself so I could ask, and now I had the opportunity, it didn't feel right.

Would it ever? Maybe when I'd settled into my job. Maybe when I'd had a chance to come to terms with what had happened between Andrew and me. Maybe when my focus wasn't splintered between the present, and every moment I'd ever spent naked in Andrew's arms.

Maybe, maybe, maybe.

THIRTY-SEVEN

Sofia

I had less than seven minutes before Andrew arrived. Seven minutes before I had to present my ideas for changing *Verity, Inc.* back into the publication it had been in its heyday. If that wasn't enough, I had to do it without having slept since Andrew ended things between us. I was almost dizzy with a combination of fatigue, adrenaline, and frustration. Obsessing about Andrew and how he'd managed to walk away from us without a second glance was another reason why I hadn't gotten around to reading my employment contract until now. I'd run out of time. I was supposed to hand it to Douglas when he arrived with Andrew. I scanned the papers again. This couldn't be right. I punched the HR director's number into the desk phone.

"Hi, Wendy, it's Sofia. I have a couple of questions on my contract. Mostly around salary and bonuses."

"It wasn't what you expected?"

It was far more than I'd been expecting. My salary meant that not only was I able to save every month—even with the astronomical rent I was paying and my student loan payments—but I was going to be able to put a dent in the fifty grand for my mother's operation. If my father didn't end up paying out, then within a couple of years, I might be able to pay for her procedure myself. "I just wanted to check how this works. The bonus is on top of the annual salary, right?"

"Yes, you have an annual bonus and a rolling three-year-long term bonus."

"Two bonuses? That's normal?"

"Yes. You've got a very typical executive compensation plan. It's the same across everyone at your level at Blake Enterprises. Obviously, you have to be employed in the company in three years for the long-term bonus to pay out."

If my mom could hold out until I got my annual bonus, I could definitely afford her knee replacement. Maybe I could even pay her some money every month so she didn't have to work two jobs.

It was a dream come true. There'd been too many recently.

First Andrew, then the job offer, now the bonus. I kept telling myself that it made sense that Andrew and I hadn't lasted. I couldn't expect too much. A job and a prospect of some savings was what I'd needed when I'd come to London. Wanting more was just tempting fate.

My assistant popped her head around the door and pointed animatedly in the direction of the *Verity* meeting room.

Apparently, Andrew had arrived.

"Thanks, Wendy. Gotta go."

I scooped up my papers and sped along the corridor.

I took a deep breath and opened the meeting room door. "Andrew, Douglas, how are you both?"

It had been just over a week since I'd last seen or heard from Andrew. He'd been true to his word and hadn't been in touch at all since he'd offered me the *Verity* job. I'd even stopped by Noble Rot the first three days after my promotion to see if James made an appearance, but he'd disappeared too.

I was equal parts angry at and grateful to Andrew. I understood that sleeping with the boss was a cliché and that he, more than most people, had an incentive to keep walls up between his worlds. But wasn't it worth a shot? Weren't *we* worth it?

I thought so.

Seeing him made my stomach rock like I was on a row boat in the middle of the Atlantic. How had we shared so much in such a small space of time and now, sitting opposite each other across a boardroom table that felt wider than an ocean, it was like we'd never been anything more than professional colleagues.

My mom was right when she told me that there was no such thing as a free lunch. This was my sacrifice: I'd given up Andrew for this job. A man for my mother's health. What other choice was there?

"What have you got for us?" True to form, Andrew didn't want to waste time chitchatting. I wasn't going to argue.

"My plan is to go from zero to sixty in two-point-five seconds. We want a big-bang launch. The readers, advertisers, and staff needed for *Verity, Inc.* going forward is so completely different to what we have now, there's no soft launch. We go in big and we go in hard."

Andrew's expression was completely blank. I wasn't fazed. I'd rehearsed this presentation fifty times before today. I was confident in my subject and my decisions, and I couldn't wait to get Andrew excited about my plans. Even if he didn't show it.

I talked them through the research I'd found, some of the market measures and relevant statistics, and a few of the branding ideas I'd been working on.

"So an entirely new team?" Andrew asked.

"I've read in three key creative people about our plans. They're enthusiastic and talented. I want to keep them. Some of the back office can stay if they're on board, but unless people have the skills and experience we need for the future, keeping them on is just prolonging the agony."

Still no reaction.

"Moving on, I've put October first in the diary as the launch day. Key for launch is getting free advertising from other media. We want to go out and talk about your grandmother and her legacy. We'll need to have tight communications on why we're switching from celebrity gossip back to real news. So that's also what we're going to be talking about in the first issue—the rise of celebrity gossip and its impact on politics, power, and the real news media. Hopefully we can get people talking."

Andrew didn't so much as nod throughout my hour-long presentation. Douglas spent most of the meeting with his head down, scribbling notes.

Had I expected anything else?

As I wrapped up my presentation, Andrew checked his watch. He asked a couple of questions on the financial model and then stood.

"I'd like a sensitivity analysis on the cost exposure. Work with Douglas."

He swept out, and Douglas pulled his papers together and scurried after him. Before he closed the door, he turned. "Great job."

I'd take that from Douglas, especially since it was more than I'd ever get from Andrew. I'd have Andrew's verdict based on whether or not I had a job next week. At least I knew how he operated. Still, I couldn't help but focus on the rush of air from my deflating heart as I stared at the back of the door.

THIRTY-EIGHT

Andrew

My new assistant, Trudy, knocked on my office door at exactly ten thirty-three. She'd asked me three times yesterday whether or not this meeting was a mistake because of the time. Other than that, Trudy was shaping up quite nicely. She was almost as irritable as I was and clearly had no desire to discuss anything but work. She was efficient and didn't seem to be offended by my monosyllabic responses to her questions.

She wasn't Sofia, but she'd do.

"Come in," I said, standing and rounding my desk.

"Aryia Chowdhury," Trudy announced as the writer followed her inside and then appeared from behind her, holding out her hand.

I took it, careful not to crush her tiny fingers. "Aryia."

"Thank you for making time to see me. From what I've read about you, I'm sure you're very busy."

"Verity Blake was important." I guided her to one of my guest chairs as I took one opposite her.

"We have a real plot twist now you've gone and invested in *Verity, Inc.*" She pulled out her tape recorder and pad. "Do you mind?" she said, placing the recorder on the desk beside us.

I shook my head.

"I think this is the first interview you've ever done, isn't it?"

I pretended not to know, but she was right. "I'm not a celebrity."

"But you're kind of famous in your world."

I pulled my mouth into an almost-smile. "We're all kind of famous in our own worlds."

"Good point. Was your grandmother a star of your family as well as the publishing industry?"

"Absolutely," I said, my body starting to relax. I could talk about how amazing my grandmother was until the cows came home. "She was the matriarch of our family until right up to her death."

"And as a child, did you have a sense of how important she'd been as a journalist and as an example to women?"

I thought back to the woman I'd loved. "Not as a young child. I just saw her as a warm, fun woman who I loved. As I got older, I was drawn to her because she was one of the rare people in my life who talked to me about complicated, difficult things. We'd often discuss the articles in *Verity, Inc.* around the family table.

"What did she pass down the generations?"

"A fire in my belly. Her work ethic was incredible. She stayed contributing editor right up until we sold the magazine, and her passion for what she did showed me what work should be. If you *have* to work—not for the money or the status or the power, but because you feel you are on a mission—that's purpose. We all have a purpose in life, but many of us never find it. My grandmother made sure I knew that whatever I did, I should feel passionate about it. I should feel like it was my destiny."

The journalist paused and looked at me. "And your purpose is to help companies become more efficient?"

"Among other things." I wasn't here to talk about me. I wanted to talk about my grandmother. "My grandmother's purpose was journalism. To find buried truths and bring them into the light."

"I like that," she said. "Truth into the light."

"But she was also passionate about her family. Yes, there was truth and light—it was simply her nature to illuminate the dark spaces in life—but there was also warmth and happiness and laughter. Everything was brighter and more exciting when she was around."

"And her husband, did he feel outshone by her?"

I smiled. "Absolutely not. He was lit up by her. We all were." I thought about it for a minute. The running of *Verity, Inc.* had been passed to my mother when my grandfather died. "He wanted to see her shine."

"For a man of his generation, though . . ." She stopped herself. "Even for a man of your generation, it's sometimes difficult to be near powerful women."

"I can't speak for men of any generation," I said. "But my grandfather's shine wasn't dimmed by my grandmother's light. He basked in it. And my father encouraged my mother's ambitions as if they were his own. I'm built the same way."

It was one of the reasons I had to end things with Sofia. She should know she got the *Verity* job based on her talent and ability. Not because she was fucking the boss. I wanted her to be incandescent.

"Andrew?"

"Sorry, what did you say?" I never zoned out in a meeting, but the personal nature of Aryia's questions made it too easy for Sofia to interrupt my thoughts. I wondered what life would be like with her. She had the same passion as my grandmother. I saw it in Sofia's mother when I met her, too. I could imagine us around a kitchen table debating the issues of the day, teaching our children what was important in life. Living. Loving. Basking.

I'd expected to end things with Sofia and move on with a clean slate, just like I had done with every woman I'd ever been involved with. But the less I saw of Sofia, the more I thought about her. Had I been stupid to offer her the job at *Verity*? I could have just fired her. She would have found something else. And then what? Would we be together, spending our nights around the kitchen table, talking about current events over big glasses of Barolo?

"Will you excuse me one moment?" I said, pulling out my phone from my pocket.

I brought up the group chat I had with my brothers. *Consider this my bat signal,* I typed.

"*See you at six at Dexter's horrible bar,*" Beck replied immediately.

I smiled and slid the phone into my pocket.

"My grandmother taught me about family. About passion. About what's important in life. She taught me how to live." Except if she were here now, I didn't think she'd be impressed with how I'd been applying her lessons. At least not where Sofia was concerned.

THIRTY-NINE

Sofia

For the first time since Natalie had returned to New Jersey, I felt homesick. I kicked off my shoes, nudged the front door shut with my butt, and padded into my bedroom to change. Up until now, London had kept me distracted. First it was finding a job, then Andrew, James, Bob Goode, and finally *Verity*. I hadn't had time to notice how lonely I felt.

As if she'd heard me from three thousand miles away, my cell flashed from where it had been discarded on my bed. Natalie.

"I miss you," she said before I could say anything.

"I miss you too."

We hadn't actually spoken since she'd found out that I was sleeping with Andrew. There'd been texts here and there. I'd told her about my new job. She congratulated me. I'd told her that Andrew and I weren't sleeping together anymore, and she offered to call. I'd assured her I was fine.

I wasn't fine.

"I'm sorry I was so down on Andrew," she said. "You obviously saw something in him that I didn't."

Even now it felt like I saw a side of him that he didn't share with most people. And that's why it was so hard to understand why he'd just ended things. He hadn't even suggested we try being together and working together. Maybe I'd been wrong about thinking what was between us was special. I'd assumed he felt the same. If he had, though, he would never have been able to walk away so easily. What I'd had with Andrew had been different from anything I'd ever had with someone else. He'd been the first man I'd really trusted be true to his word—the first man I'd been so completely and utterly myself with.

"Don't worry about it. It's over now anyway."

"Over? You want to talk about it?"

"Nothing to talk about. He doesn't mix business with . . . anything. So, here we are." I pulled on my favorite Yankees tee and slipped off my skirt.

"But he promoted you, so that's nice."

"He did. And I love the job. It's impossible and stressful, but I still love it." Sweatpants on, I shuffled the four steps to the kitchen. A life with no money in New York had me well trained for living in this tiny apartment.

"You don't sound happy," she said.

"I'm fine." I had my dream job. What didn't I have to be happy about? I was making more money. I was getting along with my father. I even had time to go and see some of London now I wasn't job searching or sleeping with my boss. I had nothing to complain about.

"How are things with Des?"

"Good. He's . . . He's a nice man. Not the monster I expected." If he'd been a monster, it would have been far easier to ask him for the money, take it and get my mom better. But he was a good man who had just made mistakes. Maybe I would find the right time to ask him. Just not yet.

"Is he going to give you the money?"

"I haven't asked him yet." I didn't tell her about the will. "It's harder than you think to ask someone for fifty grand. Even if they owe you."

"I imagine it is. Especially if you want to have an ongoing relationship with them." She didn't ask it like a question, but it was one—and I didn't have the answer. I knew I wasn't ready to close the door on my father. I had too many questions. Too much I wanted to know. I didn't know how long that would last.

I collapsed with a glass of wine onto the sofa that had been my bed for my first few weeks in London and told Natalie what my father had told me about his parents, my mother disconnecting her phone and him trying to find us years later when he came into his own money.

"Do you believe him?"

"I do. He defended my mother. He doesn't blame her. He holds himself accountable and he's . . . sorry."

"Have you told your mom?"

I needed to tell her I'd made contact with my father. At some point. I just didn't know when.

Or how.

"She doesn't need to know. Not yet. It would only hurt her, and what purpose would it serve? I don't need her feeling guilty or full of regret for cutting him loose. She did what she had to." I didn't blame my mom. She'd described the situation and my father as honestly as she could. There was always more than one version of the truth. My mother had hers; my father had his.

"Right. So what's next?"

I sighed and put down my glass. "I have no idea. I

suppose I keep spending time with my father and wait for the right moment to ask him. I just hope . . . I hope by asking him, I don't undo what we've built. I came to London to manipulate him into giving me money. That's not a very nice thing to do."

"You had your reasons. And like you said, he owes you."

"I know but it feels . . . I just wish I could pay myself. With the new job, if I save hard, work hard, hit my targets and get my bonus, I think I can get the money in a little over a year."

"That's amazing." Natalie bit at her bottom lip, a nervous tell she'd been unable to break since we were kids. "Listen, I've been wondering whether I should tell you this, but . . . you remember Caterina Costa from—"

"I remember." Who could forget Caterina Costa? She was one of those girls all Italians in New York knew. She'd gone to Harvard on a scholarship, and the rest of us would never live up to her accomplishments.

"I ran into her yesterday. She said her mom ran into Mamma Isabella at church, and Mamma Isabella said she'd been talking with your mom, and your mom had mentioned her knee was so bad she was going to have to leave her job at Christina's because—"

"She has to take the subway to that job." My heart pulled in my chest. Stairs had been a problem for a while.

"Right. And it's been a problem for a couple of years but apparently it's gotten worse in the last few months."

"How much worse?" Irritation pinched at me. Why hadn't my mom told me? Probably because she thought I'd rush home. She thought I'd come to England to follow my dreams. She didn't know I was here for her.

"Apparently she's going to give notice at the end of the month."

· · ·

IT WAS like a brick had dropped through my stomach. Mamma had been dreading the moment she wasn't fit enough to work but not ill enough to qualify for the surgery under her insurance. I wanted to book the first flight home and cook meatballs for her, take care of her—but that wouldn't help in the long-run. I was going to have to suck it up and ask Des. There was no other way. Yes, I could probably supplement my mom's income to cover the second job, but her knee was clearly getting worse more quickly than I expected. And what would happen if I got fired? "I'll figure it out. That's what the Rossi girls do."

"You couldn't ask Andrew?" she asked.

I laughed. "No. He's my boss, not my friend."

"I heard your mom met him when you came to New York. Did she like him?"

"Maybe. She worries about me."

"She just wants you to have a better life than she did."

"I'm not nineteen. And Andrew would never—" I didn't need to defend him. We weren't together. I wasn't going to end up pregnant and penniless.

"You seem sad."

I sighed. "I know you don't want to hear this, but I miss him. I wish I didn't need this job so much." Not that it would have mattered if I'd turned the job down. The fact that Andrew had chosen having a CEO rather than me told me everything I needed to know. Sure, Goode had wanted me as CEO too, but he hadn't made it a condition of the sale. Andrew could have pushed back, but he didn't. He wasn't the man for me.

"I just know you're going to meet someone."

I didn't want to meet just anyone. I wanted Andrew to

want me more than he wanted a vacancy filled. I wanted him to want me like I wanted him.

My mother had warned me about men who seemed too good to be true. The ones that made you feel like princesses. They were the ones who had the power to break your heart when they walked away.

"Come visit me," I said.

"I will. I promise. Tell me you're coming back for Thanksgiving." How could she be thinking about Thanksgiving? We were barely in May.

I laughed. "Honestly, I haven't given it a lot of thought. I can't imagine not being—"

"Wait a second," Natalie interrupted.

"Honestly, I'll try and make it. I just haven't—"

"I'm not talking about Thanksgiving. I'm talking about an idea. I mean, it might be crazy but it might—you said that what you're earning now means that if you save hard enough, you might have enough money to pay for your mom's surgery in just over a year, right?"

"Right," I replied.

"And you haven't asked you father for the money yet because there hasn't been the right moment, or you feel awkward and because . . . Well, you're not great at asking for help at the best of times."

"I'm not asking someone for directions or to loan me an umbrella. I'm asking someone to cough up fifty grand. This is not about me being bad at asking for help."

"Okay, but—"

"And," I said, not finished rebutting her character analysis, "I asked to stay on your couch."

"Well, I have two things to say about that. First, I don't count because I'm your best friend. Secondly, I'd give you fifty grand in a heartbeat if I could. But I do have about seven and a half."

"I'm not taking your money." It was so kind of her, but like it or not seven and a half wasn't going to get it done. "It's lovely of you to offer though."

"It's not enough by itself, but what if you asked for an advance?"

"From my father?"

"No, silly. From Andrew. Say you'll commit to staying there for however long if he gives you an advance that you have to pay back if you leave."

"A salary advance? Is that even a thing?"

"I don't know, but what does it hurt to ask? You say he wanted you as CEO because this other guy liked you. So use your leverage."

"For fifty grand? He'd never agree."

"Not fifty. Forty-two and a half—just over thirty thousand pounds, or whatever it comes to. If he gives you less than you ask for, offer to give up bonuses. Maybe you could make up any shortfall by saving every month."

My brain fought to catch up to what she was saying. Obviously, it was impossible. There wasn't a solution to my mom getting her operation immediately without me getting the money from my father. Was there? "You think I just go in and ask him for my bonus in advance? He'll laugh me out of the building."

"Maybe he won't. He needs you. Even if he refuses, you've lost nothing."

"Just my pride."

Natalie laughed. The sounds warmed me from the inside-out, even across an ocean.

"Maybe he says no the first time. But maybe after a month

or so, when you're proving what an asset you are, you ask again. He'll be more willing the second time. This way you're not asking for a favor. You're asking for what you deserve."

"I'm asking for what I might deserve a year from now."

"It's just a change in timetable."

Maybe she was right. Asking my boss for money in advance seemed easier than risking a relationship with my father. And I wasn't asking for anything that wouldn't be mine eventually anyway. I'd be committed to London for the next couple of years, but that was true regardless. There was little chance of me securing a job in the US earning the kind of money I was now—at least not until I could boast a proven track record. A couple of years at *Verity* would give me the experience I desperately needed.

I tried to imagine Andrew's face when I asked him. He probably wouldn't even look at me. I'd just get a terse no and be dismissed. But Natalie was right—it was worth a shot. I just needed to be as determined as I had been that first dark, cold morning waiting outside his office. He'd relented then. Maybe he would again.

FORTY

Andrew

I was the first one to arrive at drinks, which had never happened before.

There was still five minutes to go until we were due to meet, but there had been no point staying in the office. I'd not been able to concentrate on anything since my meeting with Sofia.

"Hey, mate, what's going on?" Dexter said, sliding into the booth next to me.

"I didn't see you come in. You want a drink?"

Dexter gave me a look like he thought I'd lost my mind. "I have one on order. It's not just you that have the bar staff wrapped around your finger."

I nodded just as a clatter of chairs scraping against the stone floor caught my attention.

"Tristan," Dexter said, as if an explanation was necessary.

He didn't join us right away. Instead, he started talking to the barmaid who had rushed over to help with the upturned chairs. Within a minute she was giggling and twirling her hair like she was fourteen and Tristan was Justin Bieber.

"What are we going to do with him?" I said, nodding toward Tristan.

"It's not him I'm worried about."

"I'm fine," I said, grateful that at that moment, Beck, Gabriel, and Joshua came through the door. Gabriel sat down next to me and gave me a pat on the back. The rest of them filed in, swapping hugs, handshakes, and fist bumps along with updates on whatever conversations they were partway through. I couldn't join in with any of it. I just didn't have the capacity to think about anything—or anyone—but Sofia. "Sorry about him," Joshua said to the barmaid as he guided Tristan to our table.

"You're here early." Beck glanced between me and Dex. "You okay?"

"Fine," I snapped.

Everyone got their drinks and settled around the table before a silence fell across the group.

"So where's the lovely Sofia?" asked Tristan.

I looked up from where I was staring into my glass of Barolo that I couldn't bring myself to taste and found five pairs of eyes all looking at me, but none wondering who Sofia was. "You're a gossip, Tristan."

"No," he snapped back, "I'm your friend. And something is off with you. You never suggest impromptu drinks and now we're here, you're even darker than normal."

"I'm not dark. I'm efficient. Maybe you should take a leaf out of my book."

Beck put his arm around my shoulder. "You're really good at cutting to the chase of an issue. You've always done that for us when we needed clarity. We're just trying to help you in return."

"I'm not sure I would be with Hartford if you weren't . . . the way you are," Joshua said. "Although it pains me to think you get credit for my love life."

"All I said to Joshua is that I'd never seen you so at ease with a woman," Tristan said. "I wasn't gossiping. I was excited to see you so happy."

Disappointment slid down my spine. It was easy to be happy with Sofia. She was just so completely and unashamedly herself. It was my favorite thing about her.

"And you said she was a knockout," Joshua added.

Tristan ignored him. "Tell us what's going on. I'm sorry if I did the wrong thing."

I gave a small shake of my head. "Sorry, I . . . over-reacted."

"It's a change for you," Dex said. "You're the king of underreaction. It's good to mix things up once in a while."

I'd called this meeting. I needed to walk my talk and be efficient by telling them what the hell was the matter. I took a breath. "Sofia and I are done. But . . . I'm starting to realize she was—is—important. And I'd quite like to be spending time with her." There. I'd said it.

I glanced up to find Tristan had his eyebrows raised. A grin threatened at the corner of his mouth.

Gabriel gave my shoulder a reassuring squeeze.

As I scanned the faces around me, it was clear they wanted me to go on. But I wasn't sure what more I could say.

"I've never—I have—I was thinking—" What was the matter with me? I couldn't get the words out. I didn't quite know why I was here or what I wanted them to say or do. But I knew there was no other place to be.

"We've been there," Beck said. "It hits you like a freight train, doesn't it?"

That's how it felt. Like I'd been in a near-death accident. Surely there was something wrong with me that a woman could make me feel like this.

"I bet you can't concentrate on anything," Joshua said.

I shook my head. "Not a thing."

"And you can't find the words for how empty you feel because she's not with you," Gabriel said.

I exhaled in relief. They got it.

"You're all nutters," Tristan said. "But Sofia's hot AF so I get it. Sort of. So why did you two break up?"

I explained about how I'd offered her the job but told her that we'd have to keep things professional if she took it. "She's perfect for the role and I sleep better at night knowing someone so talented—someone I trusted—is at the helm. Sofia has the same fire in her belly my grandmother had. The magazine needs that."

"But maybe so do you," Gabriel said.

I sighed, unable to contradict him because he was right. When she'd accepted the offer, I couldn't entirely smother my disappointment. She'd made a choice, the right choice, but a part of me wish she'd said no—or at least hesitated when I'd told her of my stipulation.

"I'm lost," Tristan said. "I saw you less than a week ago and you were practically beaming. And from a man who can barely raise a smile on a good day, that was something. You offered her the job. Okay, I'm following you, but why did you end things?"

"Obviously we can't be sleeping together if she's such an integral part of my team. We agreed to keep things professional."

"I agree you can't keep sleeping together if you're her boss," Gabriel said.

I nodded and sipped my wine, trying to dull the ache that crept up my throat at his words but it only made things worse—made me miss her more.

"But if what you had was more than just sleeping together, it's more complicated," he added.

"Agreed," Beck said. "If you're just fucking her, it's a terrible idea. If you're committed to each other, it's not the worst thing you can ever do."

"It's not—" I stopped at the growl in my voice. Beck didn't mean anything by it, but the idea that what Sofia and I had was *just fucking* turned my stomach and made me see red. "What do you mean, committed?"

"You've had a lot of girlfriends over the years," Beck said.

"Coming from you?" I asked. "Are you serious?"

He held up his hands in surrender. "Hey, no judgement. I'm saying you're a serial monogamist. Nothing wrong with that but if in eighteen months you're going to get bored, you won't want to deal with a bad situation at the office."

"I'm not going to get bored." Not in eighteen months. Not in eighteen years. "Life with Sofia could never be boring."

Dexter grinned like he knew exactly what I meant.

"I got me one of those," Joshua said. "Sometimes I wonder how I ever put up with such a dull existence before Hartford."

"Yep, none of the women we decided to commit to are boring. That's for sure," Beck said.

"So if you're saying you're committed to this woman for the long term, you might find working together makes things easier," Beck said. "At least you know how each other operates, and you trust each other."

I shook my head. "I can't be with her and be her boss. It's not fair. You all know that I've learned that lesson." I'd come so close to coming apart after being fired, I knew I could never go back and make the same mistake and I was certain I couldn't inflict that on anyone else.

Silence circled the table. Everyone knew my rule on not dating at work was hard and fast.

Maybe part of me was hoping one of my friends around this table would have an idea that I hadn't thought of, but when I looked up, all I saw was concern. Not a solution among them.

"I'm sure you've thought of everything, mate," Dexter said. "I just know that if I hadn't broken the rules for Hollie, my life would be . . . I can't imagine me without her."

I wasn't Dexter. I didn't bend rules. For a few days, Sofia had convinced me that boundaries could be redrawn but the reality was, the foundations of my rules were too deep to undo. Sofia had just been a temporary crack that needed to be repaired.

"I get that you don't want to repeat history," Tristan said, then took a sip of his beer. Yep. He got it. I wasn't going back there. "But if I remember correctly, it wasn't the fact that you were fucking your boss that was the problem." Scratch that. He didn't get it at all. I could feel the blood in my veins heat. He'd seen the state of me during that time. How could he forget? "The issue was the person you were sleeping with—a woman you cared about, from what I recall —gave you up, sacrificed you to save her own skin. She betrayed you."

I pulled in a breath, trying to keep the memories from flooding back. My past was in my past. I was trying to make sure I didn't go back there. "I don't want to talk about it."

"Would Sofia ever do that to you?" Tristan said, not willing to let me be. "Would she betray you in that way?"

"Of course not," I snapped. "Sofia isn't anything like—" I couldn't bring myself to utter the name of the woman who'd almost destroyed me. "She's loyal and loving and the most trustworthy person—" I stopped midsentence as I started to process what Tristan was saying.

"And you're nothing like that woman from before," Tristan continued. "You're loyal and trustworthy. You're a little irritable here and there, but you're a good person. You'd sacrifice yourself before betraying anyone. You're not her. Sofia's not her. You're not going to repeat history. It's impossible."

"It's a good point, Tristan," Gabriel said. "The issue isn't intra-office relationships. It's about the people having them."

If what Tristan and Gabriel were saying was right, then my rules and lines in the sand had all been misplaced. Had I really been so adamant about guarding against repeating history, I'd been fighting on the wrong front?

"So what problem have we solved?" I asked. "It's still not great to be dating someone who works for you."

"You're telling us that Sofia is the person you want to spend time with, spend your life with," Beck said. "If she's that special, it's worth finding a way through."

"She's the exception," Gabriel said. "And when you marry her, your relationship will always be exceptional because she's your wife."

I was going to marry her? I let Gabriel's words sink in, half expecting them to feel ridiculous and uncomfortable, but it was just the opposite. It felt so easy.

Of course I wasn't going to repeat history, because it was Sofia.

Of course I was going to marry her, because she was Sofia.

Of course she was exceptional, because she was Sofia.

"Is this how you lot felt when you met . . ."

"Hollie?" Dexter asked. "Absolutely. I knew from the moment I laid eyes on her."

"But it's not always like that," Beck said. "Sometimes you have to get to know a woman's heart first."

"In my case it took over a decade," Joshua added. "But there was a moment—or a series of moments—when I knew I didn't want anyone but her. Ever."

"And that life without her would be . . . unthinkable." Gabriel nodded. "Completely and utterly unthinkable. I mean, my hearing would be better because I wouldn't have to put up with the tuneless musical numbers all the time, but I'd give up my hearing for her happily."

"God, she really can't sing," Dexter said.

"Not a note," I agreed.

"You lot," Tristan said. "You're such saps. Look, Andrew, you want the girl, find a way to make it work. You've done that your whole life. You made millions turning around businesses everyone else thought were done. You make the impossible possible for a living. Just apply it to your love life."

I winced. "But what I do for companies is go in, fix them up, and then move on. It's been a bit like that with my girl-friends. We date and then we're over, no second look back."

"The past doesn't predetermine the future," Tristan said. "You've proven as much by buying *Verity*. You committed to one business because it was important to you. If Sofia is important to you, you'll make that work, too."

Well, when he put it like that.

"Life is really on its head if I'm taking dating advice from Tristan," I said.

"This isn't dating advice," Gabriel said. "This is life advice. You don't want Sofia to be just another girl you dated."

I nodded. He was right. Sofia was my future. I'd known it since before I kissed her. Before I'd met her in the bar. Not because she was the sexiest, most beautiful woman I'd ever seen in the flesh, but because she didn't let me get away with anything without letting me know she was letting me get away with it.

"I don't want to lose her."

"Sack her and she'll find another job somewhere else. You have plenty of money you can give her to cover her expenses," Tristan suggested.

That was never going to work. "She would cut off my balls if I suggested that."

"God, Tristan. You're a neanderthal," Beck said. "No wonder you're single."

"What? I'm suggesting she give up one job, not trek up Everest naked." Tristan shook his head as if he were surrounded by idiots.

"Why should she give up her job for me?" I asked. "She's right at the beginning of her career."

"So sell *Verity*," Tristan said.

"No way. I've fought too hard for too long for that business. And it's not just a business to me. You all know that."

"Maybe she'll have an idea if you talk to her," Tristan said.

If she had, wouldn't she have shared it with me already? "Maybe she's moved on," I said, the words bitter on my tongue. "I was adamant about ending things."

"I'm not being funny," Tristan said. "But I saw the way she looked at you. It's not been long. She's not moving on this quickly."

"Thanks, mate. Maybe the solution is for her to start job hunting and for us to work together in the meantime. If it's short term, that's . . ." The idea of being her boss felt uncomfortable, but anything was possible if it was just for a few months, wasn't it? "Maybe that's an option."

"Talk to her," Gabriel said. "Tell her you can't live without her."

"So dramatic," Tristan said on a sigh.

"Just you wait, Tristan," Joshua said, patting him on the shoulder. "It will happen to you."

Tristan chuckled. "No way. I'm not wired like you lot. I'm not sitting here waiting to fall in love."

I hadn't been either but that's what had happened. Sofia had come into my life fully armed to disarm me. It was the last thing I'd been expecting. Now I had a visceral understanding that I was meant to be with her. Like Tristan said, I just had to figure out how.

FORTY-ONE

Sofia

I was fired up and ready to wrestle an alligator, or at least ask Andrew for an advance on my bonus. There was no way I was going to try to appeal to his soft side—in business, he didn't have one. I had prepared myself for a boardroom battle.

I climbed the steps to the Blake Enterprises offices just like I had that first day. Now, like then, I needed something from Andrew. I hoped I'd be as successful today as I had been that cold March morning, what felt like a thousand years ago.

I headed right through the outer office where this had all begun, but pulled up short. My old desk was occupied.

"Hi, I'm Trudy," Andrew's assistant said. "Can I help?"

I glanced at my watch. It was ten to twelve. I was early. But I wasn't going to stand around making small talk. That's not what Andrew would do.

"I'm here to see Andrew." I swept past her desk.

"Excuse me, no visitors—"

Ignoring her as she pushed out of her chair and headed toward me, I opened Andrew's door and shut it behind me.

Andrew jumped up out of his seat like I'd given him an electric shock.

Shit. Why did he have to have those big, soulful eyes and such touchable hair? He looked tired. I wanted to ask him what had been going on and what I could do to help, but the sound of Trudy crashing through the door behind me brought me back to the moment.

"I barged in," I said. "It wasn't Trudy's fault."

"I know," he said, not taking his eyes off me.

"I'm sorry, Andrew, I didn't—"

"Leave us." Andrew shoved his hands in his pockets. We both waited as Trudy retreated.

"You really should be nicer to your assistants," I said.

"Thanks for coming by."

What was he thanking me for? "You don't know why I'm here yet."

He shrugged. "Go ahead."

Something was off. Andrew should have yelled at me for barging in here before twelve, or at the very least ignored me like I was one of the abstract paintings on the wall. Maybe the dark circles under his eyes were thanks to more than basic exhaustion. I took a step toward him, my body instinctively wanting to soothe him and be soothed by him, but abruptly, I remembered who we were to each other now. He was my boss. And he was responsible for deciding my bonus. I wasn't going to mess this up. I had to stay focused.

"I'm good at my job," I said.

Andrew nodded.

"That operational plan I produced was excellent. I

know you liked it. And Goode really likes me. That's why I've got this job in the first place."

Andrew frowned. "One of the reasons, but go on."

"What *Verity* needs now is stability. Commitment. Long-term thinking."

I paused, but Andrew remained silent.

"I want part of my salary and my full bonus in advance. Specifically, I want forty-three thousand dollars or the equivalent in pounds. We'll draw up a contract that covers all the details—a payback penalty if I leave before the three-year mark, for starters, and any other assurances you need."

Still no reaction from Andrew.

I slumped in one of his visitor chairs like all my energy had drained away from my body, leaving me with limbs too weak to hold me upright. I'd done it. I'd asked him. It had taken more from me than I expected.

"For your mum's operation?" he asked.

"It doesn't matter what it's for. It's a business proposition, nothing personal about it." I knew that he didn't like to mix personal and professional. I wasn't going to make the mistake of trying to appeal to his human side. That didn't wash with Andrew.

"Okay," he said. "You can have half of everything."

I glanced up at him. "Half?" Half might work. If I saved my salary and moved to a smaller apartment, I could come up with the rest some other way. "What about thirty? Can I have thirty?"

"You can have half of everything I have."

He came to sit on the visitor chair next to me, leaned forward, and tried to catch my eye. "I don't mean that. It sounds clinical. I mean . . . I want you to share it all with me."

He wasn't making any sense. His voice had a weirdly soft edge to it. "You want part of my bonus?"

"No . . ." He leaned back on his chair and pushed his hands through his hair. "I'm galactically bad at this. I wasn't expecting you today. I've been trying to figure out a way of . . . saying that I want—"

"Half my bonus? Is the business doing badly?"

He started to laugh. "This is ridiculous. Let's take the bonus out of this conversation."

"No!" I said, standing. "That's why I'm here. I want my bonus now."

"You can have your bonus, Sofia."

I was entirely confused now. "I can? Like, the entire forty-three thousand?"

"Let's make it an even fifty. That way, wherever you got that seven, you can give it back."

I had to sit again as the energy drained from my legs. It was like I'd been heaving against a locked door with all my strength, only to have Andrew open it and let me in. "Okay," I said, lifting my hands in the air. I'd given up trying to understand what was going on.

"But I'm serious, Sofia. I want to share everything with you."

I don't know whether it was because he looked at me like I was his entire world, or because my entire body flushed with heat at the realization that we were so close, but suddenly I realized that we weren't talking about business anymore.

"Share everything?"

He nodded. "Everything. My life. My day. My . . . bed."

I shivered at his words. What had changed? "But the separation of business and—"

"Everything."

Frustrated by his eerie calm, I felt a sizzle of irritation coursing through my veins. "I'm going to need more than one-word answers, Andrew. Tell me what's going on."

"I wasn't expecting you today. I've not figured out exactly what I need to say. But I do know that I don't like being without you. I can't do it. I won't."

I sighed. "Well, that makes two of us."

"But it's more than that. Since you starting at *Verity*, I've realized how . . . God, I'm trying really hard not to sound like I'm negotiating a business deal, but I'm not good at this stuff." He banged his fist on his desk.

I covered it with my hand. "It's me, Andrew. Just talk. We'll figure it out."

He looked at me and swept his fingers over my cheek-bone. "I'm in love with you."

My breath hitched in my chest and my heart fought to free it. "You're in love with me?"

He chuckled. "Yes. I don't want to be without you. I want to wake up next to you for the rest of my life."

"But what about the separation between work life and—"

"Honestly, I'm not sure I have a solution to that yet. I still don't think me being your boss is a good idea. Even when we're married."

I stood up like someone had stuck a cattle prod up my ass. "Married?" I'd come in here for a bonus, not a husband.

He stood up too, those soulful eyes fixed on mine. "I mean *if*. If we—I mean . . . Even if we're—unless." He stopped himself. "I'm fucking everything up. I hate being unprepared." He marched around his desk and sat in his usual chair.

My mind was racing, trying to keep up with what the hell was going on.

"These are the facts," he said, bouncing up to his feet again. "I'm in love with you. I can't stop thinking about you. I want to be with you. I've never felt . . . No, that sounds trite." He cleared his throat and tented his fingers on the desk. "When you're not with me, I feel like a piece of me is missing. Like there's a life I should be living somewhere and I'm in the wrong place. I've always been so certain about everything and now . . . everything with you is new and terrifying and completely comforting. Life with you is where I was meant to be all along and finally, I've found you." He took a breath, clearly preparing to go on. I wasn't used to so many words from Andrew's mouth all at once. "You get me and seem to like me anyway. Being together and working together will be a challenge, but if that's what you want, we'll make it work. If you want to get another job, one where I'm not your boss, we'll make that happen too. I want to do whatever it takes to be with you."

He finished and pushed his hands into his pockets.

The warmth of familiarity circled me like a blanket, and a creeping realization from my soul told me that from this moment forward, Andrew and I would be linked forever.

I got that this was the part where I was meant to speak. I just didn't know what to say. "I get it." I forced out past a throat so dry, I felt like I'd just trekked across the Sahara. "Same."

He started to laugh. "That's unusually concise for you."

"Give me a break." I rolled my eyes. "You've been thinking about this."

He circled the desk and leaned next to me, our legs barely touching. "You haven't?"

"I've been focusing on the things I can control and trying to push away all my feelings for you. You were so adamant that we were done."

He rubbed his hands over his face then shook his head. "I know. I'm sorry."

"This is a lot and it's taken me by surprise. It's not a bad surprise," I added quickly, seeing his face start to fall, "but I'm a little scared. You seemed to walk away so easily last time."

"It wasn't easy to end things, and it was even harder to stay away." He cupped my face with his hands. "I'm sorry. I know it must be triggering for you because of what happened between your mother and father. But I promise, I will never walk away again. We can fly to Vegas right now and get married if it will help drive the point home. I'm not going anywhere."

"My mom will kill me. She'll want us to get married in a church."

"Is that a yes? You'll marry me?"

Had I just accepted a marriage proposal? "It's a no to Vegas. You haven't asked me anything beyond that and until you do, I'm not saying anything at all. Are you even Catholic?" I couldn't believe we were talking so matter-of-factly about getting married, but it felt entirely appropriate.

"I'll be anything you want me to be." He snaked his arms around my waist and leaned his forehead against mine.

"I just want you to be you. You, the man I'm in love with. And the father of our future twelve Italian bambinos."

He pushed his lips together in the way he did when he tried not to smile.

I slid my arms around his neck and he pressed a kiss to my mouth.

"I've missed you," he said. "Too much. And now I'm impatient to get started on what's next. What time are you going to finish work this evening? Shall I come to you and help you pack? I need to call Dexter. I bet he already has a selection of rings put aside."

This guy was travelling at warp speed.

I moved his chin so he was looking at me. "Andrew, you are usually so patient about everything. This time, you might have to be a little patient with me. It's been just me and my mom for a long time. I've learned to rely on no one but myself and her. I'm still strapping on my training wheels, and you're entering me into Olympic time trials."

"I'm sorry. You're not alone on those training wheels. I've never lived with a woman. I don't know how to compromise. I'm blunt and surly and used to getting what I want, when and exactly how I want it."

"You are?" I feigned a shocked face.

He grinned. "But you love me anyway."

"I do."

"Then we'll figure it out."

"I know we will."

Andrew kissed me again, and neither of us said anything for a long time.

FORTY-TWO

Andrew

I glanced up at the window to the bedroom of Sofia's flat before pressing the bell. I wanted to skip this bit and just be married. We'd only officially been a couple for a few hours, but I was the luckiest man alive and I didn't want to waste time. I didn't want to take things slow for the sake of it. I'd tried to persuade Sofia to ditch work for the day but she'd refused. Why did she have to be so bloody professional?

She poked her head around the door as I got to the top of the steps. "You're early," she said.

"Where do you want to live?" I asked, following her into the sitting room. She was fiddling with an envelope.

"Yeah, I've been thinking about that. My mom is . . . I miss her."

I'd already done a bit of thinking about Sofia's mother this afternoon. "I think we have several options. She can come and live over here full or part time. We get her her own place, so she can come and go as she pleases."

"Wait—"

"Nothing needs to be decided right away." I needed to be more patient or I was really going to piss her off.

"What is this?" she asked, scanning the piece of paper she had just retrieved from the envelope she'd been playing with. "Did you do this?"

I shifted to look over her shoulder. "Student loans? What's the problem?"

"My account has been cleared. They've all been paid off." She turned and looked at me.

"Nothing to do with me," I said. "I didn't even know you had student loans."

She handed me the letter. "Maybe I got it wrong. Will you read it? Tell me I'm not going crazy."

I took the paper from her and read through it. "It shows that the balance was paid off ten days ago."

"Ten days ago? How? It's over a hundred thousand dollars. Oh God, do you think it was—no, it can't have been."

"Your father?"

"Who else? But he hasn't said anything."

"He doesn't need to. It was his job to pay that money. He's a wealthy man."

"How ironic that I was going to pretend I needed help paying off those loans to get money for my mom's operation, but he's paid off far more than I ever needed, and I never asked him for a cent. I should be able to get a personal loan now for the surgery. I don't think I'll need that advance anymore, or certainly not all of it." She turned to me. "Can you believe it? My mom is going to get her operation and I didn't have to ask my father to pay for it."

"You're not going to get a loan. We have plenty of money to cover the operation. I don't think you're getting it. Whatever I have is *ours*. Whatever you need, I will provide." Sofia provoked some kind of primal need in me to provide for her. To care for her. To make the world a better place for her. I'd grown up among powerful women, but Sofia's power over me was on a different scale. I would do whatever it took to make her happy. "You'll never want for anything ever again for as long as I'm alive."

She smoothed her palm across my jaw and lifted herself out of her shoes to place a kiss on my cheek. "I want to go to New York to see her and tell her in person about us, and about my father. And about her operation."

"Then that's what we'll do."

"You'll come?"

"Absolutely. Let's go this weekend. We'll take Friday off and get the red eye back Sunday night."

"Wow, it's all so fast. I should call my father, shouldn't I?"

"You should do whatever you feel is right."

"I want to call him. I feel hopeful about our relationship. Not because he's paid off my loans—although it's very generous of him—but more because of what that represents. It's like he wants to make amends. And honestly, I like him and I'd like to know him more. I probably didn't tell you but I had an opportunity to ask him for the money. Something stopped me. Maybe I wanted him to offer it to me willingly. And now he has."

"So now you can get to know him because you want to. Not because you need to."

"I'm exhausted," she confessed. "It's been a day."

"We should get married in Italy," I said, trying to work out what we had to do first to start our lives together. We needed a list. "We should contact a wedding planner. Someone good."

"You haven't asked me yet. And I haven't asked you. No putting the cart before the horse."

"You see?" I turned to her. "This is why I love you. You challenge me, make me see the world in a different way. Don't ever stop."

"You can count on it."

FORTY-THREE

Sofia

A warm, comforting breeze blew as we looked across the New York City skyline at the Chrysler building, the Met Life building and the Empire State building.

"So this is why we're at a different hotel and not your usual Mandarin Oriental," I said. "The view. You can see the whole of Manhattan from up here."

"This roof terrace is the perfect place . . ."

I turned to him when he didn't finish his sentence. "The perfect place for what?"

He cupped my face and swept his thumb over my cheek. "I love you."

"I love you too," I replied. Even though we said it to each other incessantly, like we had to make up for lost time, a thrill still chased up my spine whenever I heard it from him. I'd gone to London to find fifty thousand dollars and ended up with a different life and everything I could have ever wished for.

"A few months ago, you accosted me in the middle of

the street and gave yourself a job as my assistant. Little did I know, I'd finally met my match in every sense of the word. I want to spend the rest of my life with you." He dropped his hand from my face and took a step back. Then he bent on one knee and pulled out a ring box. "Will you marry me?"

His proposal was positively *wordy* for him. I couldn't see anything but that look in his eye that told me I was his queen. I ignored the ring, stepped forward, and sat on his knee, wrapping my arms around him. "I knew the moment I followed you up those stairs on that first morning, your tight butt directly in front of me, that you'd rock my world one way or another. And you have. In the best way. Although it's your heart that can take most of the credit. You're a good, kind, sensitive man. I'm lucky to see that side of you. Your belief in me has given me everything I ever wanted and I want to spend the rest of my life trying to make you feel as special as you make me feel. Will you marry me?"

"Every day of the week for the rest of my life." He stood, taking me with him, and I wrapped my legs around his waist as we kissed. He'd chosen the perfect background —it was the land of my roots and the place that had given our relationship wings.

As Andrew lowered me back to my feet, I spotted the hot tub. "I brought my bikini. Shall we celebrate?"

"You won't be needing your bikini. Just this."

He grabbed the ring box from where it had been discarded on the floor.

"Oh god, I didn't even look at it."

Andrew grinned like it hadn't bothered him at all.

As he opened the box, I gasped. It was the most beautiful ring I'd ever seen. It was a huge rectangular diamond that kind of reminded me of New York itself—all angles, and not to be missed.

"Dexter gave me a few options. I picked this but we can change it."

"Are you kidding me? It's gorgeous."

"Dexter has a talent for knowing what people will like." He pulled it out of the box and slipped it on my finger. It fit like I'd been wearing it my entire life.

"Anyone who wouldn't like this is an idiot."

Andrew chuckled. "So, you're ready to tell your mum you're getting married?"

"I'm ready to tell everyone. Everyone's going to hear how happy you make me and how happy I want to make you."

"You already do," he said.

"Hot tub?" I suggested.

"Naked?" he asked.

"Absolutely."

FORTY-FOUR

Andrew

"That ring was pretty in the box, but on you, it's something else," I said as Sofia slipped out of her underwear. She was naked in the New York moonlight and I'd never seen anything so breathtakingly spectacular.

"I don't think you're looking at the ring." She laughed as she climbed the first step into the hot tub.

I grabbed her hand and pulled her off the step toward me. "I'm never looking at anything but you if you're in the room."

"Same," she replied. I skirted my fingers up and down her arms. I wanted to bend her over the hot tub and fuck her so loud the entire city could hear me, but I knew I'd regret it. I was going to take my time tonight. Not to torture her, but to remind her that we had our whole lives to be together. For as long as my heart beat in my body, I was going to worship her.

"You're beautiful," I whispered. "My fiancée."

She shivered. I bent and placed a kiss on her shoulder.

I cupped her face and pressed a kiss on her lips. Threading her fingers into my hair, she deepened our kiss, our tongues pressing together, urgent and purposeful. She was so soft and warm and perfect, and the occasional scrape of her ring against my scalp sent a bolt of desire right to my dick. She was going to be my wife. That was the best aphrodisiac I'd ever experienced.

She pulled away.

"I don't think we're going to make it to the hot tub," she said, glancing down at my erection straining between us.

"You think I'm going to pass up an opportunity to get you even warmer and even wetter?"

I bent and scooped her up, then slipped her into the bubbling water before sliding in next to her. I positioned her so she was straddling me, face to face.

"You're perfect."

She shook her head. "I'm anything but."

"You're perfect for me. And I love you."

I glanced around, looking for a condom.

"Let's not," she said, the look of contentment and trust in her eye better than every award and pat on the back I'd ever gotten.

"You want to get pregnant?" I asked.

"Maybe," she said. "We probably should have talked about this before getting engaged."

"No need. I'm happy if you're happy. I seem to remember you saying something about you wanting fifteen kids or something. If you decide you don't want any, that's fine too." I never thought I'd hear myself saying I wanted children, but the idea of a family with Sofia felt right. It felt like destiny.

"I'm not sure about fifteen, but I'd like to be a mother.

And I don't just want one. Everyone I know comes from a big family and . . . I want that for my kids. For me."

She'd make a fantastic mother. Her passion and honesty, combined with her work ethic and determination? Our kids would run the world.

"Let's start with one." I pressed my lips onto her collarbone and she wriggled on my lap, impatient as ever.

I grinned against her skin before pulling her down onto my cock. She tipped her head back, exposing her long neck, her breasts jutting in front of me, begging for attention. So much for making her wait.

The warmth of the water, the lights of the New York City night, and the understanding that the woman in front of me was the woman I was going to be making love to for the rest of time was almost overwhelming.

Sofia shifted so she was leaning back. The change in angle—the pressure on my dick, the sway of her breasts, the short sharp pinch in my balls—encouraged a growl from deep in the base of my throat. This woman was wicked. She knew exactly what she could do to me, body and soul. I'd never felt so entirely vulnerable with someone but also so completely cherished. She knew she held my heart in her hands and I knew she'd do anything to keep it safe.

The feeling was entirely mutual. I'd do everything I could to make her feel safe and loved. And I knew that whatever I did, I'd always be pushing to do more.

"You're so fucking sexy," I said.

She brought a trembling hand to my neck as she bucked up and down on my cock. She was close now, her movements less controlled, her breathing shallow and desperate. I grabbed her hips and took over. As much as I needed to release inside her, I wasn't going to make it entirely easy.

I squeezed her arse and then moved us so we were both

standing. "Bend over and enjoy the view," I said, positioning her so she enjoyed the uninterrupted sight of the Empire State building. I pushed into her again, this time from behind. With our bodies out of the water, the friction between us increased and I almost boiled over right there and then. Deep inside her, I stilled, then reached under her and found her clit. She screamed as my fingers made contact. Maybe it was my imagination but it felt like her scream reverberated off every skyscraper surrounding the hotel. *Yes*, I thought. *I can make the sexiest woman in the world make those sounds.* I began to thrust, over and over, deeper and deeper.

"Andrew, my god, you feel so good."

Fuck. What was it about her screaming my name? It was like I was pulling out her most base, animal instincts.

I upped my relentless pace as she screamed again. Her legs began to shake and she clawed at the side of the hot tub as she came violently in front of the entire city of New York.

But I didn't stop.

I pulled in a breath and kept going, pulling her up so she was standing, her back to my front. I reached around, one hand pulling and kneading her breasts, the other working her clit. I wanted all of her. I wanted to fill myself up with her, quench my desire, satiate my constant need for her. I never would, but I was driven to try.

"Andrew," she choked out, breathlessly. "I love you."

Fuck. It was like she'd poured petrol on my fire and the flames licked up my body, engulfing me in desire. I exploded into her as she melted, desperate and shaking against me for a second time.

My legs couldn't keep me upright any longer. I collapsed back into the hot tub, holding Sofia firmly against me.

We let the bubbles soothe our aching bodies and drown out the sounds of our heavy breaths.

"Well, if that didn't get me pregnant, I don't know what will." Sofia slipped off my lap and rested her head on my shoulder.

"We can't leave anything to chance," I said. "We'll have to repeat that a few more times to make sure."

"Tonight?" Sofia said, slipping her hand into mine.

"Tonight and every night."

"I'll have no energy for work or cooking or . . ."

"Wedding planning?" I turned and pressed a kiss to her temple.

"That either."

"Then leave it to me. I don't want to wait."

She turned, leaning her chin on my shoulder. "You're so impatient, it's not like you. What's the rush?"

"The rush is I want to be your husband."

The corners of her mouth flickered and turned up into a smile. "You're so cute."

"Cute?" I asked her.

"And sexy," she said.

"You didn't think that when I was your boss."

"You're still my boss and yes, I did. I told you, that tight ass of yours has been my undoing."

I chuckled. If I was going to be objectified, nobody better to do it than Sofia. "Coming from the woman with the arse sent direct from heaven, I take that as a compliment." I pulled her onto my lap and brought her in for a long, lingering kiss.

"You're a good kisser," she said. "Especially in the moonlight."

"You inspire great kissing."

"Can I take credit for your incredible penis?" She

reached beneath the water and circled her hand around my cock. I groaned and pushed into her fist.

"You can take credit for the fact that I'm almost permanently hard whenever you're around."

She slid off my lap and kneeled at my feet in the water. "I want you in my mouth but I don't want to drown. Can you sit on the side?"

I lifted myself out of the water and perched on the edge of the tub, watching with wonder at Sofia as she took me whole. She swallowed when I hit the back of her throat and I couldn't contain a sharp hiss. Shit, I hoped she didn't plan to tease me like I teased her. The urge to come was almost immediate. I didn't know if it was the talk of getting her pregnant or just her mouth around my cock. Grabbing my thighs, she worked up and down my shaft, her teeth bordering on too sharp, her tongue firm and insistent.

If I hadn't already proposed . . .

Despite her protestations, she *was* perfect. But I wasn't ready to come.

I shifted and she released me, confusion in her expression.

"I want to come inside you. I'm going to get you pregnant tonight."

"I want that . . . but maybe we should get married first. After all, I'm an old-fashioned Italian girl."

I knew it was more than that. Her father leaving her mother was a bruise that she would wear forever. Hopefully, after a lifetime with me, it would fade. "Then let's go and find some condoms."

I guided her out of the tub and we padded inside, naked.

"There," she said, pointing to my wallet on the side table.

I grabbed my wallet and led her to the bedroom. If she wanted old-fashioned, we could do that too. When we'd toweled each other off, I lifted her onto the bed and pushed her knees apart while I stood between them. "I like to see you," I said. "I love watching every long blink." I rolled the condom over my cock. "Every bite of your lip, every desperate plea in your expression." I pushed into her again. There it was, that look that told me she loved me. I'd never take that expression, that feeling she had for me, for granted. I'd work harder than she'd ever know to deserve it.

"I love you," I said. "Forever."

EPILOGUE

Sofia

I was far more nervous now than I had been introducing Andrew to my mom the first time, or when we told her we were engaged. Maybe because we'd left it so long before seeing them all together. Of course I'd met Tristan, and we'd had dinner with Beck and Stella, but we'd been busy figuring out the wedding and where to live. The time had flown since our return from New York.

"They'll love you," Andrew whispered as we got to the top of the stone steps.

"They love *you*," I reminded him. "Your friends don't have to like me."

"Trust me," he said, ringing the bell.

I did trust him, so I took a deep breath and plastered on a smile.

The large black door that looked like it would withstand bullets opened and a girl with long dark hair grinned at me. "Americans only," she said, pulling me inside and hugging me. "I'm so excited we have another one in our gang. Let me see the ring on." She gasped at the rock on my left hand as I held it up. I didn't need to be asked twice. "Dexter said it was a stunner and he was right."

Right then a man with dark curly hair came around the corner. "You did good, honey," she said, pulling him into a kiss. This must be Dexter and Hollie, the owners of this incredible house.

"Oh, I didn't introduce myself. I'm Hollie." She took my hand and led me through the hallway. I glanced back at Andrew and he just shrugged as if he were entirely powerless. "Dexter's my soon-to-be husband and this—" We entered a huge space at the back of the house which was full of people. Another woman pulled me into a hug. "This is my sister, Autumn. She's engaged to Gabriel," she said when Autumn released me.

"Three Americans," Autumn said. "Thank God. We can talk about Twinkies without getting dirty looks."

"I can honestly say I never wanted a Twinkie before I came to London," I replied.

"I know, right?" Autumn said. "I crave so many things about Oregon, even though I love being here."

I'm glad it wasn't just me. "Yeah, I miss New York sometimes. And my mom."

"We should go!" Hollie said. "I'd never been to New York before I met Dexter. He always has to go for work and I tag along as often as I can. We could charter a plane next time and make it a girl's trip."

"Charter a plane?"

"The money is a lot to get used to," Autumn said. "But you will. Hollie got there quicker than most."

I honestly doubted I'd ever get entirely comfortable with Andrew's wealth, but he was so generous, and completely transparent about what he had, which made it a little easier. Agreeing to let him foot the bill for my mom's surgery was a no-brainer. It was all booked in to take place next month. She was coming to London to have the procedure and staying with us while she recuperated. I hoped she would fall in love with the city and I could persuade her to stay.

Hollie laughed. "Life's to enjoy, right?"

"No argument from me on that score. So . . . which ones are Joshua and Hartford?"

Hollie and Autumn wasted no time pointing them out and giving me the rundown on how everyone had met. The fact that Joshua and Hartford had known each other since they were kids but only just fallen in love was the best story ever.

"Tristan's not here yet," Autumn said. "He's the only single one in their friendship coven."

"I wonder if we can get him to fall in love with another American," Hollie said.

"He's determined not to fall in love with anyone," Autumn said, laughing. "But we'll soon see about that. Do you have any friends who might like an outrageously flirtatious British guy who . . . What does he do, Hollie?"

She shrugged. "No one knows exactly. Whenever I ask Dexter, he tells me it's something with computers."

"My best friend is single. But she lives in New Jersey."

"We need to find someone in London for him. Though Tristan is a bit of an enigma. When you first meet him—"

"Oh, I met him already. He was in New York when Andrew and I went the first time." He'd had a laptop with him and hadn't come across as particularly flirtatious. "He seemed nice."

"The thing about Tristan is, there's a lot of . . ." Hollie turned to her sister. "How would you describe him?"

"There are two sides to him. One where he's willingly the butt of everyone's jokes, and a deeper side he keeps hidden away."

Gabriel approached and introduced himself, kissing me on both cheeks. "What are you lot talking about?"

"Tristan. We're trying to find an American girlfriend for him."

"Good luck with that," Gabriel said. "He's never shown any interest in settling down."

Autumn slid her arms around Gabriel's waist. "You were sworn off women, remember? And I would have bet the farm Andrew was going to be a bachelor until the end of time."

"Maybe," he said. "But you are exceptional. And no doubt, so is Sofia."

"Hey, brother-in-law to be, what about me?" Hollie asked.

Gabriel laughed. "It doesn't even need to be said how exceptional you are."

She laughed like she and Gabriel were already related. That was the atmosphere tonight—a family of people who had chosen each other. These were bonds I was familiar with and could relate to. It was like the Ferrara family and my grandma and grandad's neighbors, who treated my mom and me like we were their own. All my nerves dissolved and I was filled with warmth as I was welcomed with open arms into this carefully constructed group of pseudo-siblings. Maybe I was going to settle in more easily than I expected.

Andrew came up behind me and snaked one arm around my waist, his palm resting over my stomach. "You okay?"

I shifted so I could meet his eye. "I am. And so is she."

"Wait, *what?*" Holly screeched. "Have you got something to tell us?"

Andrew groaned and I couldn't do anything but laugh. Apparently, we'd been way too obvious.

"A girl I think," I said. I'd just had my six-week scan, and although they couldn't tell me anything about the sex of the baby, when I saw her, I just knew.

Gabriel gave Andrew a look like he was a proud big brother, and tears welled in my eyes. Andrew was going to be the best dad.

"We're going to be aunts! Stella, get over here," Autumn called. "Hartford, come and meet your niece."

I turned to Andrew. "For the record, if I wasn't Italian American, this would be overwhelming."

He rolled his eyes. "I know."

My move to London was supposed to be temporary, but now I couldn't see myself anywhere else. My future was here, with Andrew. Soon our daughter would join this family, and I hoped my mother would, too. I'd miss New York, but London felt more and more like home.

Andrew

Sofia didn't make it over to the Blake Enterprises offices very often, so when I heard her talking to Trudy, I sprang to my feet and pulled open the door.

"What are you doing here?"

She shook her head. "What a welcome! It's eleven fifty-five. I'm waiting patiently for the clock to strike twelve."

I pulled her inside the office and closed the door, then gently pushed her against the door and pressed my lips to hers. She sighed and her body sank against mine as our tongues met. We explored each other like it had been weeks, not hours, since we'd last seen each other.

"That's a better welcome," Sofia said as she slipped under my arm and headed to my desk. "I have documents you need to see."

"Documents?"

"Yes, we need to go through some things before my mom arrives tomorrow. First, this is my resignation." She slid a cream envelope onto my desk and sat in one of the guest chairs. "I made up my mind this morning after all our conversations. It's just easier. I'll stay until we find someone else. I've done all the rebranding and the launch, and now it's just about growing the circulation. It's time to move on."

I sat across from her and took the envelope, shoving it in my top drawer. "Careful, Miss Rossi, you're starting to sound like me." We'd talked a lot about the advantages and disadvantages of Sofia continuing to head up *Verity*. I'd told her it was her decision and I would stand behind whatever she'd prefer.

"Never! But I do like the idea of working for myself. That way, I never have to worry about people thinking I only got the job because I'm married to the boss."

"No one who met you would think that."

"You're biased. Anyway, my mind is made up. I'm resigning. Leave date to be decided. I'm going to talk to HR about hiring a search firm to find a replacement."

"Okay," I said. "Next?"

"This is the list of wedding venues you sent me. I crossed out the ones I don't like." She tossed a sheet of paper. "But honestly, when my mom comes over, we should have a small registry office wedding with just a few friends and family."

I nodded, happy to go along with anything she wanted. As long as she married me, I didn't care how we did it.

"Then after the baby's born, let's have a proper wedding with a big party. We can have a blessing in a church. That's easier than a full-blown wedding too, because you're not Catholic. It works out for everyone: you'll stop hassling me to marry you, and my mom will be happy because we'll be married before the baby's born."

Sofia seemed to have forgotten the most important person in all this. "Would that make you happy?"

She sighed. "Honestly, I want to get married in New York, but you have so many friends—"

"Then New York it is. My friends can travel."

She smiled a half smile. "Thank you. London is fine."

"No. New York. We can hire anywhere you like—the Plaza? The Ritz?" I could tell by her expression that she had a place in mind.

"Well, if you're sure . . . What about the library?" she asked. "It's really pretty there. I snuck in to a ceremony once when I should have been studying."

"Done."

"Really?"

I shook my head. "I don't say things I don't mean."

She grinned and her shoulders lowered as if I'd just taken some of the burden from her. It was the best feeling in the world.

"That's done," I said. "What's next?"

"This," she said, holding up an envelope. "From my father. He's set up a trust fund for me. He says each of his daughters has one."

I'd met Sofia's father a couple of times. Despite his wealth, he was a humble man, well aware of his failings where Sofia was concerned. As far as I could see, he did nothing but try to make up for them. Not just with money, but with the way he made time and space for her in his life.

"That's nice," I said, cautiously. Sofia's emotions around her father were ever-changing. It was my job to just support her, however she felt.

"It is nice. It's also weird. I didn't exactly grow up as a trust fund kid."

"I get that it's weird. And we don't need it. Maybe you could transfer it into our daughter's name?"

Sofia rounded her hand over her gradually expanding stomach. "Oh she gets one too." She shook her head like it was the most ridiculous thing. "I told my mom." She winced. Sofia had come clean about the reason she'd come to London—and the fact she'd met her father, his wife, and their two kids—when we visited her mother to tell her about our engagement. There had been tears and fights and more tears and hugs and eventually, everything had settled down. Sofia's mom was sorry she'd cut Des out of their lives. Sofia was sorry for lying about why she'd come to England. Now mother and daughter were as close as ever. "It was fine. I think it would be less fine if I hadn't met you. I guess because his money will make less of a difference."

"That makes sense. Has she agreed to move to London?"

"Not permanently. Not yet. But she knows that wherever we move, there will be a place for her. Speaking of which, that brings me to the next thing." She pulled out her phone and brought up a picture of a house. "It's thirty minutes to the center of town. And it's got a garden and a pool and even an annex where my mom could stay."

"Okay. Looks nice."

"Great." She jumped to her feet. "Let's go see it. We can time the journey. It's in Kenwood."

"Now?" I asked.

"Yes, I've cleared your diary and we're due in forty minutes."

My soon-to-be wife was always a step ahead of me. Long may it continue.

Have you read

Mr. Mayfair Beck & Stella's story
Mr. Knightsbridge Dexter & Hollie's story
Mr. Smithfield Gabriel & Autumn's story
Mr. Park Lane Joshua & Hartford's story
Mr. Notting Hill Tristan's story

It's the most embarrassing night of my life. Not only did I *literally* run into the hottest guy I've ever laid eyes on in a hotel lobby, but the ice-cold water and whipped cream I'm carrying (don't ask) end up all over me.

When I finally clean myself up, that same guy--the hottest one of all time--donates twenty-five thousand pounds during a charity auction... *to win a date with me.* Things must be looking up, right? After all, a crazy-gorgeous guy just bid a ton of money on dinner with me. But when I see him sit down right next to my father, I know he's not interested in me. He just wants to do business with my dad. FML.

I'm determined to make the situation work. If he really wants to impress my father, the handsome stranger can marry me... for three months. It's all I need to get access to the trust fund so I can fund my charity. Tristan will be able to get what he wants from my dad, and my father will stop hounding me about getting a life. Everyone wins.

Soon it will be over. Until then, I've just got to ignore the rock-hard muscles I felt when I ran into him, the look in his eye that tells me he tastes as good as he looks, and the chemistry that fizzles between us whenever we're together.

Grab Tristan's story, **Mr. Notting Hill now!**

The Empire State Series

The Gentleman Series
The Ruthless Gentleman
The Wrong Gentleman

The Royals Series
King of Wall Street
Park Avenue Prince
Duke of Manhattan
The British Knight
The Earl of London

The Nights Series
Indigo Nights
Promised Nights
Parisian Nights

Faithful

What kind of books do you like?

Friends to lovers
Mr. Mayfair
Promised Nights
International Player

Fake relationship (marriage of convenience)
Duke of Manhattan

Mr. Mayfair

Mr. Notting Hill

Enemies to Lovers

King of Wall Street

The British Knight

The Earl of London

Hollywood Scandal

Parisian Nights

14 Days of Christmas

Mr. Bloomsbury

Office Romance/ Workplace romance

Mr. Knightsbridge

King of Wall Street

The British Knight

The Ruthless Gentleman

Mr. Bloomsbury

Second Chance

International Player

Hopeful

Best Friend's Brother

Promised Nights

Vacation/Holiday Romance

The Empire State Series
Indigo Nights
The Ruthless Gentleman
The Wrong Gentleman
Love Unexpected
14 Days of Christmas

Holiday/Christmas Romance
14 Days of Christmas
This Christmas

British Hero
Promised Nights (British heroine)
Indigo Nights (American heroine)
Hopeful (British heroine)
Duke of Manhattan (American heroine)
The British Knight (American heroine)
The Earl of London (British heroine)
The Wrong Gentleman (American heroine)
The Ruthless Gentleman (American heroine)
International Player (British heroine)
Mr. Mayfair (British heroine)
Mr. Knightsbridge (American heroine)
Mr. Smithfield (American heroine)
Private Player (British heroine)
Mr. Bloomsbury (American heroine)

14 Days of Christmas (British heroine)

Mr. Notting Hill

This Christmas

Single Dad

King of Wall Street

Mr. Smithfield

Sign up to the Louise Bay mailing list here!

Read more at www.louisebay.com